BADK ᴐ ISLAND

Amanda Nicol

AGENT
PRESS

Published in 2013 by Agent Press
PO Box 370, Hastings, East Sussex, TN34 9HP

A catalogue record for this book is available from the British Library

ISBN 978-0-9571449-2-7

www.amandanicol.co.uk

*For Agnes Nicol OBE, Janine Nicol, Marie Carbery,
Anne Murray and all the women in my family*

RACHEL JAMESON'S RULES OF EXISTENCE

Rule No. 1: *Wanting what you don't have, chasing it till you've got it and then finding out that you didn't want it after all. In fact you still want what you don't have, i.e., the thing that you once had when you wanted the other.*

Rule No. 2: *Work comes when you could do without it.*

Rule No. 3: *You will be absolutely knackered on all the most important days of your life.*

Rule No. 4: *However sorted you think you might be, when it comes to this particular issue, you're lost.*

Rule No. 5: *When solitude is craved, company will call, and vice-versa.*

Rule No. 6: *Dreams are dreams and reality is reality and never the twain shall meet.*

Rule No. 7: *Things that are for the best always feel like utter shite.*

Rule No. 8: *Feeling any degree of smugness is just asking for trouble.*

Rule No. 9: *There's always a perfect time for making matters worse.*

Rule No. 10: *A broken heart is preferable to a broken head.*

1

Badric's Island

I'm thumbing through *Battersea, Then and Now* when my phone bleeps.

CARLA
Walkies?

I pick up the book again.

> *Sunday was the day of the weekly fair. With its donkey races, prize-fighters, conjurers, fortune tellers, gamblers, drinking booths, dancers, theatres, comic actors, hawkers and vendors it incited 'immorality and debauchery of the vilest kind, rendering the place positively disgraceful'. It became known as a 'carnival of folly' and dominated Battersea Fields in the latter half of the eighteenth century making 'right minded folk shudder with horror'. People flocked there in their thousands. To the point that the Government had to intervene such was the sheer number of riff-raff.*

Hmm. Some things never change.

OK c u in the field in 20

I haven't got to grips with predictive texting. I can live without it.

According to Harold West, author of this slim volume, a century later bicycling was the new craze and if not enticed by the other entertainments on offer, the riff-raff were there to watch this quaint new pastime, forbidden as it was in Hyde Park.

Those were the days. It's not allowed now. Except on the perimeter path. And don't think for a minute that you'll get away with a quick flit across the diagonal. The Parks Police will be onto you as quickly as it takes them to get into their cars. It's dangerous apparently. I know this because I've been banned from riding my bike in the park; name and address taken, the lot. If you're in a primetime soap and having a bad day, the best way to exercise your long-suffering dog is to belt round the park on your rusty bike – bought from neighbour Miss Jackson for forty quid, a Humber Sports Model, WW2's answer to the mountain bike, sit up and beg style, complete with white paint on the mudguards for blackouts – with your baseball cap on. And who'd be a Parks Policeman anyway? I feel a soap coming on ...

> Sorry son, you've failed. I know you wanted a career in the Met, but what can I say? If you really want a career in uniform may I suggest Group 4, Traffic, or … there's always the Parks Police …

Or:

> Oi, you there! I am charging you with riding a two wheeler across an empty expanse.

2

Even:

> Madame, would you come with me? We have
> reason to believe that you have failed,
> quite deliberately, to clean up after
> your dog. This is very serious, Madame,
> since the offending matter proceeded to
> adhere to the shoe of one of our most
> senior officers as he was going about
> apprehending a cyclist.

Maybe not.

> *There is evidence of habitation since before Saxon
> times. Taking its name from a Saxon ruler, it first
> appears in 693 in a charter granting Batrices Ege
> (Badric's Island) to the Abbess of Barking. Objects
> dating from the Stone and Bronze ages have been
> found, mostly in the river. The most important
> archaeological find to date is the Battersea Shield,
> which now belongs to the British Museum.*

When Plan A fails, i.e. Acting, I fall back on Plan B for Book
or Bar job; Plan C for Course in Something Useful (teaching, usually) or Plan D for Dole and Daytime telly. D is
out: the re-run of *Wives* is imminent. The world is soon to
be reminded of my existence and there's no way Shiraz
would be seen dead in the dole office. Seriously, signing
on is not an option. Not with my credit limit, it just doesn't
seem right. And who knows? Maybe the work will come
flooding in. That means C is out too. Plan B, therefore, is
the only option. It's also a lesson in how to justify endless
procrastination in the name of research whilst attending
proactively to the vexed question of non-existent career.
So I shall continue to study (I use the word lightly) *Battersea, Then and Now* by Harold West which will inform my

updated guide to SW11, ironically titled *Badric's Island*, a homage to my dog, my home and a nod to history, an interest in which is the 'positive thing to be gleaned' from my doomed affair with David. Yes, keeping busy's the answer; multitasking. Don't know where I'd find the time for a job even if I had one.

Badric knows his time has come when I put on my jacket: keys, cash, poo bags. His four paws pound parkward with a determination that can only be described as dogged.

This is my version:

> *On Sundays there are dog walkers, duck feeders, footballers, cruisers, loiterers, sad solitaries, happy couples, not-so-happy couples, families, babies, children (some on scooters with one over-developed calf muscle) and joggers. Some of these pushing buggies made for perambulating up mountains, complete with pale infants forbidden to focus on anything in the outside world until old enough to walk, or jog for themselves if not jiggled to death by paternal joggery, making right minded folk shudder with horror. People flocked there in their thousands, to the point that the Government had to intervene such was the sheer number of riff-raff.*
>
> *Rollerblading was the new craze in the late twentieth and early twenty-first centuries, and if not there to jog, the urban male provided much entertainment whilst endeavouring to look as cool as his considerably younger counterparts, by attempting to go backwards.*

Up ahead I see the black swan gliding along, neck in its graceful curve, red beak a dot of colour in the grey day. Nina told me that in Poland there's a saying, 'As rare as a black swan.' For the one left on the park lake there was never a truer word. According to Barry, the local twitcher, the authorities decided a while back that the black swans were too aggressive and had to be rehomed. They managed to catch the female and the cygnets, but the male wouldn't have it, and eventually they gave up trying. Last year he was seen defending a mallard and her ducklings from a dog. Call it anthropomorphism or whatever; that swan's lonely.

> *Ducks flocked there in their thousands, to the point that the authorities had to intervene such was the sheer number of dabblers and divers. This was before the great Bird Plague of 2010 when despite the several tons of stale bread thrown into the green water on a daily basis, huge numbers perished. Scientists remain divided as to the cause: A bacterium found in mould (organic bread)? A build-up of artificial additives in the water ('value' varieties)? The results remain inconclusive.*

You don't feed ducks if you've got a dog. Duck feeders have to be given a wide berth. Dogs like to snatch pieces of bread out of the hands of babes, making them cry and ruining a family walk. There's Carla. Dodging buggies and balls we make our way towards the café. It's packed.

> *People flocked there in their thousands, to the point that getting a hot drink could take longer than you would think possible.*

Giacomo waves at us.
   'Eh, Rachel, Carla, 'ow are you today?'
   'OK, and you?'
   'Don't encourage him, for God's sake,' I say, under my breath. He keeps asking me out and with every free

doughnut it's harder to refuse.

'Eh, I am happy now I see two beautiful ladies, cappuccini, bacon sandwich?'

'Just ordinary coffee for me thanks.'

Giacomo shrugs petulantly.

'Hot chocolate please,' says Carla.

We take our drinks out into the weak February sunshine, untie the dogs and find a seat next to the lake.

'It's bloody freezing Rach. Can we go in?'

'Let's stay out here.'

Last time I sat inside he came over and started to give me an uninvited massage. I was with Nina and Thai, who was yelling his head off until we gave him a cheap nasty biscuit, full of junk; an act, which if witnessed by his mother, would have got Nina the sack. As his thumbs bore in, I felt my shoulders, up pretty near my ears anyway, rise even further.

'Justa relax, Rachel, you are very, very tense.'

'You're making her very, very tense! Leave her alone!' said Nina, eyes flashing, cleft in her forehead deepening. Giacomo leaned over to her and hissed, 'You know lady, you are a jealous bitch!'

'Well?' says Carla.

'Well what?'

'The date. When is it?'

'Tomorrow. Got a few more possibles too. When's yours?'

'I chickened out.'

'Hang on. That's not allowed! We had a deal!'

We're doing this Internet dating thing together so we can pretend it's a laugh and not the desperate measure that it really is.

'Sorry, I went off him when he said that he liked women to be "feminine", and by that he meant not doing "grungy things" like rolling fags.'

'Oh well, his loss.'

We watch as a cormorant on a buoyed rope hangs out his wings to dry in the chilly air. It looks prehistoric, foreign like the black swan. Or the mandarin duck, as wooden as a decoy hand-painted in Hong Kong. Forget native species, this is the twenty-first century. This is London. If you can get here, you can be here. If you're a bird. Then you don't have to get yourself up inside the landing gear of a Jumbo Jet and freeze to death.

> *On Sundays, there were spinsters, bachelors, widows, widowers, black, white, grey, the heartbroken, the homesick, the passport hunters, the cynical, the bitter and twisted, the ever-hopeful, the hopeless and the lovesick offering all kinds of sob stories. They flocked there in their thousands, to the point that the Government had to intervene such was the sheer number of lonely hearts.*

> *From Badric's Island by Rachel Jameson.*

2

Options for the single girl

Plan E is another useful time waster. This is the proactive attending to of the emotional issue, i.e., Internet Dating. (You will notice that it comes after the career issue.) Also useful for those 'it's over and I mean it this time' moments, experienced with tedious regularity by the bit on the side. And whatever you may have heard about this being a perfectly acceptable mode of modern courtship, forget it. If you are lucky enough not to be familiar with the routine it goes something like this:

> *1. Log on to one of the thousand sites. Are delighted to discover that there are approx. 2 zillion blokes within a radius of 25 miles of your computer who are gagging for it (a meaningful relationship,that is). Immediately you panic, knowing that Mr Right may well be amongst them, but that you are going to be menopausal by the time you find him.*

> *2. Begin to trawl through personal statements along the lines of, 'I am a sensitive, funny bloke into usual stuff. Likes include reading, cosy nights in by the fire ...' etc. After seeing this fifty times realise that it has been taken from the new*

*bestseller, 'How to pull online', under the section
headed, 'What she wants to hear.' Avoid those who
add LOL to unfunny statements such as 'Can't say
I'm a dancer LOL' (let's save the laughing out loud
till we see you dance, shall we? Then I'll decide).*

*3. Give up on the personality bit and squint at
2,000 or so photos instead. (Of course, you've done
this already, but being female you have convinced
yourself that looks come well down the list.)
Remember – THIS IS THE BEST AND MOST
FLATTERING PICTURE HE POSSESSES. Do not fall
into the trap of thinking it's just a bad photo.
Is it a profile shot? Or three-quarter profile? If so,
assume that he only has one eye or an unsightly
ganglion or such on other side of face. Is he behind
the sofa, or behind anything that obscures his
enormous beer gut?*

*4. Examine the backdrop. This could well be his
front room. Can you picture yourself there? Is the
sofa hideous? Does the carpet defy description?
What do the curtains say about him? Can you see a
book anywhere in the room?*

*5. In the description of self, in the 'Build' box, has
he ticked: a) muscular, b) average or c) small?
For a) read 'I am fucking amazing, I love myself'.
For b) read 'I am considerably overweight'.
For c) read … well, honesty must count for
something.*

6. If he has specified a religion, he's a nutter.

*7. For 'smokes occasionally' read 'when the
occasion allows'; i.e. dope (this may suit).*

*For 'smokes socially' read 'smokes in company',
and when not in company there is no one there to
tell him he is a liar.*

8. Knock 10k off stated income immediately.

*9. Examine what he says he is looking for. If he
doesn't specify, he is really desperate. If he does, he
has no right.*

*10. If he writes, 'What ever your looking for
Im you're man!!!!!!!' or 'I am definately a good
catch!!!!!!!' or 'My kids live with they're mother,
were their very happy,' then MOVE ON SISTER!
MOVE ON!*

*11. Do the sensible thing and narrow the field.
Enter under 'Preference', 'No children'. Out of
7,569, 11 remain. Bear in mind that 3 of them
probably just 'forgot.'*

*12. If one has been found who sounds in any way
normal, has a basic grasp of spelling and grammar
and whose front room looks passable, then send
a message along the lines of, 'Hi, I'm just like you,
so therefore I must be nice. And, like you, I am just
doing this for fun/as bet/I'm bored/nothing on
the box/lonely as hell tonight and crying into my
drink over lost youth/haven't had a shag for so
long hymen has grown back (thus ensuring prompt
response).*

13. Wait. Check email every five seconds.

*14. PING! 1 new message in inbox from Okbloke@
plonker.net. 'Thats wierd – just hapened to be*

checking my email!!!!! On my way out now!! Catch ya l8r!! xxx

He's not going anywhere. The football is on. Spelling aside, the 'ya' and the !!!!!s have already sown the seeds of doubt. DO NOT IGNORE SEEDS OF DOUBT.

15. Having ignored seeds of doubt, after three days or so arrive at the dizzy heights of Stage 2 i.e., the live and direct real voice stage. Give him mobile number, allowing you to say, 'Sorry, you're breaking up, I can't hear y ...' as you press End Call. Do NOT give him your land line number. This is as good as saying, 'You can have me on a plate', whilst handing him the knife and fork. Do NOT fall in love with a voice. Remember that the brain is very good at making a pretty picture from what little information there is available. Remain focused on hideous radio presenters.

16. Move on to Stage 3, the meeting stage, to save on mobile bill and get the whole sorry business over with as quickly as possible.

17. Arrange to meet somewhere where no one you know would ever dream of going.

18. Get ready. Hard to pitch it right. Opt for casual, with decent knickers.

19. Sit and wait, in calm fashion. Prepare for the arrival of Forever Man/Complete No-no. Rehearse excuses along the lines of, 'Sorry, dog was sick earlier/ Sorry, I was sick earlier/ Sorry, long lost friend turned up/ Sorry, impromptu family reunion to get to owing to sudden violent death of ...' etc.

20. Complete No-no appears. Bottle out of
employing excuse. Endure excruciating evening.
Go home to drink and smoke socially on your own.

(From the subsection Options for the Single Girl,
Badric's Island by Rachel Jameson)

Not that I'm bitter or anything. Otherwise I wouldn't be
doing it again today, would I? The thought fills me with
dread shot through with a touching glimmer of hope, despite knowledge of the above. (Yes, I've done this before.
It didn't work out.)

This time he works in telly, so we've got something
vaguely in common. He's called Geoff, he's my age, and
he's single. He didn't see *Wives* last time round and I want
to meet him before he does, just in case he confuses fact
with fiction. We've spoken a few times and, heeding my
own advice we proceeded to the meeting stage without
further ado. He has described himself as blonde and OK
looking. He hadn't uploaded a photo, but then, nor had
I. I suggested meeting in the park, thinking that then at
least Badric will get his walk, and I won't have wasted any
of my not-so-precious time should he not live up to the
expectations which I am trying my best not to entertain.
After all, Monday afternoon's hardly a time to have high
expectations.

As I turn the corner and approach the café I begin
to wonder why I described Badric in so much detail. If
I hadn't, I could have sized him up and then hurried on
past if I didn't like the look of him. It's unlikely that another young black Labrador dog with tartan collar and a
dark-haired mistress in tow will be at large, giving me the
escape option. Instead, I see the two people I would have
put at the top of the list that reads; 'People I would not
like to bump into on a blind date', namely Ben and Steve,
heading for the café. Ben and Steve work for Foyle & Fa-

gherty, the 'famous' ad agency. I met them just through hanging out in the park and we've had some good laughs. They adore Badric and, unlike a lot of folk round here, they're friendly and even remember who you are; even if they are paid fortunes to think up crap and have the cheek to call it 'art'. They talk through programs and sit glued to the adverts. They know about camera angles and laugh conspiratorially at 'in' jokes. It's their religion. Carla and I know this, because once they invited us round for what we might have guessed would be a TV dinner. Carla didn't want to go, but then decided to treat it like reconnaissance. Know thine enemy. We call them the 'Fagarties,' for obvious reasons. They look up as I approach.

'Rachel! Hi! Looking forward to the re-run?' says Ben.

'Come and join us!' adds Steve.

This distracts me from scanning the environs of the café for the owner of the nice voice. And then I hear it, stage right.

'Rachel?'

'Oh, hi!' I say, feeling heat creep up my neck as disappointment free-falls from my heart to my trainers. Ben and Steve are waiting for an answer so I mutter something about next time as they give me looks that say, 'Darling, who he?'

I'm not going to rip the guy to shreds. Appearance isn't the issue; the fibbing is the issue. The 'slightly overweight', the 'hair starting to thin', these little hints at something only slightly less than perfect: what the hell's the point of lying? If you're going to meet the person then they are going to catch you out. It's strange. It really is. It's worse than estate agents' spin. Or maybe some people actually believe their own hype, in a sort of inversion of an anorexic looking in the mirror and seeing a fat person. Anyway, all I'm going to say is that he didn't tally with the voice... as predicted. Better then just to email before meeting, leave the voice out of it. Deep breath.

'Shall we head for the river?'

All that is left is to make conversation for the next half hour or so. I ask him about his work. He'd said he made docs, which sounded promising. These turn out to be minority sports docs for obscure satellite channels.

'You know, angling, pigeon racing, ferreting, that sort of thing.'

'Oh right. Sounds interesting.' Not.

'Yeah, it is,' he said, and with that picks up a large stick, and putting the full weight of his impressive bulk behind it, throws it for Badric, who manages, unbelievably, to get right in the way of the backswing. A horrible clonk and a sharp yelp and more yelping sends me into a maternal frenzy, down on my knees before my poor animal, whimpering, but (as if he needed to remind you just what sort of a fine fellow he is) still wagging, a graze evident above his right eye.

'My God! I'm so sorry! Is he okay? Oh God, fuck! How did that happen?'

I don't answer and ignore him as the apologies continue to stream out of his mouth to the point that I was tempted to pick up the stick, and then it could have turned into an incident for the Parks Police. I did feel for him though. Of all the things that could happen on a blind date, I bet he hadn't thought of this. He'd have paid good money just to have gone arse over tit in the mud.

'I think I should take him to the vet.'

He says we'll go in his car, miles away, naturally, on the other side of the park. I put Badric on the lead as he looks a bit wobbly. I am trying hard to be calm, when it becomes farcical. Firstly, he asks if I have anything on me that I could use to wipe his paws (I am speechless). Secondly, the wheels of his car start to spin in the soggy leaves in the car park, round and round they go as the engine squeals. Badric is sitting in the back seat of his car (on my jacket) with tears running down his face. Eventually some kind soul attaches a towrope to our man's car and off we go. His apologies couldn't be more profuse. I want him to shut up. The vet is closed. Surgery is not till later. We head for the emergency vet in Victoria. He offers to pay. I know about the emergency vet and know that he will regret saying this. At last we arrive. By this time Badric appears to be absolutely fine, but nevertheless we go in and wait for a short eternity till eventually a terse woman in a white coat sees us and shines a light in his eyes and assures me that he is fine. I am relieved, but that's nothing to the relief of my date. He almost bursts into tears. His mood changed slightly when presented with the bill, but he was as good as his word. Outside my house he said, 'I don't suppose you're going to invite me in for a coffee.' I reply as politely as I can that a quiet night in nursing my dog's sore head is all I'm capable of.

I am worried when Badric doesn't fall upon his food as if half-starved, but eat he does, then goes to his basket to sleep off what must be a colossal headache. He's taking it pretty well, considering. I'm not. I ring Carla immediately, she tries not to laugh despite her concern for Badric. I laugh too, but when I put the phone down I feel awful. I decide to terminate any budding correspondence with any hopeful Internet dater immediately. Anyway, all it does is make me want to call David, which, after a large glass of wine I am seriously considering when I am saved by the appearance of Ferdie.

Ferdie is my lodger. He's from Brazil, he's the percussion player in Carla's band, but really he's a dancer, just back from a tour in Germany with *Danse de la Lune*. He just about pays the mortgage, and he can fix things. He wears white 501s, which look extremely fetching, and clean shirts under stylish jackets. He's got the DNA of every beautiful and exotic person that ever walked the planet, eats a lot of fruit, doesn't smoke (cigarettes), doesn't drink (one beer, once in a blue moon), he doesn't smell, or listen to loud music, or eat my food, or use the last bit of washing powder without replacing it, or try it on ... usually.

But there was just the one time. That one beer must have gone to his head, because it happened. It was New Year's Eve. I should lock myself in my bedroom on New Year's Eve. I have an alarming tendency to ruin the end and beginning of the year by doing something injudicious. You can forgive yourself a Millennium Eve indiscretion, greeting the dawn of a New Century with a stranger from a drunken party might not be such a bad thing, what else could you do with that strange mixture of anti-climax and expectation of imminent annihilation, whether by the millennium bug resetting the sights of our nuclear arsenal on Central London, or being cut down by a vengeful God who existed after all? No such excuse with Ferdie. I wasn't even particularly drunk. But whatever the encounter lacked, it was more than compensated for by aesthetics alone, if you get my drift. He seemed happy enough at the time, but the next day he was ... well, we both were ... a little quieter than usual. He didn't say anything. I didn't say anything. The atmosphere was slightly strained for a while – he knew I was seeing David – but soon he was touring, and it was never mentioned. In that we've never spoken about 'it', it's as if it never happened. Almost.

'Hey, Rachel, what is wrong?' I tell him and he gives me a hug. And another hug. I drink some more wine and he stir-fries some veg, which we share. I drink some more and we smoke a joint, and Badric wakes up, shakes, and is on the scrounge, i.e. is fine. I celebrate with another glass of wine and Ferdie cracks open that once-in-a-blue-moon beer and... God it's been a while, and the rest, as they say, is history. Actually, it's a bit too now to be history just yet.

'Rachel, you are a beautiful woman, so, so ... natural,' he says, before falling asleep in my bed.

Natural? My mind is racing now. I'm wide-awake.

When did 'natural' start to sound like an insult? Not that he meant it like that, but ... But then there's more plastic surgery *per capita* in Brazil than anywhere else. A soft breast in Brazil must be like ... I don't know, but it sounds like a good title for a TV series: *A Soft Breast in Brazil.* One woman's desperate struggle to raise the money for cosmetic surgery by prostituting her children. No, change the title to *The Last Soft Breast in Brazil,* or maybe just, *The Breasts From Brazil.*

You don't scatter the ashes of dead women in Brazil. You get a hard lump of ash mixed with silicon to chuck off the Copacabana Beach, and you have to watch out for the swimmers. Actually, there's something in that. There's a business opportunity, a gap in the market. When I was little I had a kit that you could make your own paperweight or jewellery with. You could get a shell, or a leaf, or an ant and set it in this molten plastic stuff ... You could have a pendant with a bit of mum in it. It would be a sort of immortality.

Natural. It implies neglect. You haven't been working hard enough at the gym. You are, quite naturally, getting on.

I've given up going to the gym. I couldn't stand it any longer. It was the music that got to me in the end. If I had to hear *Eye of the Tiger* one more time I was going to scream. Heroic music, for all the heroes bravely approaching the step machine like it was the final ascent of the Matterhorn, standing before it with head slightly bowed, exhaling slowly with cheeks puffed out. I tried, but I failed. The only part of me that was responding was my legs, and they were OK in the first place.

I can't believe I just did that. That was so not a good idea. I love Ferdie, but not in that way. He's gorgeous, but we don't have a great deal to say to each other, really. He's the perfect lodger, but I've known for some time that he liked me a bit too much. I've tried to be sensitive, you know, kind yet firm, tough love and all that. I feel guilt-ily glad that he is off again with *Danse* in the morning; France this time. All right for some.

I lift his arm and wriggle away, get up and go down-stairs, pulling on my dressing gown. My head is starting to throb. Badric gets up and stretches and looks up at me hopefully. I let him out the back and put the kettle on. It's not even late, just after eleven. The phone rings. Must be Carla, or David even, I think, with a rush but it's Mum. Mum at this time of night means bad news. She tells me that Granddad has died.

3

The big wheel

The scene in the function room at the Duntochter Motel
is surreal. It's not 21st century Glasgow, it's the Berlin of
George Grosz. A cabaret, not a wake. A circus act, a hall of
mirrors, the place that you come to dance and drink as
you morph into the next generation. Walking the plank. A
few grandparents to go, parents edging forward, you lot,
the kids, following behind with kids that have become the
kids. They're everywhere, they're tiny, some in nappies,
just past the point of not being alive, having just come in
where Granddad had just gone out. He hadn't even seen
some of them. Just missed each other, so to speak. I'm
feeling very drunk. Shouldn't have turned down Jeannie's
tatty scones and square sausages after all.

'Rachel! Rachelle ma belle, if incest was legal darlin',
you'd be in big trouble!'

Uncle Rab, my favourite uncle. Older, everyone's older.
Then, very quickly the brain adjusts the picture, or the
picture adjusts the brain, whatever, something happens
and then he's the same as he always was, and ever will be,
Amen. It's weird, as if a dance with an uncle was actually
a set-up, inescapable; one of those parties that you go to
catch chickenpox on purpose. Only this virus is deadly.
You go to funerals to catch death. If you're lucky it takes

a lifetime to incubate. Some people are more susceptible, catching it while they're actually still alive.

Like Aunt Ellie over there, long dead. Sometimes the long dead take a bloody long time to die after the initial death-whilst-still-alive, as if death doesn't have to bother with them. It's the ones that are busy having a good time that it sneaks up on and wham! Game over. It's the watched pot syndrome. It's a generalisation, but that's whisky for you.

God, she's coming over, as pale as death. Death's modelled itself on her. As pale and dried-up as the fish paste sandwich on the paper plate, lipstick fleeing from her mouth down a million Silk Cut creases.

'Aw, pet, ye were a just wee bairn last time I saw ye! Sick aw doon ma anorak so you were!'

I feel queasy at the mention of the word. I think I'm going to be...

'Excuse me a minute Ellie...'

Little cousin Louise is already in the loos, red-eyed and blotchy-faced.

'Oh, Rach...'

'Hang on a minute, Lou...'

I stick my head into, thankfully, a disinfected haze.

'God, I'm going to be sick too.' I hear the clickety-clack of her heels in a hurry as she follows suit.

'Rach, is there any loo roll in yours?'

I pass a wad under the door. Louise has got a toothbrush.

'How much do you want for that?'

'If you can bear to use it after me, you can.'

Well, we are cousins, even if it does take death to get us together. No, that's not quite true because she's another *émigrée*. We meet up in London for all sorts of reasons. Not always what you'd call happy, these occasions. Usually it's because something nasty is going on, a 'life event,' i.e., parental cancer, abortion, end of an affair. These things are either too much of a downer for friends (cancer) or you just can't face the 'I told you so/to be careful' (affair, abortion). Extended family is good for this. Cousins are especially good, and aunties. One or other of them is bound to have been there, done that.

Lou and I are the 'posh cousins'. The traitors, the would be Sassanachs. It's not true. There never was a choice. Other people's decisions shape our lives. We peer at ourselves in the mirror.

'God! I'm Mum – it's official.'

We're catching it, no doubt about it. Death. It's there on our faces, round our eyes, tell-tales in our roots, still far off, but there, there, accusing us of not getting on with it, of not being married, pregnant, sorted. Of not playing our part, of pretending still to be the kids when we're so obviously not. Let's get out of here. Get back to Euston. Stride purposefully down the platform, disappear into black cabs and be swallowed up by our own lives, into the swirling currents of the city to buy some more time, tread water.

'How's things?'

'Oh, you know, OK I guess, I hate seeing Mum upset.'

'I know, it's horrible.'

'How's that lovely doggy of yours?'

'He's fine. Carla's looking after him. He'd love it up here.'

'Heard from the history freak again?'

'No, not for a while now. I need to move on, Lou.'

Ellie is waiting for us, holding out a plate of biscuits.

'Would ye just look at you two! Busy wee bees! Dinnae forget to have kiddies noo will ye! I dunno where I'd be without ma Dougie!'

Dougie. There he is, propping up the wall, three sheets to the wind: twice divorced, poached in drink, living with his mum, gone to pot.

'Yeah, he must be...' Louise's words tail off.

21

'A great comfort to you, Ellie.'

Cousin Angus approaches; Uncle Rab's son. He's in love, big time. This time it's for real.

'Yeah right,' says Lou.

We know Gus quite well because he comes down to London for work now and again. He's a laugh. He's brought the love of his life along to meet the family, lucky girl. We all go outside and sit on a bench. The Duntocher Motel. Squat, red brick, flat roofed, ugly; the waiting room for the crematorium. Gus takes a ready-rolled joint out of his top pocket.

'Not for me, thanks.'

Louise passes as well.

'Aye, it's the big wheel, that's what it is,' he said.

'Aye, aye...' Aye, Lou and I can still say 'aye', can't we? We were born here. We love it up here. Sort of.

Yesterday I hired a car, drove up to Loch Lomond, stared at the still blue water and tried to feel something. Ate a Tunnock's Snowball, found my old primary school, remembered the day I forgot to put on knickers and was so upset I had to go home again, saw the old house, thought about Mum sunbathing naked, here, in Scotland! Dad demolishing the generator when we got put on the mains, taking me into the garden very late at night, pointing to the moon and telling me that a man had been there. Concorde on a test flight over the Highlands, the sonic boom splitting the sky as we blocked our ears. The holidays in Harrow, at Louise's, before mum and dad had taken the leap, the riverboat trips to Battersea Fun Park.

'I want to live here when I grow up.' Well, who wouldn't? A fun park and a dogs' home. Perfect. And it happened, even though by then the Fun Park had been condemned and pulled down, and the dog wasn't from the Dogs' Home, but the gift of a history freak; a black Labrador puppy for my thirtieth birthday. The last of the litter. If I didn't want him he'd keep him himself.

'Let's call him Badric.'
'OK.' Whatever you say.

Dragging myself back to the present, it occurs to me that they should wire these places up to the National Grid. The bereaved could take comfort from that, even get a discount on their electricity bill to the tune of the price of a cup of tea. You could claim it like Nectar Points or something. Green Solutions. God knows we need them.

'Look,' says Gus as a puff of white smoke from the tall chimney of the crematorium is lost to the grey sky, 'There he goes.'

4

And so you're back

The train journey is as blurred as the landscape outside. One hangover later and it's gone, the homeland, the birth-place. Lou and I say goodbye, promise not to leave it so long, and go our separate ways. I'm glad to be back to the brake lights and electric blue flashes, the glittering web of Albert Bridge. Neon scribbles in the flat black water. Wakes of colour held for a moment by the river. A gull being carried downstream, living flotsam, going with the flow, unlike the traffic on Chelsea embankment. It's crawl-ing, a pitiless struggle to the death, or the M4, whichever comes first.

'Just here's fine, thanks.'

The cab squeals to a halt. He's done one of those infuri-ating all-round-the-houses jobs.

'I think it would be quicker if you went...'

'You want to drive, love?'

Bloody rip-off. I hand over twenty quid.

The man in the shop says hello. Sometimes he does, sometimes he doesn't. Moody git. At last, home sweet home ... I'll just dump this lot then go and get Bads, have a bath, watch *Newsnight*. Hang on, there's a light on ... Did I leave a light on? Yeah, the hall light, but that's the sitting room. Ferdie's not due back yet ... shit... There's someone in there, pacing around, on the phone. It's a bloke, he's putting the phone down, he's having a drink... Right, I'm calling the police. Hang on, he's running his hand through his hair like... David. It is David! Bloody hell!

I fumble with my keys. He's opening the door ... letting me in as if he owned the place!

'Rachel!'

He looks tired, thinner. Then that brain thing happens and he looks the same as he ever did.

'Why? Who else is coming?'

'It's so good to see you! Here, let me take those.' He reaches for my bags.

That fucking song comes to mind, *'I should have changed that stupid lock, I should have made him leave his key ...'*

'Get off! What the hell do you think you're doing?'

I push past him, take the bags to the kitchen, put them down, and look around. How long's he been here? Not long by the looks of it. No cups in the sink, a bottle of whisky on the side.

'Would you like a drink?'

'David! Stop behaving as if this is normal! What the hell are you doing here? I told you to stay away and I meant it!'

He sinks onto a chair, head in hands, muttering something about needing to see me, to talk.

'Bit late for that isn't it? I'm sorry, but whatever it is it'll have to wait. I've just got back from my Granddad's funeral and I've got to go and get my dog.'

My dog, not our dog, not the dog you gave me, my dog. Adrenaline and anger. It's a good mix. Brings the blood to the boil. Instant hangover cure.

'I'd like it if you were gone by the time I got back. Goodbye.'

Slam.

Bastard.

Carla opens the door, resplendent in purple headscarf

and fluffy slippers.

'Bloody hell! What a nerve! D'you want me to come back with you?'

'Yes... no, I don't know. What does he want? God my head's splitting. Got any painkillers?' Badric is beside himself.

'Yes, I've missed you, yes I have!'

Funny how we try to hide dramas from our dogs, as if they really were our children.

'Has he been a good boy?'

'Yeah, course he has, and Jess has loved having him here.'

'Anyway, you're not exactly dressed to go out.'

The bottom's dropped out of her leggings and her T-shirt is an uninteresting shade of pinky-grey.

'What, do you think he'd fancy me? Hey, d'you remember when I had Ian round for the first time and Nina appeared all done up?'

'I can't believe she did that on purpose. How is she anyway? I haven't seen her for ages,'

'She's off in wherever-it-is with what's-his-name.'

'Oh yeah, you mean Suffolk, with Adrian. Good luck to her. Anyway, I suppose I better go and face it, whatever it is. What am I going to do?'

'Just get rid of him!'

'What if he's dying or something?'

'Just get rid of him! And ring me.'

'Thanks, Carla.'

David. I must have summoned him by reading the books he gave me. I suddenly have an image of him, reading aloud. Harold West getting poetic, comparing the river to an artery, its tides a pulse, its past so many layers of memory. Chapters of an epic, its beginnings forgotten, its end never in sight.

'A bit like *The Archers* then.'

He'd hold up his finger, 'No listen, this is fascinating...'

As we near home Badric cocks his leg in all the leg-cocking places to make up for lost time. He's still there, of course. I didn't need my female intuition for that. Asleep on the sofa. Not even the dog sniffing round him makes him stir. Good. I can't deal with this tonight. I close the door. I'll carry on as normal. Bath, gallon of water, telly. Badric's asleep on the bed already. Forget the bath, forget telly. Necessities only. Text Carla.

**It's crashed out on sofa. Will sort it 2morrow.
Thanx 4 dogsit xx**

My bed resembles Tracey Emin's. I bloody hope David hasn't been snooping around. Then again, serve him right if he has. Ferdie's beer bottle and my dry wine glass are where we left them. I reach for them and step on something unpleasant. Yuck! The condom. I pick it up and hold it out at arm's length. As I go to wrap it in loo paper and put it in the bathroom bin I notice with horror, that it's ripped like a burst balloon and minus any content. The tear is at the top though, not the bottom, so I don't absolutely have to freak out. I count to ten, and keep calm. I go back to where I found it and, yes Miss Marple, I think its dried contents are on the carpet. Thanks a lot, Ferdie. This is still reason enough to lie awake calculating dates in the moments when I am not considering running downstairs to murder (or just look at) David.

Morning. That moment when it's so nice, home, the light through the curtains... Happiness is a warm Labrador. What time is it? GOD! DAVID'S DOWNSTAIRS! I smell burning. I leap up, throw on yesterday's clothes and rush downstairs to see the kitchen thick with bluish smoke. Two slices of charcoal are stuck in the smoking, broken, toaster. I turn it off and open the back door.
    'DAVID!'

The loo door opens and he emerges. He's got *Battersea, Then and Now* clutched to his chest like the eponymous shield.

'I see you keep all the books I gave you in the lavatory.'

Hmm, I wonder why. 'Yes, you know, I like to dip into them, when I feel like it.'

You taught me how to do that. And there's talk of a loo paper shortage. It's bloody freezing in here now.

'What's that smell? Damn it! The toast! I was going to bring you breakfast in bed.'

'Excuse me? Look, you've got to tell me what is going on right now or I'm going to ...'

The doorbell rings. Post, probably.

'Don't answer it!'

'Of course I'm going to answer it!'

A huge 4-wheel drive is idling in front of the gate. A woman is standing in front of me. I feel the sting of her hand on my face. Badric is wagging his tail. Wagging his tail! Thanks a lot, biscuit-for-brains. To think you made me feel safe!

She, Fiona, that is to say David's wife, is turning on her heel, getting into her enormous car, if you can call it that. Whatever it is, it's totally bloody unsuited to a nineteenth century residential street. Even if the four wheel drive does mean it handles jolly well over the humps or 'sleeping policemen' as they are also known and if ever I ... I ... I'm losing it.

5

The enemy within

'NO! I'm going on my own, but when I get back I want to talk. OK?'

I need to go and look at the river and calm down. Outside I see Teresa (Teraysa, not Tereesa). There she goes, getting away with it again. She parks in the disabled bay every day, every night, as if it's hers. Maybe it is, maybe Daddy works for the Council. One day I just had to say something.

'You do know that you shouldn't park there, don't you? Miss Jackson needs that space.' It was one of those things that just popped out of my mouth, with no basis in fact whatsoever, borne of a sense of injustice that the rest of us had forked out a small fortune for residents' parking. Mrs Jackson doesn't even have a car. This was her reply, 'Well, God bless the old lady, but...'

You just have to rise above it. Float up to the moral high ground and stay there for as long as possible.

This morning it's bleak, wet and cold but this doesn't deter the squaddies. The squaddies are people who make time in their already gruelling schedules to be humiliated publicly by a Sergeant Major from Chelsea Barracks. They are made to run up and down, do press-ups till they are blue in the face, then touch their toes 100 times. And they're grateful for it. As the squaddies recede into the distance the t'ai chi-ers come into view, East meets West. All things considered, I'm being pretty cool about this. Not as cool as a t'ai chi-er, but who is? They're doing their thing, very slowly, very, very slowly, with the Peace Pagoda as a backdrop. What is it that they remind me of? It's watery ... something in an aquarium, squid perhaps, or seaweed. Joggers panting and sweating come up from behind, tss, tss, from their headphones, iPods strapped to their hot arms like little battery packs and they're gone, leaving the t'ai chi-ers standing. Well, not standing, but as close as you can be to standing whilst actually moving.

> *People flocked there in their thousands. To the point that the Government had to intervene such was the sheer number of keep-fit fanatics.*

Ben and Steve said they really wanted to be Buddhists. Didn't wanting to be a Buddhist defeat Buddhism from the start? How could Buddhism ever fit in with life, life anywhere, let alone London? If you wanted to be a Buddhist so much that it was making you suffer, then surely you'd have to rid yourself of the desire to be a Buddhist?

This is my flick around with the remote way of dealing or not dealing with stuff. Fiona just slapped me. Flick. David is in my house. Flick. Ferdie. Flick. Granddad. Flick, flick, flick. Squaddies, T'ai chi-ers, joggers. Flick. I must tell Lou. God, didn't I sound so sorted on the train? I was positively preaching. Couldn't stop going on about how great it was to be David-free, how I could buy a castle in Scotland for my house, about things being OK despite the lack of work, about freedom and choice and all things nice ... Must have been the mix of most of the things we'd bought for our friends (apart from Carla's Edinburgh Rock and that was only because it was so horrible), whisky and more whisky and the 'life's is too short' talk that funerals can inspire. We had the man chat too. They're OK, by and large we even like them. And we agreed, nodding sagely, that it's OK to look for love. Everyone does that. Men aren't the enemy. We know who that is. The enemy within. Buddha knew it and the advertising folk know it. The constant state of desire. You can make a hell of a lot of money out of it, or you can get over it. Yes, you have to ask just how hard a time you're having if you own a house in SW11, even if you did pay for a large chunk of it by getting your tits out. Sorry, I mean by getting a good part in a popular TV series. It's hardly a tragedy.

Flick. It's just not that simple, the man/woman thing, otherwise lesbians might live happily ever after. Gay men might mate for life. And as for the rest of it, the nitty-gritty, it's a regular minefield. Deciding whether to park in a disabled bay, to clean up after your dog or to visit Miss Jackson when you'd rather watch *EastEnders*, all that stuff. It's power, of a sort. Moaning about not having a husband and children when women have spent hundreds of years complaining about just that, it's nuts. It's one of those irksome Rules of Existence.

> **Rule No. 1:** *Wanting what you don't have, chasing it till you've got it and then finding out that you didn't want it after all. In fact you still want what you don't have, i.e., the thing that you once had when you wanted the other.*

It's a joke. Might apply to the David situation if I was sure I didn't want it. My phone jumps in my pocket. Shit, it's Jenny Scary-Agent.

'Hi darling, you back in civilisation? Good. There's a little job I think you'd be perfect for. See? I said things would pick up! Casting at three, it's an ad, OK? '

> **Rule No. 2:** *Work comes when you could do without it.*

31

Not that I'll get it anyway. Pencil, paper, have neither; so pretend to write down the address whilst desperately memorising it. Acting. That's what it's all about.

'OK, thanks Jenny.' Grovel, grovel. 'I'll be there.'

It's ringing again, Carla, thank God.

'Is that the wee lassie from across the border?'

'I take it you mean Battersea Park Road?'

'Well, come on, what's occurring?'

'Oh nothing, I've just been slapped in the face by his wife and stormed out, and I've got a casting this afternoon. You know ... business as usual.'

'Blimey, are you OK? What's going on?'

'I don't know yet, I'm pacing myself. I'm just walking Bads.'

'Hurry up, mate, the suspense is killing me!'

It's clearing up, the sun's trying to come out. Down the squirrel run, head for crocus corner, it's all starting to happen, the magnolias will be out soon. It's pretty, this bit. It's where the pigeons come to do their courting.

'Just take 'er down crocus corner mate, works every time, believe me!'

There's Miss Jackson, pockets full of nuts for the squirrels, heading for the high bench. It's high for the old folks, see? So they can get down easily. Funny thing that. Sitting on one of them makes you feel old and young at the same time, because your bum's so high off the ground that you can swing your legs, as if you were a child. It's a nice feeling. Maybe that's the real reason that the seat is high, give the old dears a chance to be young again, or to confuse them. The high bench is like a symbol. Old ladies become little old ladies. Old men become little old men. They shrink and benches grow. Badric rushes over to her and she makes a fuss of him. He snatches a monkey nut, but spits it out, unimpressed.

'Hello, Miss Jackson. How are you?'

'Hello, dear. As well as can be expected, you know. Got a new lodger dear? I saw a man go into your house yesterday.'

I bet you did. I bet those nets were twitching like nobody's business. And if you didn't recognise him he really must have changed.

'Er, no, that's just a friend ... He's not staying. My lodger's away at the moment, but he'll be back any day now.'

And if I know life at all, it will be sooner rather than later.

'I told my friend Josie at the Bingo about you dear!'

'Oh yes?'

'She wants your autograph. She remembers you in *Chefs' Wives*. She thought you were ... well actually dear, she didn't think you looked very well.'

'Oh. Anyway, I must be off, I'll pop in soon, I brought you back some...'

Oh, no I didn't, because I ate it on the train.

'Did you dear? You shouldn't have. Something sweet is it?'

Oh well, Carla won't mind.

'Yes, Edinburgh Rock! It's delicious! Not very good for your teeth though!'

What did I say that for?

'Won't do these teeth any harm, love!' she said, tapping an obvious denture with an arthritic finger.

'Ha, Ha! Good! I'll drop it in later then. Bye for now.'

I'd like to think that I was a good neighbour by my own volition, but really, Badric has to take the credit. He never forgets he or she who gives him a biscuit, and this she did, when we first moved in.

OK, here goes, can't put it off any longer, turn the key in the door. Silence. Go through to the kitchen. It's tidy. There's a note on the table.

> *Had to do a few things, sorry about all this, will make it up to you. What about dinner at the King's Ransom? 8 pm. D x*

6

The casting

Well, well, the King's Ransom. He must be feeling guilty. No. I'll just stay in and have beans on toast.

As if!

That's what that smug creature perched up there on the moral high ground would do, but not me. She wouldn't have got herself into this mess anyway, because she would never have had an affair with a married man. You have to ask yourself whether parking in a disabled bay is such a crime after all. The thing about an affair is that you can be both victim (as seen by single women/your friends) or Jezebel (married women/their friends). You're neither of course. You're just a mug.

The bath is a good place to think. The dirt floats to the surface of your mind and then you cry, to wash it all out.

Tears! The great new Braincleanser from Cloreal!

I haven't even thought about Granddad once: the quiet blacksmith's hammerman, who smoked half a Woodbine on the way to work and half on the way back. Who worked in a place where it always rained. That's what mum had thought when she'd met him on the corner of the street every night. He worked hard all his life. Came home drenched in sweat every day. He liked a wee dram, watching Celtic, looking at photos of his family. Eight children, shot to the corners of the Earth like arrows; not to get away from him, but to have better lives. That's what he wanted. That's what you expected for your children. And now he was dead. And Nana would be lonely. And the children who'd stayed would worry, and the children who hadn't would worry, and the grandchildren wouldn't. Because it's not our problem ... yet. I must ring Mum, and Lou, and Nana. No, a card, a letter for Nana.

I'm drying myself when I hear a noise downstairs. Please, not now. I thought it was on hold until the King's Ransom?

'David?'

'Hi Rachel! It's me, I's back!'

'Ferdie! Hi, how was it?'

Damn. Oh for an empty house tonight. What am I thinking of? Fickle heart, I hate you. He puts down his bag and comes over to give me a hug, asking me how the funeral went. I feel myself wince. Shit. I don't feel good about this at all. I'd like to ask him if he was sure that the condom had done its job. Instead I ask him about the trip and tell him I've got a casting. Fickle heart, why can't you just love Ferdie?

He goes to his room to unpack and sleep. I've got time to make some calls and check my e-mail. Ooh, one from Haden. He's in Australia doing a film; a decent one too, all right for some.

Hi darling,
How's life back in freezing cold London? Things are going great. Didn't think I'd like it but it's fantastic. They've just had Wives out here so I'm a star! When does the re-run start at home? At least we'll get some dosh! Work OK, haven't got a lot to do at the moment so I've just got to sit by the pool and admire the scenery. (You know me!)
Haden x

Yes, I do. And the scenery would have a great tan and a six-pack.

P.S. Guess what I'm drinking? Shiraz!

Haden Marshall is my opposite number in *Wives*. He's got it all, looks, talent etc., etc. Scenes that found him pacing around in his Calvin Kleins (and there were plenty of them) reduced the women on the set to a bunch of simpering ninnies on a Diet Coke Break, including me.

But more than that, he was nice. He didn't give a lot away at first, but after a while we got to talking. He was actually Greek. His real name was Yannis Theopolis, but, face it, that wasn't going to go down well with a casting director, so he took the surnames of two of his friends, *et voilà,* a star is born. He'd been to a grammar school and sounded as English as they come. 'A social migrant'. That's what he called himself. And why not? It sounds a whole lot better than a social climber. Acting was the obvious choice. If you can change your accent, back and forth, and not because the voice coach at RADA was telling you to, but to avoid being beaten up, you could act. It had been a bit like that for me too, coming down from my cosy Scottish primary school to a huge terrifying open plan modern Harrow comp. I lost the wees and the ochs before you could say milk time.

He plays Ricardo, top chef extraordinaire, with ambition to match Hitler, and I'm Shiraz, his wife and accomplice. It's The Scottish Play transposed onto the London restaurant scene, sort of. It's got it all: glamour, sex, money, power, revenge and (and this is the clever bit) food. It's genius. Or so the writers like to think.

It paid ludicrously well. It was like one long advert; one long advert, made bearable by working closely, sometimes very closely with Haden. I didn't fancy him. It was something far more grown-up than that. It was desire. Desire! Powerful, physical, you know, that thing that makes you lose half a stone overnight and keeps your pupils permanently dilated. The object of your desire might be oblivious to it, but other men aren't. They start sniffing around as if you're on heat. The crew actually used to break into spontaneous applause after our bedroom/Jacuzzi/against the deep freeze scenes because I was so convincing. Method acting, see?

'What? You mean you get on really well, you're soul mates, you've seen each other naked from the bottom up and nothing's happened yet? Get real,' said Nina (that's how good her English is), 'He's gay.'

No. He was ... just being a bit old-fashioned, a bit cautious. He respected me. He was getting to know me first. Mustn't mix business with pleasure and all that. Yes, destiny is a funny thing. It was to be a soap opera that was to change my life.

A few days after this conversation we were walking in the park when the Fag-arties came along and saw straight through my cunning disguise. You see, my huge celebrity status (joke) meant that baseball cap and shades were the order of the day. Otherwise I was spotted, by little girls mostly and I didn't really relish the bulimic tart role model thing. When they asked for my autograph I always made a point of telling them how stupid Shiraz was, causing them to look at me as sceptically as they would a smoker telling them not to start. Didn't fool the Fag-arties though.

'Hi, darlings! Rachel – saw you on the box last night. You were fabulous! Lucky you getting to roll around with Haden Marshall! Very few women have had that privilege you know! Is he still seeing Franco Felucci? Wouldn't kick him out of bed either! Must dash!'

'Don't say it, Nina, please.'

The celebrity status has long since worn thin. A haircut,

some different clothes, and people forget. They move on. Something else is soon tickling the nation's fancy. *Secrets of an Opera Singer*, or *Tales from the Dentist's Chair*. As long as it's got plenty of beautiful people in it, and sex, of course. How I ever got to play Shiraz in *Wives*, I'll never know. It's guaranteed that a night before a casting will be a sleepless one.

> ***Rule No. 3:*** *You will be absolutely knackered on all the most important days of your life.*

It must have been down to meeting Haden; that moment, that pheromone-infused moment just before I went in must have swung it.

I don't miss being recognised. The joke got a bit stale. I wonder what it'll be like this time round. Hopefully no one except casting directors will bother to watch it.

'Alright Shraz!' They'd call as I passed, workmen mostly, whistle, stick two fingers down their throats, then give me the thumbs up ... because Shiraz was bulimic.

In a sort of ongoing revenge against Ricardo, with a large helping of self-loathing on the side, every time he shagged another young foreign waitress she'd throw up his superb food. Girl Power! Clever writing or what?

Today however, it's the usual situation, even though I had a pretty good night's sleep, all things considered. I still look like I've been beamed down from Planet Frump to do a research project.

I wonder what today's ad is going to be for. The last one I went up for I didn't get, thank God. It's just come out. I saw it the other night. It's for 'feminine hygiene', you know, because we are so dirty. The actor is about a decade my junior. She has her period and is getting ready for a hot date. You know she's got her period because she rubs her unfeasibly flat stomach with a pained expression on her face. As she rummages in her knicker drawer in her dressing gown, the voiceover quips, *'Going for a thong?'* Hilarious, isn't it? But, period an' all, she opts for the sensible big knickers. Cut to her looking despairingly at her rear view in the mirror, at the shame-of-it visible panty line through her skin-tight bootcuts. At that very moment her flatmate walks in and empathises with this terrible dilemma. But not to worry! Out of her fashionably cavernous handbag she takes an itsy-bitsy box and hands her friend something that looks like a bandaid for a mouse. Oh come on! How come they haven't heard of tampons? Anyway, our heroine is overcome with gratitude and gets changed again. The lacy thong is donned, with this thing now in place, totally invisible beneath her figure-hugging cream trousers. Thinking-caps on girls, here comes the 'science'. Watch as this scrap of nappy miraculously absorbs a pint of fluid (nice, clean, hygienic, inoffensive blue fluid), whilst staying firmly in place thanks to its tiny 'wings'. And they really are tiny. They are about the size of a gnat's. 'Toot, toot!' The hot date's arrived in his hot car and off they go into the sunset.

Things for Thongs! Another lifesaver from Dr John.

Dr John. A man presumably. It's not that you wouldn't wear a thong, or string, when you've got your period, but whether you'd be going on a hot date is another matter. You might be wearing one; in fact you were more likely to wear one when you've got your period than on the days immediately preceding it. If suffering from water retention, thongs are even less comfortable than usual. You may as well put some dental floss between your legs and be done with it. But, we've got used to uncomfortable undergarments over the centuries, like carthorses with buckles and brasses digging in all over the place. Maybe it's a ploy so that when a man finally divests you of these objects of gentle torture, you'll be even more grateful to him than you supposedly already are. And boy, do you feel naked when you're naked. Not like men. They can hang loose all day long in their baggy boxers if they so wish. Maybe that's why nakedness isn't such a big deal for them –there's not so much contrast with the dressed state. For women, however, it's a bit like taking the mould off a jelly that hasn't quite set. Thongs, strings, whatever, you just have to be careful to pick the right days to wear them, otherwise you can look like a cross between a sumo wrestler and a baboon in oestrus. Which, reassuringly, is not unlike how I feel today.

OK, ready, looking sufficiently off-putting to any casting director. Better ring Shelley.

'Hi Shell, how are you? Could you walk Badric for me today? Great. Yeah, I'll catch up with you later.'

Shelley is Carla's daughter, she's nineteen, three years older than Carla was when she had her. She's lovely, tall, towering over Carla, with huge eyes and frizzy black hair that she's always straightening. She doesn't think she's lovely, but she's happy to be tall. She told me that even if you're ugly, if you're skinny and tall you can be a model and that there's always the possibility that a scout from an agency could be sitting next to her on the number 49. She's doing catering at college and was an avid follower of *Wives*. She's happy to walk the dogs for a fiver, and a Barcardi Breezer or three.

Keys, make-up, which coat?

Badric gets up, stretches, shakes and looks at me hopefully.

'No, you be a good boy and go back to your basket. Mummy's got to go and see if we can keep you in high-class dog food for another six months. Auntie Shelley will come and take you out later.'

I'll probably have time myself later, but I've got work to do. That's what a ten-second turnaround in a small room in Soho is; a day's work.

The casting's alright, as they go. Go in, register, hang around eyeing the competition, wait, wait, and finally get called in. Grovel, grovel, do my bit. Try as hard as I can, for me, for Jenny, for the credit cards, for the dog. It's a car ad, and it shoots in Cape Town. It's all over in a flash, I've no idea how I've done. Years ago I'd have done a painstaking post-mortem on the thing, but these days, I try to forget about it as quickly as possible; ego-damage limitation. It's just luck, a numbers game. Either you look right or you don't. Either you sound right or you don't. Either one of them fancied Shiraz or they didn't.

As the bus chugged its way as slowly as a motor vehicle could down the King's Road I wonder about David and what the evening would bring. David. Mr History. The funny thing is that since we split up, I've started to get into it. History makes more sense than now. Probably didn't to the people that lived through it, but that's distance for you. But it's hard to get the facts into your head without drama, without people. Shakespeare knew that. That's it! Soapumentary! Forget prose. Write what you know. A script. And where to begin? The year 693, naturally. I can see it now, see the words on the page ...

Badric's Island
by
R.L.Jameson

Badric, our hapless Saxon King sits by the banks of the river polishing his shield.

B: Damned be that accursed Abbess. Over my dead body shall I grant her my pretty Ege.

41

> Cut to an Abbey where we see a beautiful
> woman, writing a letter to a friend.
>
> (her voice)
> Dear Sister, Greetings from this vile
> place they call Barking. For barking is
> what I shall be lest soon I have what is
> rightfully mine, that swamp they call
> Badrices Ege, so handy for Chels Ege.
> That fool Badric swears that he shall
> never leave, I shall have to employ all
> my womanly wiles to make it mine without
> giving up my abbey and resorting to
> hideous matrimony...

Obviously all the major female roles would be played by me. I'd finally get the chance to wear that absurd 'balcony' bra that David gave me, because it's a well-known historical fact that in the past women's breasts resided somewhere up near their clavicles, and they were always half-popping out. It might even be in Olde English with subtitles, but a general sort of *Blackadder*-esque, Old-ish English will do for now.

A phone is ringing. Several people in my area of the bus fumble in their bags.

Sorry, all you folks with phones that never ring; it's for me. I've got a life!

'An ad? Shame on you traitor-woman!'

'I know, I know. Just filling in till I get that call from the RSC.'

Carla wants to know if I'm up for a spot of DA later, after their rehearsal. I can't tonight. I've got to sort this thing out with David.

DA. No, not Disco Aerobics, Direct Action, and I drive the getaway car. Have you ever wondered about those

'THIS ADVERT DEGRADES WOMEN' stickers on bill-boards? OK, so you don't get as many as you used to but they're still there, and the big ♀s? Well, that's what Carla, Mica (her keyboard player) and I do for kicks. Me, the woman who lives off adverts. But what can a girl do?

As for *Chefs' Wives*, OK, it's hardly Shakespeare, but it is a study of madness isn't it? A sort of modern madness; madness-lite, all artificial ingredients and totally fat-free. Anything too real might have detracted from the glittery appeal of it all. Might have put people off their food, if it hadn't already. But, a girl can dream, and an idling bus is as good a place to do it as any. Beats thinking about David, anyway.

Oh yes, it's just a matter of time – the day my definitive Ophelia is eulogised on *Late Review*. Kirsty Wark's chin propped in her hand, smiling as Germaine Greer announces that this is the Ophelia she'd waited for all her life, Bonnie Greer nodding vigorously in agreement. Tonight it would be unanimous: Tom Paulin would say that he couldn't remember the last time he was so moved by a single performance. And God, would I be busy! Jenny would be on the phone constantly telling me about this or that interview. Off I'd go to Manchester to the BBC to say the words I've rehearsed so many times, 'Thank you, Jenni.'

Just to clarify, this isn't scary agent Jenny, this is Jenni-with-an-i Murray, and it's *Woman's Hour*. We've just finished discussing said definitive Ophelia at length.

'Thank you, Jenni,' ever so 'umble, like, 'I'm just a normal working mum...' (OK, this may be taking the fantasy a little too far.)

'Thank you Jenni,' bold, proud, not quite so 'umble, 'I'm just a pioneering child-free woman...'

'Cheers Jenni!' Chummy, as if we hang out in the BBC canteen every day in droves, we women of the moment.

'Thanks Jenni.' As if to a good mate in the full knowl-

43

edge that I'd be back again soon to discuss my next ground-breaking performance on the West End stage. Or maybe my rip-roaringly funny, devastatingly witty and supremely ironic soapumentary, soon to be made into a full-length feature film and heralding a new dawn in the women's movement; 'neo-feminism,' or somesuch, because you're worth it, in case it slipped your mind for a millisecond.

Badric's Island: it's not about historical fact, just an exploration of how to wrest power from the powers that be, with nothing but a pair of cantilevered breasts at your disposal. Or that's what the men like to think. No, I retract that, Jenni. That's not what neo-feminism is about at all. Mustn't generalise. Unless referring to advertisers or superpowers.

Where were we? Oh yes ...

Hildelith *(the Abbess)*, and nine of her nuns have come to terrify Badric into acquiescence.

H: Hey-ho my Lord, I've heard that a fine dwelling is going for a song in the parish of St. Reatham, soon to be the most sought after address in these parts. It's some way hence by cart, but a mere stone's throw as the crow flieth. *(Tittering from the nuns.)*

B: *(aside:)* But she's a damned fine woman and no mistake. How I long for knowledge of her frontispiece ... 'tis pity she's a nun.
Dear Abbess, prithee sit awhile and discuss this matter. Allow me to relieve thee of thy cloak. The Lord would not

```
wish for thee to hide the bounty with
which He in his wisdom hath thee so
adorn-ed. (He makes a grab for her
garment.)
H: Unhand me, Sire! (More titters.)
B: Damn thee woman! Conspirest thou to
unhinge me?
H: (aside:) Yea forsooth, unhinge thee
from this place, which is mine by the
decree of destiny!
```

Hey, there's Nina. I'll get off and walk. It'll be quicker anyway.

'Nina! NINA!'

She's pushing Thai, the überbaby in his superbuggy, dressed top-to-tootsie in Poppy and Sam which, try as it might and despite the astronomical expense, doesn't manage to make him look cute. But it's not his fault. That's the problem with lifestyle choices. Nature doesn't give a damn, but give it time ... The day will come when you can buy the perfect infant to go with the gear from Poppy and Sam with interest-free credit for the sleepless years.

She's only been Thai's nanny for a month or so. She was sacked from her last job. The wife was convinced that something was going on between Nina and her husband. It's a shame really because nothing was. He was only giving her a few driving lessons. Or that's what she told Carla and me. Little Charlotte was inconsolable, because she'd spent more time in her short life with Nina than with her parents. And if the husband didn't fancy her then he must have been the only man in South West London that didn't ... apart from Giacomo that is.

Nina is Polish, with a certain Eastern European glamour on a budget. She always looks good. She's the queen of the second hand shop. She really should be doing something very important in Brussels, she can speak Russian, German, pretty good Spanish and her English is better than mine.

'Hi, Rachel! How are you?'

'Fine, I think...' I say a cold 'coochy-coo' to Thai, and we walk together over the bridge.

It's high tide under a sullen sky, the river is swollen and angry. Looking down at the grey-brown of the depths I see that it's already on the turn, little eddies and bubbling whirlpools marking the change of direction. A drake, who thought he might just hitch a ride down to Hammersmith is just about to be pulled back in the direction of Vauxhall. It's good to live by the river. It's so reassuringly uncontrollable, but don't tell that to the Thames Barrier.

I tell her about Scotland and the casting.

'How was Suffolk?'

'Oh, it was beautiful, really beautiful...'

'And ... how's it going with Adrian?'

Adrian is some bloke she met whilst doing a cleaning job. Adrian must have thought he'd won the lottery when, expecting a Hilda Ogden lookalike, Nina walked into his flat. Suddenly, the ironing didn't seem quite so pressing (pardon the pun).

'It's going really well, actually.'

Actually? I sense a 'but', but she's not going to expand. Well, you don't do you? You blank any 'but' that rears its ugly head for at least a month. You're not defending him of course, you're defending yourself; defending the choice that you made, all by yourself ... with a little help from a hormone or two.

'Good, that's great. What's his place like?'

She says it's idyllic; it's the England of a holiday brochure. In fact, it reminded her a bit of her grandmother's place in Poland where she spent all the happiest days of her childhood.

Uh-oh, sounds fatal. I tell her about the David situation and she gets inflamed in that ferocious Slavonic way of hers.

'The bastard! God! Why aren't you furious? Don't you dare sleep with him or I'll never speak to you again!' One of these things is likely, the other isn't.

And why wasn't I furious? It's a good question. I explain that every time I start to think about it, my brain just goes off at a funny tangent.

'That's because you still love him.'

We hug and say goodbye. She turns off down Thai's street and I head for home, thinking about what to wear for dinner. Bad. Bad thought. Maybe she's right.

7

David

Shelley's sitting on the sofa watching telly with Badric snuggled up to her when I get in. He gets down dutifully and sidles over with one of Ferdie's surprisingly inoffensive trainers in his mouth, just to reassure me that I'm still his Number 1.

'Hi, Shel, thanks ever so much. Nice walk?'

'Yeah, how are you? I'm really sorry about your granddad,' she says, looking down, embarrassed.

'Thanks.' For some reason I also look down, embarrassed. I give her a fiver and tell her to hang around if she wants, while I have a shower.

'Can I?' she says, like it's a treat.

'Course you can! Is Ferdie in?'

'No, they're rehearsing tonight aren't they?' Oh yeah. Goody. There's a space in the hallway where the bongos or congas, I can never remember which, the big ones anyway, usually are, covered in take-away menus and junk mail. A ball of dog hair drifts around the vacancy like tumbleweed.

Thou shalt not make a special effort. Thou shalt not shave thine legs. Thou shalt not deliberate over underwear. Thou shalt not tidy thine bedroom.

*Thou shalt not check to see if that ancient condom
is past its use-by date. But thou shalt, thou shalt.
And thou shalt tell yourself that it is force of habit,
that it is for you, that you may be run over crossing
the road on the way to the restaurant and that
to be caught without an approximation of a
matching set would bring unendurable shame and
dishonour upon thine house.*

I'm feeling guilty now. I want to stick the hair back onto my legs. I want to pull on some horrible old pants and scrape my hair back. I want to go to the King's Ransom as nature intended with my genuine femaleness there for all to see; nature red in tooth and toenail. I shall not wear a bra. I shall not wear perfume or jewellery or anything else that shall hide my true vileness. Natural woman I shall be, and proud of it. Because what the world sees as female is actually a lie, a damned lie to which we all conform. We've been made to feel so guilt-ridden about the fact that we do not look like Barbie; that we are such complete failures because our bosoms do not defy the laws of gravity; that we spend fortunes on trying to cover our shame, because we're worth it. And now I feel guilty for not being able to throw all that stuff out, to liberate myself from the tyranny of the tweezers. Germaine! Did you really want me to feel guilty? Did I really need more guilt? Can a bit of mascara be as bad as putting yourself under the knife? Does it have to be all or nothing? Please Goddess, let a little bit of feminine frou-frou be OK. If not, then I'm just going to pretend that I'm a drag queen trapped in a woman's body, and that make-up for me is what it is for Eddie Izzard.

The King's Ransom looks like a set from you know what. David's there already, peering at the wine list. You don't get any old house plonk with David.

He gets up.

'Hello again.'

And it happens. The tide turns. Yesterday's fury forgotten and fondness floods my sad female heart as I remember a million starry evenings in extortionate eateries all over the South East and beyond. Suddenly the things that infuriate me about him become all part of his strange, overgrown boyish charm. I can hear Nina's voice in my head, 'Don't you dare sleep with him or I'll never speak to you again!'

'Hi,' I say, in a-couldn't-care less, petulant sort of a way. Because it wouldn't do to let him get away with it that easily. As if I eat at the King's Ransom every day of the week, as if I'm not hungry anyway. He doesn't notice this display, or doesn't react, which is just one of the many things that makes me adore and want to throttle him simultaneously. We um and ah over the menu and order. The *maître d'* knows my face, although he can't quite place it, thank God.

'So, how have you been?' he asks, innocently.

'Look, David, can we cut the pleasantries! Why did your wife slap me yesterday? I can't believe she's just taken all this time to get round to it. I want to know what's going on, if that's not too much to ask.'

I know that her name is Fiona. But 'your wife' is better. It's nice and bitter; it dehumanises her whilst emphasising the wanton breakage of vows. I can't call her Fiona. I can, however, call her 'bitch,' 'cow,' or anything derogatory that comes to mind. She is my rival. This is where sisterhood goes out the window as quickly as hair up the hoover. It's awful, horrible, foul, hateful, because I know in my heart that, in another life, Fiona could be my best friend. I could so easily be sitting with my arm around her saying, 'God, what a little, whoring, immoral bitch!' Because one day it could happen to me. It has happened to me, albeit without the wedding. I know exactly how it feels; betrayal of those exclusive rights to someone's flesh for the duration of the relationship, or 'farce', as it's now become known. I know, because he went back to her, and while I may like to imagine that they went to straight to Peter Jones and ordered twin beds for their new sex-free union, somehow I don't think so.

But I knew the facts, had the choice, and that's what makes me guilty too. Worse than him perhaps because, well, men are men aren't they? They can't control themselves; absolute slaves to it, poor dears. We should think ourselves lucky that they aren't dragging us screaming into the bushes every two minutes. Thank God for civilisation. Yep, I knew the facts. But since when did facts come into it? If he's got the right bits of the immunity jigsaw that your DNA is seeking, you've had it. You can smell it, allegedly. It doesn't matter if the bloke with the lovely house and the double first from Cambridge is down on one knee, if Mr Rightgenes walks past carrying a hod laden with bricks and *The Sun* newspaper under his arm (or has a wife at home for that matter), you're doomed.

But what about love? Love at whose flower-strewn altar we humbly worship. It puts an end to every argument, every gruesome fact-filled argument, which finds you spelling out the reasons why this man must be expunged from your existence, can be quashed by four little words; 'But I love him.' You can't argue with it. And it can't be just down to the hormone that keeps you together for as long as it takes to have a baby, because it can last for years ... supposedly.

> ***Rule No. 4:*** *However sorted you think you might be, when it comes to this particular issue, you're lost.*

Carla's mum used to be a Relate counsellor. She told her that, after everything she'd heard and seen over the years, she honestly didn't believe men and women were meant to be together long-term. She realised she had to quit the job when she started recommending that people cut their losses and split up.

'She's upset at the moment...' he says nodding at the waiter who's just given him a taste of the Sancerre.

'Oh well, that's OK then.'

'Well, I've had a lot on my mind lately, been a bit distant.'

'Oh for goodness sake, David, will you just tell me why?' I look at him and then realised that in his book, which is a fairly tightly closed one, what he's just given me passes for an explanation. 'Do you mean you're in a spot of bother?' That should cover it. David's an Englishman after all, the sort of person that refers to terminal illness as 'a bore', the family home and contents being razed to the ground as 'a nuisance', or the violent death of a loved one as 'unfortunate'. This could be seen as a virtue when contrasted with the unholy stampede for therapy, to deal with the fact that you just found out that your mum used to flush the dead goldfish down the loo and get another one before you came home from school. I don't know.

'Fiona and I...' I give him a look so terrible that he changes tack. '... and I'm being made ba ... ahem ... ahem.'

'Sorry, I didn't quite catch that'

'Bankrupt. Bankrupt.' He says it twice so there could be no mistake.

'Oh.' I don't really know what to say to that, not really knowing what it means. 'So, how come I'm the chosen one?' Surely his accountant might have been a better bet. 'Well, I'm sorry to hear that David, really.'

He always seemed to be doing good business; hence our weekend trips to sites of historic interest; part of our relationship that wasn't a relationship because we never got past the exciting bit. David's an antique dealer, which suits a man like him because it affords plenty of opportunity for ducking and diving, subterfuge and lies. And when the big deals didn't come off there was always a hungry market in the States; people who just couldn't wait to tuck their home entertainment system (telly) into a crappy Edwardian wardrobe, to which no one in an Edwardian conversion back in London would give house room, even if they could get it up the stairs.

But I can't keep up the nasty act. One glass of Sancerre down, three or four to go. Or maybe we'll go on to red.

'I can give you some cash, as rent, just for a week or two, and I wonder if I could leave a few things with you for a while,' he says.

'David, I can hardly charge you to sleep on the sofa!' Then again, I don't see why not. That's when he looks at me in that rather attractive way of his and I start to feel myself blush, and I nod, muttering, 'Yeah, whatever.' Treachery – that's what it is. Treacherous body of mine, I should have left you at home.

David is now asleep, the years have fallen off his face in the moonlight and he looks like a boy. I don't want to go to sleep. I want to talk and laugh and put on some music. I want to read out all the interesting and funny bits from the pile of books by my bedside. I certainly want to smoke. I feel energised and alive. Not like him. He is spent like a match, dead to the world. Oh how the mighty have fallen! Not *veni vidi vici,* rather, *vidi veni snori.* Conquered? Not me. I feel like running naked round the park. In fact, that's what I'm going to do. No, not naked, don't worry. Wouldn't want to scare the rapists.

I get up, put on some tracksuit bottoms and a jumper and go downstairs. It's half-past two and Ferdie's sitting in the darkness with the TV on. Shit. I'd forgotten about being a heartless philanderer. I didn't hear him come in. I should just sit down and tell him that the other night didn't mean anything and that David is here, and that I am really sorry for hurting his feelings, if indeed I have, which I may not have done at all, in fact I could just be a complete ego-maniac to assume that it meant any more to him than it did to me, but God, it's tiring even thinking about it and I am in some sort of post-David state that I wish to prolong so I say nothing.

'Hi Ferd!' 'Hi Rach!' We both whisper as you do when there aren't any lights on.

Badric comes through from the kitchen, banished as he was from my room earlier.

'How was rehearsal?'

'Oh, not bad, but Lien was an hour late.'

'God, Carla must have been livid!'

Lien, pronounced Li-en is the lead singer. Lien is Neil backwards. That's how cool he is.

'I'm taking the dog out.'

'I come with you ... is dangerous for you...'

'No, really, I've got the dog...'

He makes me tell him the exact route I'm going to take and says if I'm not back in half an hour he's coming to get me, and to take my phone. In fact, I'd say the same to him, because more blokes get jumped in the park than women.

London belongs to the night now, and it's quiet, magical. The park gates are locked but this doesn't stop us, Badric does a limbo dance and I squeeze through the turnstile and we're off. And it's not scary or cold and it's not even that dark. It never is in London. But even so we see a fox and hear an owl hoot. Wild and free all of us, and Badric's ears flap and my hair flies about as the wind dances with the high trees and so what that David is in my bed and anyway I wanted that, for I am she, *Woman who runs with The Dog.*

8

Carla

I wake up on the sofa still in my wild woman gear and with a terrible headache. I go through to the kitchen to find that Badric has experimented with bulimia, which is not his style at all. Then I find a chewed fragment of the empty packet of Edinburgh Rock in his basket, with a few pastel crumbs left inside and I understand.

'Badric! Come here!'

He skulks over, head bowed, tail between legs, condemned, then looks up at me with his ears flattened against his head and the whites of his eyes showing. That's how scary I am. I look at him. He looks at me. And that's as far as it goes. It's funny to watch the relief flood through him, reaching his tail, which begins to wag slightly as if to test the water, then with positive ecstasy when I say, 'Poor boy, were you a sick doggy in the night?' and make a fuss of him.

I'm clearing up the revolting mess when I hear someone on the stairs. I hope it's Ferdie and that he goes straight out because I really don't want him to see David coming out of my bedroom. It is Ferdie and he's on the bottom step when noise from above makes him look back to see David coming out of my bedroom. He looks at me and raises his eyebrows.

Aargh ... surfeit of lovers in my kitchen. Go away! Be gone, both of you! And take the dog for a walk while you're at it. I want my house to myself. I want to listen to all the impossibly erudite people on *In our Time* with Melvin Bragg, and feel crap about my life. I want to have a healthy breakfast of Alka-Seltzer and coffee, followed by a long bath to wash off my big mistake.

My 'big mistake' is asking me where I got to in the night. I glare at him as if to say, 'Shut up, I don't want Ferdie to know that ...' To know that what? What he plainly knows anyway? It's devilish complex, and I can't cope with it.

'David, help yourself to coffee,' I'm going to have a bath.

The phone rings. Shit, sound wide-awake and business-like – it's Jenny.

'Hi darling! Good news! They'd like to take another look at you ...'

No. No, not today please. I know I've been a bad girl but ... 'tomorrow.'

'Great! Thanks, Jenny,' grovel, grovel. 'I'll be there!'

What a relief. I know exactly how Badric felt ten minutes ago. This calls for radical beautification.

'Darling, I'm going to go and get a paper,' says David, a little too comfortably, 'Shall I take the dog out?'

I think I brought that about by sheer force of will.

'That would be great.' Forget the bath. 'I'm going for a swim.' I can't get out of the house fast enough. Miss Jackson's curtains shift as if lifted by an internal breeze. Must remember to get her an Edinburgh Rock substitute, shortbread maybe, Tunnock's Teacake – something Scottish.

Splashes and shouts resound with that particular acoustic of the swimming pool, hard-edged smacks as the sound belly-flops against the water. Ears out of the water and I hear it, ears under and I don't. A bit of peace, a bit of quiet, off the island for half an hour or so, my goggles affording me a good view. Some way off, shadowy, clearer as I approach I see what I like to call *The Dance of the Manatees*. It's an awesome, wondrous sight to behold, and seems to happen most days at about 10am. This session is otherwise known as Aquaerobix for the metabolically challenged. Seeing these creatures move in time to *Black Velvet*, with a delay caused by resistance, you feel reassured that the human race will survive after all. That nature knew best all along, that the layering of fat was but a pre-emptive strike against the coming flood when the ice caps melt. As all the stick insects are swept to their deaths, these noble creatures will survive, line dancing down the submerged High Street without getting their hair wet.

> **Rule No. 5:** *When solitude is craved, company will call, and vice-versa.*

I get home to find them both still there. I wonder if this is some sort of territorial stake-out. David is looking though a file of paperwork. Ferdie is making a juice. The atmosphere is thick, broken only by laughter from some comedy repeat on the radio, the distance between the two men as wide as the Atlantic Ocean.

'Good swim?' asks David.

'Yes thanks, I didn't really expect to find you still here.'

'I'm just leaving, I've got an appointment.'

'Oh.'

Good.

Ferdie hands me a glass of liquid virtue, for all the good it will do me.

'Carla rang, she said could you give her a call?'

It's time to face the music, time to confess. You can't get away with the, 'But, I love him,' argument with Carla. Even though she's a self-confessed lonely heart and accepts this as a fatal flaw, she doesn't suffer fools; female fools at least. I go upstairs to ring her from my bedroom. David follows me upstairs.

'Look, I know it's a nuisance, me imposing like this...'

'David, it's fine.' Not. 'If you need somewhere for a day or two, that's OK. But as for last night...'

'Yes,' he says, advancing.

'No,' I mutter, retreating, 'Last night was a one-off. Very nice and all that but it doesn't mean ... I don't have to spell it out. If you are here tonight, it's the sofa, OK?'

'Yes, yes of course,' he says, unconvinced and unconvincing.

I've known Carla for about three years now. I met her in the park. It was one of those dead-inside, nothing's-ever-going-to-change days, in a break from filming, when there's nothing to do except go for an extra-long walk, hiding beneath my shades and baseball cap. I'd rowed with David, again, saying that I couldn't wait forever, that the situation was untenable, immoral, awful, that the nights apart were getting to me, blah, blah, blah.

These days are great for the dog. He gets an extra-long walk and you can pretend that you are not talking to yourself but to the dog—even if he is fifty yards ahead of you, as he was when I saw him stop, suddenly unsure of his eight-month-old self. I hurried forward to see a woman struggling with a bloke. They stopped when they saw Badric, and quick as a flash the man jumped on his bike and was off.

I ran towards the woman, who was shouting after him, 'YOU FUCKING BASTARD! BASTARD!!!'

'God, are you OK? Did he hurt you? I think maybe we should tell the Park's Police,' I said, trying to stay calm.

'Yeah, I suppose so,' she agreed, composing herself, 'though fat lot of good that'll do. Hey, aren't you in that Chefs' thingy?'

We introduced ourselves and made our way to the Park's Police Station, if that's not too grand a name for their Portakabin HQ.

'D'you want me to come with you?'

'No, I'll be fine.' She went inside.

Badric and I waited outside. The least I could do was offer to walk her home. After about ten minutes she came out, looking angry. I felt myself rise in her defence.

'Is that it?'

'Yeah, more or less. Made me fill in a form, describe the guy, you know. Said I should go to the police and report it, but it's probably not worth it.'

'No! Do you think they didn't believe you or what?'

'Yeah, they believed me. They just don't give a toss. They say it happens all the time and there's nothing they can do about it.'

Jesus! Talk about defeatist. I'd a good mind to go in there and make an enormous fuss. It had to be thought: if she were white would it be a different story?

'All they were bothered about was the fact that you're not supposed to ride a bike on that path!'

Bloody hell! Unbelievable!

'Are you sure he didn't hurt you?'

'Oh yeah, he hurt me alright! Cost me eighty quid, just last week too!'

What? Sorry you've lost me.'

'…Yeah, bought it out of Loot. Last one got nicked too.'

I put my hand up to my mouth.

'What's the joke?'

'I'm sorry … I thought he was attacking you!'

She put her head back and roared. 'I'd like to have seen him try! He was only about fourteen!'

She said that she'd just sat down for a minute to reply to a text from her mate when she heard him jump out of the bushes and make a grab for her bike. She was really pissed off because it was good exercise and she enjoyed it.

'Maybe you should get a dog.'

We put each other's numbers into our phones and went our separate ways.

A couple of days later she rang me.

'I've decided to get a dog. I don't know much about it … I was wondering if you fancied coming to the Dogs' home with me sometime this week?'

Of course I did. Going to the Dogs' Home sounded every bit as good as an afternoon on the sofa watching a weepy, in terms of an emotional workout, in terms of research. Never know when you might have to play someone suffering from post-traumatic stress disorder. Because that's exactly what it was – a trauma. I'd never been there before. And by the time we came out I was ready to sell up and devote the rest of my life to the cause. I don't even want to talk about it. I'll only say that no amount of *Animal Hospital* is going to prepare you for that. Happily, the outcome was that Carla got Jessie, a three-year-old collie-cross, Jessie got Carla, a thirty-three year-old Caribbean-cross, and Badric and I both got a New Best Friend.

I shoo David out of my bedroom, (twelve hours too late) and ring Carla.

'Can I come over this afternoon? I'll tell you about it then. I need to get out of here.'

The first time I went to Carla's flat I felt as if I'd entered some sort of shrine to the Goddess.

'God, Carla, this place is gorgeous!'

My house seemed like a sterile, angular, minimalist, if dog-hairy, hell, by comparison. That's the problem with minimalism, its possibilities are so limited. It's not that I'd made a special effort to be minimalist, it's just that the mortgage seemed like the ultimate luxury and I'm useless at the rest. I can't really be bothered, in truth. I try, I try, but when I casually toss a throw over a chair, it just looks as if I've done what actually I was doing, i.e., trying to cover up the dog hair. My walls are painted white not only because it's the cheapest paint, but because committing myself to a colour is beyond me. I see it as a sort of post-modern symbol; a can't decide, won't decide, too many choices, you-decide-for-me symbol, while I sit on the fence, or stepladder, with my pot of white paint.

Soft Options by Delux! Take the pain out of painting!

She asked me if I wanted a cup of tea. 'Sorry, I don't do cow's milk.'

'Oh ... don't worry, whatever you ... do ... is fine.'

She disappeared into her kitchen and I looked around. It's a council flat, ground floor, with a little garden, two bedrooms, kitchen, bathroom, and living room. She told me that she got it ages ago because she was a single mum.

'Result!'

'Innit!'

She said that when her daughter, Shelley, left, she did it up.

The walls are painted bold colours, with ethnic look-ing wall hangings and plants everywhere, piles of books and a guitar. She brought out the tea and, wait for it... a cake THAT SHE'D MADE HERSELF. I noticed a couple of framed photographs of a good-looking bloke on the wall and wonder if this is the father of her child.

'That's my brother Michael. He died of meningitis four years ago on Christmas Eve. He was ... great.'

I cross Battersea Park Road, leaving the rarefied atmo-sphere of South Chelsea and enter what is for a lot, if not most people round here, the real world: past the pub where some man got shot last month for his phone, not because it was so outmoded that he had to carry it in a paper bag, causing a policeman to believe that it was an AK 47, but because someone else in the pub wanted it. Yes, South Chelsea-ites, it happens. Past the off-licence with the metal grid over the counter, past the council finance office, past 'Ali's Kebabs,' catching sight of Ali, who waves. Carla and I go in there sometimes. Ali gives spit-roast new meaning. He's tougher than yesterday's left-overs and only a fool would mess with him. He looks like Blackbeard, he's got a patch over one eye and a cutlass under the counter, probably. Past the community centre (closed), the Afro-Caribbean grocer (closed) and another off-licence (open). Past the gigantic Lego-like blocks that the council sold off as quick as you could say scam, then down to the blessed relief of the old low-rises, made of something you can recognise as being of the earth, i.e., brick, surrounded by things which you can recognise as being of the earth, i.e., trees.

I tell her my sorry tale, full of remorse and woe and she makes some chamomile tea and we smoke some of her ropey old last year's home-grown, and she doesn't tell me off. She knows what it is to be tidal in your resolve. What it is to be lonely. I do not, however, tell her about the added complication of having been to bed with her percussion player (again). I have no idea why not, only that it implies that I feel less guilty about David, the married man, the bastard, than Ferdie, the unmarried man, the nice guy.

9

Bogof!

Badric and I walk back through the park. I'm stoned; not very, just enough to want to avoid anyone I know to whom I cannot reveal this fact. Suddenly, the world is full of such people. The shortbread I bought for Miss Jackson on the way home is burning a hole in my pocket. I had every intention of getting some fruit and veg, but I'd achieved enough.

'Hello there young lady!' It's Barry Big Binoculars. 'And hello to you too Baldrick!'

I'm going to get a T-shirt printed saying, HIS NAME IS BADRIC!

'Have you seen it?' He says, excitedly.

'Seen what?'

'The Pintail. She's a new arrival!'

'No, sorry.' Wrong response. Is he looking at me strangely or am I being paranoid?

Ruff Guy and Mush come up from behind. Badric immediately does his Ridgeback impression, but I'm glad because Ruff Guy is a perma-stoner. He feels weird and paranoid when he's straight.

'Alright Barry, Rachel!' he says, but Barry's not listening, he's off, scanning the skyline for avian UFOs.

Ruff Guy tells me some tale he's told me before about

some bloke who trashed his van. He says he's going to get him tonight and shows me the end of a length of heavy-duty chain that he's got up the sleeve of his jacket.

This place is mad. I'm tired and I'm hungry and I've got this bloody thing tomorrow and I wish I hadn't smoked that weed. Ruff Guy goes off to hunt his quarry and I get home. The house is empty. David's done some shopping. The fridge is full of luxury items and I hardly know where to begin. I open a bottle of wine, put on some music and dance about a bit with Badric and now I'm glad that I did smoke that weed... and I hope that they all stay away, because I need to catch up with myself, do some washing, some housework. I like that stuff. Probably because no one's telling me to do it, I'm no more obliged to do it than Ferdie, and he does his share, but it's a good thing to do. It marks an ending and a beginning, even if it is only the ending of a mess and the beginning of a mess. It's the expression of my inner wee wifey, and try as I might, she will not be silenced. I even write to Nana, and give my parents a call.

'Hi Dad, how are you?'

'Not too bad. I'll get your mother.' It's a cliché, but it's true.

We talk and I ask her how she's feeling. I should be there. I feel guilty. I want to ask what it feels like to lose your dad. I want to ask her if having had me makes it better, makes more sense of it. But it's not the time. She assures me that she's fine, that she's going to go and stay with Aunty Agnes for a couple of days, and that they were all happy that he didn't suffer too much. I tell her about the recall for the ad and she sounds pleased.

It's not the career they would have chosen for me; too risky, too irregular. Mum is more sympathetic than Dad. She knows all the words to the songs in old musicals and we used to watch them together some afternoons. She was a midwife, thereby an expert on hopes and dreams.

She told me that she'd wanted lots of children, but that my birth was a fuck-up (my words, not hers), some doctor bodged it and that put an end to her child-bearing years as quick as you could say hysterectomy. Carla reckons that's why I can't fight my corner; it's an only child thing. *I'm just a girl who can't say no*. Tra-la. Dad's an engineer and sees the world in terms of nuts and bolts. The first production we did at college was *The Insect Play* and I know it's a bit weird, but he didn't have to fall asleep ... and snore.

There's an expensive looking holdall behind the sofa. David's. I look inside it, and it reveals nothing other than some clothes. Bor-ing. Not even a history book. She must have kicked him out quick-time. I can't help it, I take out the navy jumper and press it to my nose for a minute then stuff it back in again. A few years back this situation would have been a dream come true, him turning up with his bag. Funny that.

> **Rule No. 6:** *Dreams are dreams and reality is reality and never the twain shall meet.*

I feed Badric, arrange some things on a plate for myself and put the telly on, flick around from make-over show (house) to make-over show (garden) to make-over show (woman). This woman wants to look like Barbie. She's already had a 'boob job', and she's working hard on her 'gorgeous' fake tan.

Her mum – yes, mum – is ooing and ahhing over her daughter's stupendous new 'boobies'. She bore her, she raised her, but she could not supply her with superboobies to order, unlike Dr Frank(enstein) Schultz. He's prodding them too, telling her that the scar will disappear, and if it doesn't, well, she can get it tattooed orange to match the rest of her.

The programme flashes back to a couple of weeks ago. Our wannabe Barbie is in tears, sore, bruised and bandaged. Let's try it this way round for a laugh. A man, his groin sheathed in gauze, tearful, apprehensive, nods deferentially, reverentially, at Dr Shultz, (a woman), who is peeling back the bandages to inspect her handiwork, telling him that it may be painful for a while, and to refrain from touching it other than when strictly necessary. Once the pain subsides, he may experience some loss of sensation.

This man, we'll call him Dick for argument's sake, is looking up at his dad for reassurance, who pats him on the shoulder, telling him that it'll all be worth it in the end. The doctor is happy. She stands back and smiles. The silicone implants to plump up and elongate Dick's penis have worked a treat. At last he passes muster.

Now it's the ads. This BOGOF thing really annoys me. And you'd have had to be on the Space Station for a decade or so not to know what it's about. In my case it's more BUY ONE GIVE ONE to FERDIE! if he's around. BOGOF really rubs salt into the wounds if you're single. You know damn fine that it's well beyond your capacity to eat two watermelons before the 'eat by' date. I know this because I've tried. I've eaten watermelon for breakfast, dinner and tea before now. I've even tried something revolutionary – *proscuitto e melone d'aqua,* considered making a delightful calorie controlled *sorbet de melon d'eau,* or even injecting the bloody thing with vodka and having a crazy party or ... sod it, chucking it into the bin. But that's not as easy as it sounds, its diameter exceeding that of your stylish slimline chrome kitchen waste receptacle.

The 'OF' of the BOGOF duo awaited its fate, accusingly. It haunted me as it dominated the fruit bowl. I started to feel sorry for it, to empathise with it as it sat there forlorn and alone, its flesh going soft, its seeds drying up, never to find their way back to the earth, never to multiply. That's what I'll do; give the poor thing a decent burial. Take it into the garden, get Badric to dig a hole for it, drop it in, cover it up, say, 'God Bless You', and leave it at that. But Dog Brain thinks it's a game, digs it up again and nudges at it with his nose. But even he doesn't want to eat it. Right, that's it. I'm scooping out the seeds and drying them, painting them different colours and stringing them together to make a necklace, a fertility symbol, and I'm going to wear it for the rest of my fucking life. And when they see Shiraz in tears (oh come on, it's not Hedda Gabler for Christ's sake! Did you think I could believe in that?), the raw emotion wrung from my very soul, they will never guess that it's not born of abandoned puppies, or lorry loads of little lambs going from Wales to Greece with no water, but from the wasted life of a watermelon. That's how sensitive I can be. One day I even caught myself feeling sorry for mould.

I pour another glass of wine and sink back into the sofa, slowly, seductively, to the libidinous saxophone music that is inviting, or should I say inciting me to indulge in Temptation by *St. Valois*. Sounds good already! First we see a besuited gent driving away from a grand house. Cut to a young, oiled bloke glistening in a sarong. He approaches a 90% naked woman lying in a hammock in the garden, reading a book (she's clever as well as pretty), one long, tanned limb dangling invitingly over the side. Not that she's interested in him, God no! He's just a slave! Probably gay, that's the only sort her ancient husband would employ. But then again ... She looks over her sunglasses and we begin to suspect that her husband may have been duped, as the gleaming hunk holds out a pot of Temptation on a silver salver, and she spoons it slowly, suggestively, into her mouth. As if to imply that it's a mere substitute for... Well I'm sure you can guess ... that's right, a Flake. Anyway, the good news is that it's virtually fat free. It's virtually virtual, this pot of chocolate air, it uses up more calories spooning it into your pouting mouth than it actually contains.

I can resist anything ... but Temptation!

Oscar Wilde would be so proud.

Next, it's skincare. Women's makeover show – no point in trying to flog them garden shed preserver. (Which does actually work, unlike the death-defying cream made in France.) Skin care products are often made in France, like the chocolate mousse. That must be why French women are so sexy and chic – they've got the scientists they deserve. A couple of pots of this love, and we'll have you looking like Brigitte Bardot aged 17. And I prefer the French when it comes to these matters. I want, nay expect, my skincare products to be made in a *laboratoire*, in a *clinique*, where flawless women weave their way between arum lilies to mix droplets of essential oil of rose with dew and almond milk. Not some nasty laboratory in Slough, full of men, animal fat, canisters of chemicals and red-eyed rabbits, oh no, that wouldn't do at all.

I put a couple of blankets and a pillow on the sofa just to underline the point, let Badric out the back, sit on my cold garden bench and smoke a cigarette, resisting the urge to have another glass of wine. It's a nice night, sharp, colder than it's been of late. I'm tired, but my mind is racing. The burning issue is demanding attention but I won't have it. Not tonight. If I go in there I may get horribly lost and never be seen again. If I try to work it out I might start something I can't finish. Which is a tendency of mine. I contemplate my gym ball, sitting redundant by the back fence, last year's bindweed unable to disguise it like a sad comb-over on a bald head. I wonder how many of these things roll around SW11, unused and forgotten, yesterday's fad. I remember Badric's attempts to get his jaws round it, like a shark at the hull of a ship. The idea was to sit on it and tone up whilst watching telly. Too much wine got slopped onto the floor, I found.

Badric and I climb the wooden hill and I can't believe that we've made it; the house to ourselves for a whole evening. I settle down in bed with Germaine Greer. Carla gave me *The Whole Woman* for Christmas. I turn to the chapter called *Manmade Women* to try to shed some light on the makeover show. I read that that Japanese prostitutes who attended to the 'needs' of American military in the 1940s had industrial grade silicone injected into their breasts (as oppose to that all-natural breast grade silicone, I suppose). Jesus. I turn the light out and consider positioning *The Whole Woman* in front of the door to act as a sort of ideological shield against possible intruders, i.e., David.

I think about tomorrow, about what to wear, then totally weird and unrelated thoughts tell me that lovely sleep is approaching when ... the doorbell rings. Badric leaps up and barks and I put on my dressing gown, cursing he who forgets his keys. But it's not David or Ferdie, it's my enemy Ter*ay*sa. I say 'enemy' with feeling. The parking is one thing, but the regrettable poo incident is quite another.

I was taking Badric out for his morning stroll soon after we'd moved in. He was very excited to be living so near to the park, and obviously felt that the whole world was his friend, being so blessed. I didn't yet know her name, so when my neighbour exited her front door at the same time as us, I felt it would be a good time for us to introduce ourselves. She was about my age – we could be friends!

'Hello, I'm Rachel, and this is Badric,' I said. At that moment, Badric's lead slipped out of my hand and he bounded happily towards her, to say hello, and hopefully not to jump up on her white trousers. As he did so, she swung her handbag at him, hitting him around the head, not very hard, but hard enough.

'Get him away!' she cried, 'I hate dogs!'

'There's no need to hit him!'

'I'm glad I've caught you,' she said, coming closer now that Badric was firmly back on the lead, 'I thought you might be able to explain this.' She raised her eyebrows at me, whilst pointing at the pavement. I look down.

'Well?' she said.

'Well what?'

'It's dog shit!' she declared, triumphantly.

'I can see that.'

'Well it's a bit of a coincidence that you move in and a day later there's dog shit outside my house!'

I looked at her. I had just learnt that she wasn't a dog lover, but even so, a basic grasp of biology, anatomy or whatever would prevent most people from equating that, which was so small as to be evidence of a desperate Chihuahua, with a Labrador.

'You don't think Badric is responsible for that, do you?'

'Well, he's the only dog along here.'

'But it's too small!'

She looked at me as if I were a poo fetishist, a dog shit expert, someone who likes nothing better than to measure do-do and to thereby deduce from which breed it has emanated ... or something.

'Well someone better clear it up,' she said as she flounced towards her car.

I was speechless.

'Sorry to bother you, Rachel, I've locked myself out and wondered if I could climb over your back wall? I think I can get in through my kitchen.'

'Well, I suppose so...'

'Thanks,' she says, smiling a tiny smile. I've never witnessed this phenomenon before. I was starting to think she'd had Botox injected into the wrong place by accident.

'Come in.'

She skirts around Badric pointedly.

It's almost worth it to watch her struggling over in her

leather skirt and fabulous boots, especially when Badric loses it, barking like mad and snapping at the very high heels. Somewhere in the dim recesses of his canine mind the words 'person', 'wall', 'climbing over' and 'intruder' had got all mixed up. I really should have offered her the use of the ladder.

'Bloody window won't open! I'll have to come back... Rachel, could you please call your dog off!'

Repeat procedure in reverse.

'You'll have to break a window and get someone out to fix it.' It's quite simple, love.

'No, I can't, Mark will go mad at me. Could I wait here until he gets home?'

Why would he go mad at her? And why should she care? Strange.

'OK, but...'

Ferdie, you angel, I think as he walks through the front door.

'Ferdie, Teresa's locked herself out. She's going to hang around till her husband gets home.'

'Oh. No problem,' he says, heading for the fridge.

'Sorry Teresa, I'm going to bed, I've got an audition thingy in the morning.' For once, I'm looking after number one, because I'm worth it.

'Of course. Do,' she says, giving me another teensy smile.

Right, now it's getting serious. Beauty sleep top priority.

Now what? Something considerably bigger than Badric is worming its way under my covers.

'David?' I put the light on, and yes, it's him, there, next to me.

'Sorry, sorry, don't wake up. It's just that there's a girl on the sofa.'

The clock says half past three. Don't get angry, these things are sent to try us, just ignore him, I say to myself.

10

The foie gras episode

There's no need to explain how I feel this morning. Refer to **_Rule No. 3_** if in any doubt. Not that a recall for an ad is enough to make this one of the most important days of my life, but you know what I mean. I could do with the money though, that's for sure. Or that it's the day of the first episode of the rerun of _Wives..._ but that just might help with the casting.

I get up, and quick as a flash Badric's off the rug and onto the bed for a lie-in with David. I shower and get myself together, determined to feel rested and optimistic even if I'm not. Sometimes exhaustion brings to the face a strange, untamed quality, which is not altogether unattractive. Or it could be just your eyes not working properly.

I go downstairs to find Teresa still on the sofa. She stirs and opens her eyes, sits up and looks around.

'Oh God, Rachel! I'm so sorry, I didn't mean to...'

What? Eat the biscuits that I'd bought for Miss Jackson? The packet is nearly empty and there's another wine glass in the sink. Someone must have had a midnight feast.

'So, Mark didn't turn up?'

'No. And his phone's been off all night.'

'Oh.' Dear.

I make some coffee, take one over to her, eat the last two

biscuits, leave a note telling, not asking, David to take the dog out, say to Teresa that I hope it gets sorted soon, give her the card of the glazier that I used last time, and head for the front door.

'Good luck for your audition thingy,' she calls after me.

I've got loads of time. It's only half past nine and it's not till eleven. I could get a number 19, or alternatively I could sit in a café and have a cappuccino, then get a little private bus, black with an orange light on top, in which I can touch up my makeup to my heart's content. It's a business expense anyway. And they'd hardly be expecting Shiraz to arrive on the Clapham Omnibus now, would they?

I get there on time, go in, same routine, come out, that's it. None the wiser. Jenny rings, asks how it went. I tell her it was fine. She says that things are a bit quiet at the moment, but not to worry, it'll pick up again very soon. I can feel her relying on the *Wives* re-run. A bit quiet means dead. It gets to the point when you'd do anything: wear a giant sausage outfit for a supermarket, or accept the part of the back end of a pantomime horse, the front end being occupied by a vegan who's recently had lunch. At least I get the occasional voice-over to keep me going. Ever since someone decided that Scottish voices sell, I got lucky. I do a lovely Scottish – well of course I do. I am Scottish. Scottish, you know ... from Scotland, somewhere further up north than 'Up North'. Well out of the way.

Yes, I know what it is to be flavour of the month at Word of Mouth, the voiceover agency, or 'Gobshite' as Carla and I prefer to call it. It got to the point last year that *'Your home is at risk if you do not maintain payments of any loan secured on it...'* popped out of my mouth involuntarily now and again, and so quickly you'd almost miss it, because it's small print.

I try but cannot justify a cab for the return journey, so I sit on the bus wondering how to fill the rest of the day. I miss Haden. I can't wait till he gets back. He knows just how hard these work-free days can be; nothing to do but sit around eating and drinking, moaning about it and toying with the idea of getting a job ... a proper job, I mean. A total change of career; teaching maybe, or perhaps becoming an astronaut. It's all part of the deal. It's called 'resting', and it really would be nice to do a bit of that this afternoon, because tonight's the night for some DA. Yesterday, Carla said she saw an advert down at Nine Elms that needed sorting. I feel uneasy about it. I want this job. I always want the job, ad or not. And like it or not, there's going to be a bit of attention thanks to Sky TV, isn't there? It just feels a bit dodgy. Maybe it just gives the whole thing a new twist, added weight. Oh God, who cares? Let's face it; of late it has given meaning to my existence, it transforms me into a secret agent. That's how I've been squaring it anyway, working for Gobshite et al. Fact is, I haven't got the guts to refuse Carla and Mica tonight. After all, *I'm just a girl who can't say n*... My phone rings. I look at the screen. Angus.

'Gus! Hi! How are you?'

Gus is not happy. The love of his life has dumped him. It could be that the funeral had been a bit much. He's at Heathrow, he's got a meeting at three but could he come over later, and stay for a couple of nights just while he gets his head together?

'Yeah, of course. Great! See you at, what? About six-ish? Course it's OK!'

You cannot say to a heartbroken cousin, 'Sorry, got a bit of a house-full at the moment!' or 'Ever heard of hotels?' You just can't. But that's what I can, must and shall say to David at the earliest opportunity.

Right, no messing about. Straight into the shop, no hello from the moody git today, straight to the biscuits, to the finest shortbread FoodEtc can offer, grab a sandwich, to the till, out again and straight to her front door.

'Oh hello, dear. You've been busy!'

'Have I?'

'All those parcels and boxes that came this afternoon. Been doing some shopping for the house dear?'

Miss Jackson never did quite understand the minimalist look. She used to do a bit of cleaning and ironing for me when I was rich, when I was a huge star.

'I think you must have got the wrong house... ' And policemen might have wings. I produce the shortbread and hand it to her.

'Thank you, dear. How thoughtful of you.' I catch a glimpse of the FoodEtc price tag at the same moment as she does.

'I'm sorry, but Badric ate your present.'

'Did he, dear? Never mind,' she says, giving me that 'And your homework too, I suppose?' look.

I take a deep breath and stride up to my front door. I go in to see Ferdie on the landing outside my bedroom holding a ladder, and David's legs and feet protruding from the hatch-thing that is the entrance to my attic. I hear him thanking Ferdie and saying something like, 'All done!'

'What's all done?' I enquire, to which they both peer down at me and say 'Hi!'

David comes down the stairs first, Ferdie follows with the ladder, which seems a bit rich. Somehow I don't think this alleged delivery had anything to do with him.

'What the hell is going on, David?' Ferdie leaves the ladder in the hall and makes haste to his room.

'It's just the stuff I mentioned at the restaurant ... a few things that I need to store for a while. Remember?' No, I don't remember ... or do I? A hazy recollection of a mention of storage emerges from the Sancerre misted memory.

'I'll pay you the going rate. Whatever you like.'

I wonder what the going rate is for a bit on the side?

'Well it would have been polite to ask.'

'I just said that I did.'

Snookered. 'Whatever. Has Badric been out?'

'Yes, but just to the shop and back. How did you get on?'

I ignore him, call Badric and head for the park. I want to eat my lunch in peace. I'll get a drink from the café and then sit in the quietest, darkest corner I can find.

'Ciao bella! Come stai?'

I smile weakly at Giacomo, pay for my drink and escape. Luckily, the lunchtime rush is on, so he's busy. I head for the river and eat my sandwich as I go, causing Badric to walk impressively to heel for a few minutes. I watch a heron fly overhead in the direction of Chelsea Creek. Barry told me they go there to catch eels, drawn to the warm water outlets of Lots Power House, with its huge arched windows and tall chimneys billowing steam clouds into the sky.

I pause at the old jetty, chained and padlocked, the gateway to the Fun Park, and picture it – the tree walk and the crazy house, the colour, the smell of candyfloss, the firm grip of Dad's hand on my wrist.

David told me that Julius Caesar crossed the Thames here, to subdue the Catuvellauni tribe, whoever they were. There must be so much stuff down there, under the mud, under the shopping trolleys. We used to walk on the foreshore at low tide, when Badric was little, before he took to water. I wouldn't take him down there now though, the currents are vicious, deadly. I have nightmares about it, his being sucked away from me, spiralling down to join the torques, the coins, the rings, the daggers, the guns; the mudlark's dream hauls, as I run up and down the bank, frantic, calling him, cursing myself for ever letting him go.

The brackish smell of the muddy low-lying water takes me back. David's little outboard; nothing special, just a fibreglass job called *Boudicca*, or *Boo* to her friends, lost to a storm one night, breaking her moorings and ending up squashed under the back end of a houseboat. But before she met her fate, off we'd go, Badric's head sticking out of my jacket, and WOW! It was fantastic! Brilliant! Special to be out there, overtaking the Blue Circle cement barge, waving to the Harbour Master, his bow wave making us rock and spill our mugs of wine as we passed under Albert Bridge, then Chelsea, on to Vauxhall, Lambeth, Westminster, Waterloo. David shouting things that I could only half-hear above the motor and the spray. Past the Globe, up the slippery green ladder to the Prospect of Whitby then home in the half-light, his one arm on the wheel and the other round me because I was shivering, drifting into a cobalt blue Whistler nocturne. You couldn't not be in love.

One thing did lodge in my mind; that when Cleopatra's Needle was finally erected on the Victoria Embankment, a time capsule was buried underneath. Now, what will the historians of the future think of this? In it was placed: four Bibles in different languages; Bradshaw's Railway guide; copies of that day's newspapers; and, this is the bit that really gets me, photographs of 'twelve of the most attractive women in the country'.

Cleopatra would be so proud.

When I get home David has gone out. Ferdie is watching TV and asks me if I'm OK. I tell him that I'm fine and he asks no questions.

'What's with all the flowers?'

'Oh, the girl from next door brought you some, and so did your friend.'

Blimey, it's starting to look like someone died.

'When did Teresa go?'

'About half past eleven. Her husband is come to get her. I dunno, they were fighting in the street and she is very unhappy,' he shrugs.

'Oh dear.'

I contemplate going round to see if she's alright, but his car's still outside, so I think better of it and head upstairs for a powernap before Gus gets here. I ring Louise to see if we can't make it into a full-blown cousins' night but she's not up for it. Shame, I was half-hoping, OK, three-quarters hoping that Gus might prefer a night on the floor in her room in Bermondsey. She's got a new bloke, she tells me. We all know that you should refrain from seeing this person every night until you are ready to drop down dead with exhaustion, but...

'Don't worry, enjoy yourself!' Not adding, 'while it lasts'.

Hooray! I slept, for one hour and fifty-two minutes precisely; a more than respectable result. I have a shower and wait downstairs for Gus's arrival. Seeing the ladder still in the hallway I experience a surge of rage, and wonder whether I should go up and investigate. Before I have the chance he arrives with flowers and champagne. He looks around.

'I'm glad to see ye like flowers, Rachel! I thought they might be over the top!'

'Yes, I have to have flowers in every room, you know. It's a London thing,' I say, finding a cracked jug with a poor dead spider in it that will pass for a vase.

He opens the champagne. POP! Badric leaps up for the cork and bats it around the floor, kitten-style.

'Thanks for this. What are we celebrating?'

'Well, apart from you being on the box tonight, my lucky escape.'

We raise our glasses.

'A lucky escape!'

A lucky escape from Helena, who wanted him one minute, didn't the next, cost him a fortune, pranged his car, flirted with his mates, drank too much. Who seemed so perfect, at first. But of course.

I sympathise, spout all the requisite platitudes, refill his glass and repeat till it's all gone and he's feeling better. We giggle our way to the nearest dog-friendly pub to get some food. We say how it only feels like yesterday that we saw each other and then remember that it was only three days ago. Bloody hell! When I tell him what's happened in the meantime he goes quiet and looks concerned, but I laugh it off stoically and change the subject to his work. He's something called a 'Process Manager,' which seems to me about as complicated as organising the entire universe, but he enjoys it. The only thing is that he won't really be taken seriously till he's a bit older.

There you have it in a nutshell. You see, when it came to role models, we women pulled the short straw. They got God, the Father Almighty, Maker of Heaven and Earth, as old as the hills, looking a bit like Charlton Heston with a long white beard. We, on the other hand, got the Virgin Mary, aka Mother of God, about as old as Charlotte Church (mind you, even she's getting on a bit), whose baby, begotten by immaculate conception ends up getting crucified in front of her. That or the *clitorati*, the thousand or so crotch-rubbing love-children of the other Madonna. Great.

Gus goes to the bar and orders. I watch as he tries to make himself understood. Really, with all those Scottish voices on the telly and radio these days you'd think it would be easy by now. He comes back and says that this place isn't too friendly. I know this, but find myself defending London, as if it needs defending. One huge glass of wine costing as much as a bottle later, and I'm desperate for my food, and watch in outrage as people who came in after us get served. There's a tennis ball on the table with our number on it (it's a sport-loving place with a wide-screen TV), and I'm starting to get the urge to lob it into the kitchen by way of a heavy hint when it finally arrives. Fancy food. Posh pub-grub for the culinarily challenged, but it's OK – there's bread as well. The waitress gives Gus the eye, she's as thin as a pin, dangerously thin, ill-thin. I decline the offer of more to drink. I need coffee now. I need to sober up, I've got to drive later, but I don't tell Gus this. He thinks I'm being good, which I am, in a way. He isn't though. He's in the mood for oblivion and starts to get maudlin about Helena. What was a lucky escape a couple of hours back is now a tragedy. She was lovely, beautiful, intelligent, kind, and he fucked up, bigtime. Do I think she still loves him? Do I think there's still a chance? Do I think he should ring her? Don't know about the first two, but as for the third, no. No. Definitely not. Yes, she may well be half-expecting a call, but the sound of him slurring in a pub in South West London is not going to help one bit. Trust me on this one, Gus.

When we get home Ferdie and David are there. David said he was going to cook for me, but since we've eaten he'll ring for a pizza. He and Ferdie pore over the menu in strange, matey fashion. Gus opens another bottle of wine and Ferdie skins up. What does Ferdie think about all this? About David? What would David think if he knew about Ferdie? Do I owe either of them anything? My fingers stray to a spot that is lurking just beneath the skin on the side of my nose. I am happy about the arrival of this spot. This is a premenstrual spot. Sure of it. Everyone is settling down in front of the telly. I protest, but it's too late. Jesus, that fucking music. Never send to know for whom the theme tune tolls; it tolls for thee.

It's the *foie gras* episode.

'Oh please, do we really have to '

'YES!' they chorus; the drunk, the stoned and the bankrupt.

It's the opening of Ricardo's new restaurant in Notting Hill, to which he's invited a couple of hundred of his closest friends, all of whom he secretly despises. It's tipped to become the place to end all places. Picture the scene: the beautiful people; the fabulous décor; the tiny fried quails eggs on little hash brown cakes strewn with morsels of bacon; the three skewered baked beans on a slice of quality sausage; a fried cherry tomato on a square of black pudding; a wild mushroom astride a triangle of fried bread. The journalists are busily thinking up their articles for the Sunday supplements. 'Absolutely brilliant'; 'Po-mo party food to dine for'; 'Ricardo, in his inimitable style has forgiven the fry-up, brought home the bacon, edified the egg, martyred the mushroom, beatified the bean' and so on. And bingo! Fully booked for the next three months. The champagne flows, Ricardo surveys his new domain with a thinly disguised sneer of satisfaction on his ruggedly handsome face, before his eyes lock on to the bare back and perfect behind of Mercedes, wife of Jean-Pierre, his arch-rival in squash, cooking and life. Shiraz clocks this, grabs the wrist of her friend Angel (short for Angela) and they go off to powder their noses. Or rather, the inside of their nostrils.

'That bitch Mercedes is after Ricardo...' etc, etc.

I go into the kitchen to make some more coffee. I wish I hadn't had that wine. I look over at Gus, Ferdie and David. Gus and Ferdie are enjoying themselves, getting stoned. Gus calls over, 'God Rach, you look great in that dress! Shame we're cousins!' Like father like son. I look at David. Whereas Gus, and possibly Ferdie (although we've never really had that sort of conversation), think it's crap, but a laugh with plenty of eye-candy to boot, David thinks it's profoundly crap. I can see it offending him to the core. I have the strong urge to go over and kiss him.

The doorbell rings. That'll be the pizza. Badric goes berserk when I open the door.

The man backs away.

'Take your helmet off! Your helmet! I point to his head and mime taking a helmet off, 'Take it off! SHUT UP, BADRIC!' I hold on to his collar and he makes choking noises.

Our man gets the message. 'Sorry, I can't hear a thing with it on.'

'No, I'm sorry, it's just that when someone comes to the door wearing a crash helmet he thinks it's some sort of raid.'

'Oh, right.' No smile, he just hands over the outsize box and the bill.

'Hang on.' I put the box down in front of David and Ferdie, get cash from David and see that the scene has changed.

The VIPs are now dining, Ricardo's sourced the best *foie gras* the world has ever produced, and gently warmed it. It is sublime. He's sitting next to Mercedes and we can only hazard a guess as to what he's doing with the hand that isn't conveying the *foie gras* to his precocious palette.

I pay the pizza man. It's the usual, 'I'll make a real business of rummaging for the right change so that she'll tip me the whole lot' performance.

'Keep it,' I say. Could be a resting actor after all. I'm just about to go in when I see Teresa pulling up in her car. I want to thank her for the flowers. She's wearing big sunglasses despite the darkness and looks pale. She's half in the disabled bay, but it's not the day to challenge her.

'Hi, Teresa, thanks for the flowers!'

'Oh hello, Rachel. I just wanted to thank you, that's all.' She looks away.

'Forget it. Are you OK? '

'Yes,' she says through trembling lips, and hurries to her front door.

'Hey, Teresa, let's have a drink sometime.' She nods and goes inside. Ah, the mystery that is Teresa.

Back on the home front the viewers, including Gus, despite the pub meal, are tucking into a pizza the size of a wagon wheel. And I don't mean the eponymous disappointingly stale-ish biscuit of yesteryear.

'Rach,' says Gus, a string of mozzarella giving him some trouble, 'Why don't you go blonde again? It suits you.'

I ignore him, and he doesn't pursue it, distracted by the row that Ricardo and Jean-Pierre are having. Jean-Pierre tells Mercedes that they're leaving, grabbing her by the arm. Mercedes shakes off his arm with a toss of her dark hair, and suddenly clutching her stomach, rushes towards the loos, her tanned face distorted with pain.

'You've poisoned my wife now, have you?' Jean-Pierre smirks. 'The papers will love this!'

Now look, look closely at Shiraz, look at that tiny smile,

that knowing look, that total grasp of the situation. She knows, you see, knows all about Ricardo and his ways, but knows too that she is his rock, his safe haven from which he can stray like an alley cat, to mix metaphors. He doesn't know how much she knows, she doesn't know how much he knows she knows and so on. She'll bide her time; she's the Queen of the *Chefs' Wives* and it's not a position to be taken lightly. But don't worry, she's not going to get too powerful, because she loves him too, and it hurts. And an eating disorder will keep her in her place. And Jean-Pierre can threaten Ricardo with the press all he likes, but they all know he's got too much to hide to ever say a word. Honour among thieves.

I look at myself. That was good that bit. Blonde, I don't think it suited me at all. I remember the camp hairdresser telling me that my 'plain' colouring was great, a real bonus, I was lucky, because it made me a 'blank canvas'. Yep, that's me. Rachel the Blank Canvas. Come! Project upon me what thou will'st.

There I am again, this time in our bedroom. Ricardo is pacing about in his Calvin Kleins. I have just accused him of what I know to be the truth: that he and Mercedes have been at it again. He laughs this off, telling Shiraz she's being ridiculous. She's not sure if she is or not. He tells her to get a life.

'Get on and write that bloody book you're always on about,' he says.

'I am getting on with it,' Shiraz hisses and flounces in to the en suite, where, fingers down throat, taps running so he can't hear, she gets rid of the mini full English. She didn't touch dinner; Zsa-Zsa, her miniature poodle, sits at her feet under the table like a live waste disposal unit. She's waiting till later, till he's asleep. And of course she's not getting on with the book. Her PA, Isabella, is to do it for her, but Ricardo must not know this. Shiraz wants more than to be a Chef's Wife. She wants a piece of the pie (not to eat). She is 'writing' a lifestyle book, to include dietary tips, an exercise regime, some homespun philosophy and supper recipes, 'How to tempt the taste buds of a top chef' with gorgeous pictures of herself placing a humble yet perfect omelette, or somesuch before the great artiste. Posh 'n' Beck's style. At home with Ricardo & Shiraz. Something like that. Isabella is busy trawling through Nigella, Delia, Nigel Slater, Jamie Oliver et al, finding the recipes and mix 'n' matching till they sound like something Shiraz could have learnt at her mammy's knee (if her mother hadn't spent most of her life in the insane asylum, but that's another episode). The producers actually considered making this book in real life as a clever-clever marketing tool for the series but, in the end, nobody could be bothered, and the copyright issues were more complex than the recipe for Madhur Jaffrey's Diwali feast.

Half a bottle of mouthwash later, Shiraz appears from the bathroom ready for bed, sexy soap-star style. Ricardo begins to ravish her. I look at David's face. He's trying so hard not to mind, to suspend disbelief, but he can't. It's quite funny. I shall never, ever, tell him that Haden is gay. Any minute now Shiraz is about to learn once more what it feels like to be a *foie gras* goose. The credits roll. Thank God that's over. My audience claps and cheers. David may be a good liar but he's not so good at acting. That was nearly as painful for him as it was for me.

I leave them to watch whatever they want and go upstairs. I email Haden.

Hi darling,
Have just seen us at it. Are you really sure that you are gay because we make a lovely couple and I can talk to you about Shakespeare and you are fucking gorgeous and clever and kind and funny and I want your body.
Rachel xxxxxxxxxxxxxxxxxxxxxxxxxxxxxxxxxxxxxxxxxxxxx

Only joking.

Hi darling,
My house is full of men, are you jealous? How's work?
Hurry home, need a sanity transfusion.
Rachel x

11

Direct action

I've still got hours to kill and now I'm caffeined up to the eyeballs. I put on my tracksuit and go back downstairs. Gus has crashed out on the sofa and David is in the kitchen talking to someone on his phone. Ferdie gets up, avoids my eyes and goes to his room. I call Badric as I put on my trainers. He's happy, stuffed with pizza crust. David mouths to me to wait. I wait.

I did want to run, but a walk with David it is. The park gates are locked, Badric squeezes under the turnstile, but there's no way David can squeeze through the gap so I call him back and we head towards the bridge, turning down to the riverside walk. David reaches for my hand but I shake it off, then wish that I hadn't, then feel glad that I had. You know, the usual tedious round of conflicting crap.

'David, I really think it would be better if you went to stay in a ho...'

'Look!' He points at a fox creeping out from behind a bush, his eyes flashing in the streetlight. Badric gets a whiff of him and charges. The fox dissolves into the darkness and he gives up.

'I think it would be better if you found somewhere else to stay, if you can't go home.'

He stops and turns to me.

'I thought, I mean I was...'

'You thought that we could pick up where we left off and start living together without even talking about it? What planet do you come from, David?'

We walk on, both knowing that we are heading for the churchyard. I could just say, 'Let's go back now.' But I don't. The temptation, the lure, is too great.

This was a bad idea. I feel sick in that gut-wrenching way that I always feel when I come in here. David used to call me 'Blondini' after a certain Madame Genevieve Young, aka 'The Female Blondini', who crossed the Thames on a tightrope from Cremorne Gardens on the Chelsea side in 1861. Not because I ever attempted this daring feat, but because of my daring feat of a blonde day's filming of *Wives*, after which I'd rush back here, to *Swan*, his little houseboat that he'd had for years, since before he was married, keeping her as an office, and the rest.

There's another boat in her place now, a small Dutch barge called Trojan, and I'm glad because for her still to be there, going up and down every seven hours would only make matters worse. Or *Boo*, or his old Volvo, the only car on the planet that could accommodate a crappy Edwardian wardrobe. Just to remind myself that there are worse fates, I seek out my favourite gravestone belonging to the poor boy who roasted to death in a lime kiln.

I look up at the church clock. It's after midnight. Wordlessly, we head home and even if Gus wasn't draped uncomfortably over the sofa with his mouth hanging open I suspect we'd have gone upstairs together.

I get David off to sleep and wake myself up in the best way I know how and soon it's time to go. Washed, dressed, text Carla and back out into the night. Now I'm a Sandinista, a guerrilla, I'm wearing my combats for a reason. We three are about to meet again. Look out billboards, look out London night, here we come! While you sleep your living conscience will do its worst. Look out Foyle and Fagherty; your nemeses approach!

Shit, I should have started the car earlier. It's been sitting here for days and it's stone cold. Come on, come on! I'm not sentimental about my car. It doesn't have a name, or a little cardboard Christmas tree emitting the scent of the pinewoods, or a converted bead curtain over the driver's seat, or an amusing sticker or two on the back window. My car is really just a travelling basket for Badric, and smells like it, so I'm told. Not to me, I'm immune. Anyway, you can't be sentimental about an ancient Renault 5 with a silly bubble-and-stripe motif down the side.

The car coughs into life and I head for Carla's where she and Mica are waiting.

'Alright Rachel?' says Mica, getting in as Carla holds the seat forward.

'Hi, Mica. Not bad, and you?'

'Surviving.'

I mutter something about just having seen *Wives*, then regret it because it's naff to say you've just watched yourself on telly: a naff thing to say and probably an even naffer thing to have done. Anyway, too late. Mind you, could be a sort of passive-naffness not to mention it at all.

'Shit I meant to record that for Shelley!' says Carla, 'she's been going on about it. I think she's going to ask if she and a couple of her mates can come and watch next week's round at yours'.'

'Yeah, fine.' I say.

Mica says nothing. We get on OK now, but she used to be wary of me. I think she saw me as the enemy. She was one of the few people that remembered me from the Pasta Perfecto ad, a particularly idiotic charade for sauce in a jar that had the potential to change your life, fooling your dinner party guests into the bargain. Carla must have done a good PR job on me, because all of a sudden she seemed to change her mind.

Carla gets in and off we go. Quick as a flash we're in Nine Elms Lane. The offending billboard is at the Vauxhall Cross end. Difficult venue this; a bend is better, or somewhere less well-lit, not so busy. Even at half past two in the morning there's a fair bit of traffic. If it's impossible to park nearby, it's my job to do a loop, and pick them up as I come round again. This is the case tonight, unfortunately, because in my devil-may-care mood I'd have preferred to get a bit more hands on. I let them out and drive round the one-way system, jumping when a police car screams past, watching the night walkers, the stumbling drunks, the clubbers, the homeless. Round again and I see them, I get a good look this time, Carla's little, light as a feather, Mica's big, powerful and Carla's on her shoulders. She's finished, she's down, perfect timing, I'm there, they're in, we're off, giggling like mad. This is the best bit. Mica sticks a tape into my ancient car stereo, one of her old put-togethers, women only for the occasion. My mind flits annoyingly to David in my bed. Mica promises to do me a copy as soon as, and we bounce around in our seats as I zoom over Lambeth Bridge, up to Parliament Square, across Westminster Bridge and back to Vauxhall, pulling up on the opposite side of the road to admire our 'adjustment'. It's a triumph, it's a goodie; it's legible, loud and clear.

A woman, or should I say young girl, is looking down admiringly at her own implausible cleavage, her breasts squashed against each other by a black satin Miracle Bra. Underneath this, shouts possibly the most patronising, insulting, infuriating, little phrase, which we've all heard at some point when accused of hysteria or having a tantrum, fit, rage, whatever, *PULL YOURSELF TOGETHER GIRL!*

Oh, ha bloody ha!

Carla has superimposed two free-falling breasts onto the image, crossed out the text with a wiggly line of black aerosol paint and written under it, *LET YOURSELF GO!* ♀♀♀ You just can't argue with that.

We're at the lights by Battersea Park station when Carla says, 'Bloody hell, Rach. There's you!'

I look up at the billboard by the bridge to see my blonde self standing in the middle of a stainless steel kitchen, with that hateful creature Zsa-Zsa tucked under my arm. The fingers of my free hand are straying towards a gleaming Sabatier. There is a second's silence followed by a snort of laughter from Mica which sets us all off again, making me forget to drive when the lights go green. This is not a good idea in the middle of the night because it makes you look drunk. However, the minicab driver behind us doesn't toot, but that's not altogether surprising. It is a fact that a fair few of the minicab drivers in South West London have little or no knowledge of the area, English, and quite possibly, the Highway Code.

I drop them back at Carla's, Mica's going to stay over, she told her other half they were having a girls' night, truthfully. Carla asks me in for a smoke, but all of a sudden I'm knackered. She comes round to my side and puts her head in the window.

'You OK?' she says, putting her hand on my shoulder.

'Yeah, I'm just tired, that's all.' She looks at me knowingly.

'Have you told him yet?'

No I haven't told him yet. I don't even know if it is 'yet'. I don't know if I'll tell him at all, ever. Why should I? Why should my life be an open book and his as closed as the Great Library of Alexandria? I shake my head. She leans towards me and gives me a kiss on the cheek, and I head for home, thinking about Wives as I go.

Shiraz and Zsa-Zsa. Rachel and Badric: compare and contrast. Two women who love their dogs like children, in both senses of the phrase. Who feed them scraps; in Zsa-Zsa's case, more than scraps. If Zsa-Zsa were a real-life dog and could give thanks, it would be to the God who deemed that she should be the cherished pet of a bulimic married to a celebrity chef. If he could be, Badric would be jealous. He'd have put himself up for the part like a shot. But God forgive me, dog lover that I am, that creature really got on my nerves. Her real name was Henrietta and she came from an agency called Pets 4 Sets. She would arrive in a pet carrier and spend almost as long in make-up as me, where she was shampooed and fluffed up and fussed over by some, not all, of the crew, while she did this extraordinary thing which despite the cries of, 'OmiGod how sweet is that?' gave me the creeps. Being an acting dog, at some point in her little doggy life, she'd noticed that when humans bare their teeth it is a friendly thing, not the bad vibe that it is in the dog world. God knows how she survived if she ever did go out for a walk (which I doubt), or maybe she reserved it for humans, but the thing would smile. It would look at you and ingratiate itself with this bizarre rictus, made all the more macabre courtesy of the shiny black gums, and the fact that it was a smile never to reach the doggy eyes (as I said, she was an actor dog.) Seriously fucking weird, and when she turned this grin on me, with my knowledge of canine etiquette, I couldn't help but assume she was being aggressive, so must have given off some sort of chemical signal which she understood on some deeper level, changing her expression subtly into a true baring of teeth, which no one else seemed to notice. I'd say, 'Look, Henrietta's getting annoyed now!' eliciting the response, 'Rachel, what is it with you and that dog? You're paranoid!' On a couple of occasions she'd vindicate me by snapping at my ankles. I got a Christmas card last year bearing her image, the creature grinning her demonic grin with a halo superimposed and some wings on her back, 'with love from 'Zsa-Zsa' and all at Pets 4 Sets' … signed with a paw print.

I squeeze my car into the space behind Teresa's badly enough to nudge her bumper. Not that I'm the sort of woman who does this on a regular basis, or drives ten miles to find a parking place into which I can manoeuvre without reversing. No, I'm a 'good little driver', or so Barry told me last week when I saw him standing in the wind and rain on St John's Hill and felt that just waving and driving straight past would be bad karma. It's usually taken for granted that a man is a 'good driver' but a woman is a 'good little driver', you know, with a specially modified car with really long pedals for her ickle leggies and a fluffy pink cushion on the seat, extra-large mirrors to help with the spatial challenge and an adapter for a hairdryer on the dashboard. Actually, that's not a bad idea.

As I'm checking to make sure that I haven't done any noticeable damage, a tousled head appears at the rear window. Blimey, it's Teresa. She wiggles her fingers in an unhappy wave and disappears again. I go round to the side and see that the window is open slightly like she was a dog whose owner had popped to the shops.

'Teresa? Are you OK? '

'Yes thanks,' comes the feeble response.

'You must be freezing!'

'No, it's not that cold tonight.' Sounds like this isn't a one-off. 'You're up early,' she adds.

'Are you locked out again?'

'Something like that.'

'Come on, come in with me.'

'No, really Rachel...' But her resistance is very low indeed. 'I'm really sorry about this.'

Badric does a tap dance with his claws on the tiles in the hallway as if I've been away for a year and we all go through to the kitchen.

'That's my cousin,' I say, pointing through to Gus who is still dead to the world. I put the kettle on and Teresa fumbles in her bag for a cigarette and offers me one. I go through to the sitting room to find a light and when I get back she's in tears.

'Sorry, Rachel...'

'Teresa, it doesn't matter. You don't have to tell me what's going on, it's none of my business, but ...' But I'm dying to know.

'It's just Mark and I... It's my fault really, I'm just so scatty these days. He tells me that he's going to be away, but I honestly can't remember him telling me, so when he disappears, he says he told me and gets cross ... I know he's tired too, but the other day I heard him on the phone to someone and he said something like, "I can't talk now, she's here..." When I asked him who it was, he said that he'd been planning a surprise for me but that I'd gone and ruined it. I'm sure he's seeing someone else, but he says that I'm just being paranoid.'

Is that what David had told Fiona? That she was just being paranoid? There's not a lot I can say. I don't know her well enough and I don't know Mark at all. I don't warm to the man, and I think the feeling's mutual. Especially since he saw me watching him dancing in that particularly embarrassingly way of the forty-ish professional white bloke with a rhythm deficit, to a funky track that was booming remorselessly over the heads of the happy shoppers in FoodEtc, laughing into his mobile in front of the yoghurt and all-things-possible-in-a-plastic-pot display. Given this new information, I'm beginning to suspect that this bout of arrhythmic thrusting was because he was talking to the other woman, as he imagined spooning Temptation, by *St Valois* into her forbiddenly-fruity mouth.

I tell her that I'm going back to bed. I'm more than desperate to be horizontal, even if it is to be next to an adulterer. I tuck her up on the armchair. She apologises about five more times and I go upstairs with a heavy heart. Every time I begin to make sense of something, something else promptly gives me another perspective on the thing.

I'm starting to think that anyone who believes anything must be insane. To be fair, David never tried to justify his behaviour. He never told me that Fiona didn't understand him, or any of that bullshit. Of course she understood him; they'd known each other since university for Christ's sake. She understood that he didn't love her in the way he once had. She understood that he was seeing someone else. (That's 'seeing' as in seeing someone else's naked body.) What more was there to know? And I knew ... what? That he was weak; a coward for not admitting to himself and to the world that his marriage had become a sham, for him at least; for not getting out and finding out how it is to be alone like the rest of us? Or that he was a man trying to do the right thing by everyone, a man who'd gone off his wife? And why was that? What had she done, or not done, and if she had done or not done something, was that her fault? Or not? Was he just a man doing something stupid, but which he couldn't control because he was in love? After all, that was the excuse that worked so well for me.

I lie down beside the strange and familiar shape and instantly fall asleep. Soon I am Shiraz, driving somewhere in London, in a terrible hurry but getting nowhere, and Mum is beside me in the passenger seat. I've just told her what I've done, and instead of crying, which I'd expected, she is absolutely killing herself laughing. I'm trying to keep my eyes on the road when something runs out in front of me, I'm going to hit it... Shit! I sit up.

'A bad dream. A dream, that's all', David takes me in his arms, strokes my hair and says 'Shush, shush,' as a tear or two find their way into the crook of his arm and I sleep again.

94

12

Shiraz

Shiraz is a character in a soap opera. That's what I tell myself, or should tell other people, when they say, 'Be a bit
more like Shiraz!' Or the strangely obvious, 'You looked
just like Shiraz then.'

It's only rarely in real life that the truth, or the truth as it
appears at that particular moment, is spoken, usually after
a large amount of alcohol, to a loved one and soon to be
regretted. Loved ones are, of course, the best people for
this as the emotional investment/blood tie prevents them
from saying 'Fuck off', and never speaking to you again,
which is what friends, acquaintances and neighbours
could well say or do.

Not so in soaps. In soaps if someone has pissed you
off, flirted with your man, or worse, you plot to kill them.
You take them by the throat and slam them against the
wall, dig your nails into their necks until they bleed, throw
wine down their Issey Miyake outfit, key their car, whatever. Yes, Shiraz would have dealt with David in a different way altogether, and Fiona. Fiona slapping me was, in
fact, one of those rare real-life soap-opera moments. If it
hadn't been me she'd slapped, I might have cheered. Shiraz would have slapped her back and then stood in the
middle of the street shouting her head off as her rival's

huge car lumbered away. But then, what the audience knows about Shiraz, the rest of Shiraz's world doesn't. They may have their suspicions, and her therapist may know, Ricardo may know, or is in denial, or thinks it's all in the past, or is turning a blind eye... but we know. We see what goes on behind the bathroom door. We see the things that we do not see in real life: the Diana all alone in Kensington Palace moments; the desperation behind the bravado, sitting on the loo seat weeping. We are privy to the subplots of her life, the things we wish we could be privy to in real life. (Or at least I do. Next door being a case in point.)

All the world's a stage, and drama gives you behind the scenes. So, while Shiraz pops a couple of laxatives into Mercedes' champagne and contemplates a Waynetta Bobbit job on Ricardo, we also see her creeping down to the gigantic Smeg at 3am to cram *foie gras* and raw cabbage down her throat; ripping the last of the flesh from the delicate bones of a *poussin* with her teeth while she sucks warm, flattish Bolly from the bottle. We see her kick Zsa-Zsa out of the way, then pick up the wretched creature, full of remorse and leave what's left of her mascara all over its fluffy white coat. We watch as she staggers into the soundproofed bathroom (made so on her secret request), where she pukes and wretches over and over again until something inside is quieted. We feel for her as she creeps back to bed, tucking Zsa-Zsa up in a suspiciously cot-like basket at the end of the bed. Ricardo, still in his Calvin Kleins sleeps on, oblivious, as we real-lifers do, night after night, as our friends, neighbours and loved ones keep their subplots to themselves. In the morning, Shiraz will be truly sorry to hear of Mercedes' dreadful night on the toilet, but will quip with ice-cold comfort, 'Instant diet, darling.'

When I wake, David has gone. There's a red rose in wine

glass on my bedside table and a note.

Sorry you had a bad night. Badric's been out.
Lunch? xx

A bad night? Huh! What the hell did he know? Sleeping
till whatever times it was, relatively undisturbed, after a
triumph on the billboards is a good night, thank you very
much.

I look at the clock. 12.13. Great. Approximately half an
hour to regroup, then once more into the breach, dear
friends, once more. I have a shower, get dressed, and go
downstairs. No sign of Teresa. Oh dear, Gus is sitting very
still on the sofa with a horribly hung-over expression on
his face. He raises his hand in a 'Don't say it!' salute. Ferdie
is in the kitchen, the toaster is in bits and he's worrying
away at it with a screwdriver. He passes me a scribbled
note as Badric wags his whole body at me.

Rachel, thanks for last night. So sorry to have
bothered you again. T x

Two notes in the space of an hour. One thing I'll say for
this week, it hasn't been boring.

'Ferdie, you didn't have to...'

'Yessss!' he smiles at me, triumphant, 'It is now OK! '

'Ooh, well done!'

He grins. Guilt aside, I am totally seduced by this abil-
ity of his. He told me that in Brazil, in his family at least,
things were never thrown away, never given up on, until every possible avenue had been thoroughly explored.
Even then, the chances were that some little bit of a gad-
get's seemingly unfathomable workings would be carefully stored for the day when another torch or radio chose
to be a bastard. It must be great to feel you have the upper
hand when it comes to things mechanical. Must make you

feel that these things are in their proper place, well beneath you in the pecking order of life, give you a sense of control, an idea that you can shape your destiny. It must be great not to feel that a toaster has the power to ruin your day. You can get creative with your household appliances, settle the score, have a dialogue. The ghost in the machine doesn't have to mean a clogged-up juicer when Ferdie's around. Not so with computers, of course. I don't know a living soul who knows how they work. Computers are like life itself.

He starts putting it together as I sweep the implausible mountain of blackened crumbs into the dustpan and then into the stylish slimline chrome kitchen waste receptacle. It is filled to the brim; the underside of its lid spread with an odoriferous *mélange* of coffee grounds, ash, dog hair and primeval soup (organic). Ferdie sees this and smiles. We have a little ritual thing going on here. These bins have been designed with the modern couple in mind; there's no question of this being a one-man job, and I say 'man' quite deliberately, because It Is written that the taking out of bins is the undisputed domain of the patriarch; it's a sort of symbolic act, a good versus evil affair. Like, here, let me, I'll do this, I'll cast the demons out, I'll cleanse the world of all that is bad, of all that rots, of the filth and mire that you, yes, you woman, generate with your kitchen sorcery! Or something like that. Anyway, not even a superhero can get the bin bag out of this bin. He needs his woman to hold it down while he wrenches it free of its sticky base. They are in it together, for better, for worse bin liners. We complete this operation, as the bag shreds at the top, but Ferdie's got it sussed, knows just how much pressure to apply when and where, and when it finally starts to rise up, we cry out, 'EXCALIBUR!'

I have explained this to Ferdie. I'm not sure that he knows what I'm on about, but he joins in the spirit of it, for sure. I stare in dismay at the designated recycling corner. The eco-crime of driving the hundred yards to the bottle bank shall no doubt soon be committed ... again.

At this precise moment David walks in with a carrier bag from Peter Jones, out of which he proudly presents a box containing a brand new toaster.

'Oh, thanks,' I can see that it is chrome to match the bin. 'Actually, Ferdie's just fixed the old one.'

'Oh, right. Well, always handy to have a spare!' says David, disappointment flitting across his face. But it's more subtle than disappointment; that miniscule facial expression that belies something that you understand, but that would take a 2,000 word essay to explain in words. Maybe it's not even something you see, but something you feel, or smell.

'Hey, no problem!' shrugs Ferdie. And the same thing applies to him, but what I think I see, feel or smell, is something that I, like a fool, like the worst sort of philanderer, had not seen, or had chosen not to feel or smell before. I try to meet his eye and give him a 2,000 word essay back, but he looks away and heads upstairs.

'God, I'm so sorry,' says David, 'Did I put my foot in it?'

I say nothing, meaning 'yes, but not in the way that you think... '

'So, how about lunch?'

'No! My cousin's here, remember?'

'Rachel, darling,' he's getting closer, 'I need to talk to you.'

'Sorry, David, it'll have to wait.'

What a moment! The power! Now the shoe's on the other foot. What about the countless times when I wanted to talk? What about the times that I sat by the phone, obediently not ringing him? Or the times I naïvely thought we were in for a good long chat, when I would just nip to the loo and come back to find him sitting on the edge of the bed, trousers and shirt already on, fiddling with his cuffs, looking anxiously at his watch, the flush still fresh on my falling face. This is when you need a 9-5 job. The bleak indignity of being naked at half past three in the afternoon, two glasses of wine rendering me incapable of doing anything constructive for the rest of the day, apart from lie about what I'd been doing, should anyone call. Straightening the bedclothes, taking the glasses downstairs, having a coffee and a bath, vowing that that would be the last time, despising myself and him for making a fool of me and an unknowing fool of the world and his wife. Forget it. That's what you do. Forget that you have no integrity whatsoever and therefore you do not deserve better treatment, because you have to do right to get right. It's hideous. I absolutely do not recommend it if you have but the slightest concern for your immortal soul. But if you haven't ... well that's another matter altogether.

Let him put that in his pipe and smoke it.

'Oh, of course. Well in that case, I'll see you later.'

'Look, David, I really think it would be better if you went somewhere else, don't you?'

He looks at me with an inscrutable expression on his face, puts his hands up in surrender and says, 'Fine.'

Ferdie comes back down, grabs his jacket and calls, 'See you tonight,' as he leaves.

Of course, it's Carla's gig.

'Hey, Gus, fancy coming to a gig tonight?'

'Aw aye! Too right! Rock on!' he says, lying back down on the sofa.

David is still hovering around when the phone rings. It's Nina. She's got a couple of hours off. Do I fancy a swim?

Gus tells me to go, not to mind him. He wants a shower, and he's got a bit of work to do. I tell him that I won't be long, and to use my bed if he wants to sleep some more. You see, David? It's not *our* bedroom.

In the changing room I am shocked and somewhat dismayed to see that Nina has been about some radical depilation of the nether regions.

'Adrian likes it,' she says, turning this way and that to look at herself in the mirror. Europeans, Eastern-Europeans, you know what they're like. They don't consider modesty a virtue. There's something to be said for it, undeniably, but for us Brits, it's not quite the done thing. We love our guilt; the guilty thrill of the unknown, the unseen, the semi-clad. I'm all for it, personally. It's a great smoke screen. Still, I have to admit her attitude is refreshing. It makes you wonder. Were these people never taught shame? What the hell is wrong with them?

'But do *you* like it?' I ask.

'I'm not sure. What do you think?'

I look at this sore-looking area of skin that hasn't seen the light of day since Nina was pre-pubescent. (Oh I get it, pre-*pube*scent.)

'Well ... isn't it itchy?' This seems like a better tack.

'Yes, a little, and it's getting a bit stubbly and rough.'

Aha. Now I see a point to it. Without wishing to be indelicate, there are times when a man's attractive two-day growth can cause a certain discomfort to the inner thigh (if you're lucky), so why not use this patch of homegrown sandpaper for some gentle abrasion of our own, for a change?

I keep this thought to myself. But one day when the changing rooms were particularly busy (must have been Poledancerobix or something), I did hear a young girl asking her mummy if she was going to get hair 'down there' or not, as if it was the luck of the draw, like getting piano lessons or a pony.

We swim up and down, trying to hold a conversation over the noise and the splashing. I confess my sins. She said she knew I would anyway, and shows no sign of never speaking to me again. She tells me that Adrian had kindly pointed out that she had a couple of grey pubes. And this was after his caring remark regarding said pubic hair, 'A bit long, isn't it?' She said she did a home job on it. She didn't fancy getting naked for a beauty therapist with strips of wax. Can't think why not.

When I get home Gus has recovered. There's no sign of David, or Ferdie. Gus says he wants to take me out to eat before the gig. I reply unconvincingly, that although that would be great, he's my guest and I could cook something.

'Yeah right,' he says.

I could, I've got everything you could possibly need ... except the food. The pristine *River Café Cook Book* looks so good up there on the shelf, the deep blue contrasting so well with the white. It really would be a shame to mess it up.

First things first, there's a doggy to be walked. It's hard not to hate weekends in the park. I was getting over it, till he reappeared, but now it's happened again. The place has transformed into Babyville. They're everywhere. They're taking over the world.

> *The birth rate may be falling but you could be forgiven for thinking otherwise. At weekends you will see babies in buggies, slings, papooses, prams, in arms, at breasts, having their nappies changed in the toilets, being held aloft like trophies. To the point that the Government had to intervene such was the sheer number of stupid little books on springy coils dangling from buggies, should Clovis or Clytemnestra choose to display their unique genius and appreciation of literature aged four months.*

Still, not all the world has children. It's a relief to see the Fag-Arties in the distance. No, hang on a minute, that's Fag-Arty, singular. Fag-Arty whose gait does not have its usual 'up-and-at 'em' mad dash about it. We catch up with him.

'Hi, Ben,' I say, 'how are you?'

'Shit.'

'Happy families thing getting to you as well?'

'Something like that.' He looks Gus up and down, in the way only an advertising man can, as he identifies the target (and other) group to which this stranger belongs.

'This is my cousin.'

I introduce them and they shake hands.

'Fancy a coffee?'

'Is it licensed?' asks Gus.

While Gus gets the drinks so that I can avoid Giacomo, Ben tells me that Steve arranged a three-way for his birthday, and he just couldn't handle it at all. It was blatantly obvious that Steve was more interested in his birthday present than in him and that they'd had the mother of all rows and Steve had gone off to stay with a mate. But that 'the mate' must be that jumped-up little prick, because his phone's been off for two days. They did have one row by text, but that was it.

A row by text? Jesus, just how frustrating must that be? I can just see those thumbs going like the clappers, blurring as they did their sort of mad Morse code on the tiny keypad. Give me email for a row any day. But God, a row by text would make you so succinct, so concise. I stifle the urge to laugh. Gay men and their quaint birthday gifts.

13

Saturday night and Sunday supplement

The ridiculously stressful time that it takes to find a parking space in West Kensington on a Saturday night could have been spent at a leisurely pace on a bus. But, we Londoners like our personal space, our cocoons, our pods. Privacy. An Englishman's car is his castle. It's a class thing too. Going on the bus is by way of saying, 'I am Poor.' It shouldn't be like this, but it is. It's also to do with a feeling of control, that given just the right break, the right gap in the traffic, the right moment to hit the lights, you'll be away, off, up front. But most of the time you just have to sit there having your nose rubbed in it by other people's 'Baby on Board' pronouncements, as if the teddy sun visor wasn't clue enough. What about 'Dog on Board'? And anyway, is some infanticidal maniac really going to be pulled up short by the sight of a sticker?

We queue up till it is our turn to be looked up and down, perfunctorily searched and frisked by a Grant Mitchell look-a-like, then I say very loudly so that everyone can hear, 'I'm on the guest list! I'M ON THE GUEST LIST!!' I'm not just any old punter mate, I'm special, I'm in the in-crowd, so make way! They take an age to scan up and down the list, and eventually one says, 'Yep, Rachel

Jameson plus one.' This makes Gus important too, but not as important as me. Now they defer to us, stamping our hands gently so we get nice clear ones, not black blurs with a bruise underneath. It must be part of their training. 'Don't forget to cringe and fawn to the guest list. You never know who they might be, so gentle, gentle! The others though, the plebs, the nobodies, make sure to make it perfectly clear to them that they've only slipped through the net cos it's a quiet night. AND REMEMBER, NO TRAINERS.'

Actually, The Tangerine isn't a NO TRAINERS type place. More like TRAINERS ONLY.

We go down into the depths of the place. The official rummage through make-up bags and wallets is hardly worth the bother because the place is thick with the smell of weed. We fight our way to the bar and wait impatiently for our bottles of beer. If it wasn't for the fact that Carla was playing I'd be ready to turn round and go home by now. Getting here, parking, getting in, getting a drink. Jesus, you deserve a medal for going out in London. My mind takes momentary refuge in a memory of David, Badric and I sitting by the fireside in a quiet pub in Dorset, all three gazing at one another in devotion over a bottle of wine. Or in Badric's case a packet of Pork Scratchings.

The band that's on is not bad, fronted by a rapper by the witty name of Fly Tippa. Gus and I force our way back through to the bar for round two. Not a good idea for me because I promptly need the loo. Oh God, the bloody queue. It would probably be every bit as quick to drive home and back. This is when I freely admit to penis envy. The other band has quit the stage, and even though these things always take far longer than you think, I start to panic that I may miss the beginning of the set. I hop from foot to foot till I can bear it no more, then I take a deep breath (it will smell) and with my head held high I stride purposefully into the Gents and into one of the two cubicles as three male heads at the urinals turn to look open-mouthed. I am followed by about five other women, and we smile at each other in sororal sympathy. In and out. Fixing your face at their mirror would be pushing it.

I find Gus leaning against a pillar. He passes me my warm beer and a joint and hollers that Helena just rang his mobile, then hung up. I take one cautious drag then hand it back to Gus. It's that evil bright green skunk that's taken over the world. What is it with that stuff? Ruff Guy told me that they fertilise it with llama dung. God forbid that they should start chucking it on the vegetable patch. An innocent-looking courgette could do for you like a magic mushroom.

'Oh,' I say, helpfully, noticing Shelley up at the front with a bunch of her friends. They all look off their heads.

The band is on stage, busy with cables, kicking them out of the way, going back and forward to their amps. To whoops from the girls at the front, Ferdie removes his jacket to reveal a vest pulled tight over his muscles. Goodness, the man, my lodger, admirer and accidental lover is divine. Why can't I love Ferdie and learn to speak Portuguese? I ask myself this baffling question once more. Al and John are turning knobs on their guitars and Mica has her head down, pressing buttons on her keyboard. Carla is tightening screws on her cymbal stands and takes a drink from a bottle of water. Lien is swaggering about, tossing his locks around. Coloured lights bathe the stage, glinting on the mike stands and the drum kit. The music fades out and the hum and babble of the audience fades in. Some guy appears on the stage.

'Back by popular demand, please give a big hand to MOTHERLODE...'

Mica removes her shirt and points with both hands to her P♀WER! T-shirt, Carla counts them in, CLICK, CLICK, CLICK, CLICK.

'FUCKING BRILLIANT!' yells Gus. I watch Carla. She's

amazing. She has a power quite beyond her size. Can't see her getting Bingo Wings.

After the second song I see Shelley, swaying towards the loos. I yell at Gus that I'll be back in a minute and follow her. The queue has gone now that the band's on.

'Shelley' You OK? ' I hear a groan.

'Rach? Is that you?'

'Open the door, babe.'

She's sitting on the loo seat looking distinctly green.

'I've been sick.'

'You'll probably feel better in a minute then,' I say, fumbling in my bag for a mint. She takes a sip from a bottle of water and takes one.

'Thanks, I think I'm OK now.'

'Sure?'

'Yeah, I think I had a dodgy kebab.'

'Right.' I help her up and we go over to the mirrors. God, what fifteen years does for you. I look worse than her.

'Thanks Rachel,' she says, 'Don't tell mum.'

'I won't, but Shel, no more to drink tonight, right? ' She scrunches up her face, 'No way!' We head back out into the throng.

'Ye missed a really good bit!' Gus shouts in my ear.

At the end of their set we push our way through and congratulate them. Their clothes are sticking to them, they're already doing a post mortem.

As Lien melts into the night and the guys are getting their pints, Mica and Carla are left on the stage. Mica's keyboard weighs an obvious ton, and Carla's kit has to be taken to bits. We offer to help, but not knowing what's what, our offer is declined. We hang around for a while, then say our goodbyes and leave.

The night air is cold and sharp. I feel the sweat cool on my skin. Gus is hungry again, so we queue up for chips in a late-night food place. My ears are ringing and I want to get home. I want a shower and a drink. I want to curl up beside David and savour the prospect of Sunday morning with Badric, croissants, newspapers, the radio and him, all to myself.

Gus talks about Carla non-stop all the way home.

'How old is she?' 'Is she single?' 'God, she's amazing!' 'Would she like a servant?' I say 'maybe', but that he'd have to wear a sarong like in the Temptation ad.

'No problem,' he says, 'Wha' aboot ma kilt?'

He says he's never been out with a black woman.

'Shut up Gus!'

'What?'

'She's not a bloody journey into the *Heart of Darkness* for Christ's sake!'

'Jesus hen, you're touchy! I didn't mean...'

'That you're racist...'

'In the name of the wee man! Of course I'm not racist, I've got...'

'Please don't say you've got plenty of black friends Gus. Look, sorry, I'm tired, that's all.'

But there's more to it than tiredness. He's right. I'm touchy in that particularly fractious, friable, close to tears way that tells me that the last four weeks have gone by very quickly and that the niggling ripped condom on the carpet worry will soon be history.

The house is dark, and there's a momentary pause before Badric comes to the door, which means that he's been fast asleep on guard duty. Gus offers to take him round the block. I creep upstairs and open the door of my bedroom slowly, so as not to disturb the gorgeous man. But the streetlight shining on the bed reveals a smooth surface. I turn on the light and fall upon an envelope that is on my pillow. I rip it open and feel a horrible sick feeling as I do.

> *Darling, thought it best to get out of your way. Am going to stay with Nige for a while till I get organised. Take care, Dxx*

Nige? But Nige lives in Ireland for Christ's sake! I kickbox myself for telling him to go, and collapse on my bed like the sad fool I am for a braincleanse. When I hear Gus and Badric come in I wipe my eyes and go downstairs for that drink.

'Hey, what's up?' Gus comes over and puts his arms round me, which only makes matters worse. I tell him in a watery sort of way.

'Where's that bottle of whisky?'

'God, sorry Rach, I think I finished it last night.' He goes into the kitchen and comes back holding out a glass of wine from a bottle that's been open for too long. 'I'm sure it's for the best,' he says.

'Yeah.' I want to get to bed before Ferdie gets back. Any more sympathy and I'll kill myself. I call Badric and we both plod wearily up the stairs.

Rule No.7: *Things that are for the best always feel like utter shite.*

I don't know why I buy the Sunday papers. They are incredibly heavy and on the way back from the shop I have to stop about ten times to pick up the shiny rubbish that comes flying out. Is there anyone who is pleased to have this stuff scatter itself uninvited all over the place? It's almost worse than it coming through your letterbox. At least then you have the momentary thrill of thinking that you've got a letter. Though why I imagine I might get one, I don't know. It's not as if I write the things myself. Who does these days? But if I was ever to inherit a huge fortune from a relation who had died before I even knew of their existence, I know that this news would come in proper writing. That ... and bills.

So we have our croissants and newspapers, and Badric and each other, all to ourselves, my cousin and I. Ferdie comes down, shakes his head at the offer of coffee, then disappears back upstairs with a croissant and a litre of V8. Unbelievable.

I flick through the glossy pages of the magazine, trying to find something absorbing that will stop me thinking about David, even for five minutes. Someone I've never heard of reveals that his favourite colour is mauve, his favourite food is *spaghetti alle vongole*, his earliest memory is of being held upside down and shaken as he almost choked to death on a marble, then seeing it roll slowly across the kitchen floor and settle in a knot in a floorboard, and that he is kept awake at night by reliving the shot that won him the Open. Oh I see ... a golfer, how elucidating.

Next a big, bright, bold, double-page spread. The title reads, 'The Battle of the Boing.' It would seem that we have been underestimating the machinations behind the 'hollowed' walls of the bouncy castle. Their gay façades have been concealing something darker; bouncy castles companies are at war, and someone's playing dirty. Mike 'bouncer' Ball of Bouncy Castles r Us claims that all ten of his castles have been sabotaged by rival company Bouncy Castles 4 U, over a period of six months, obviously ruining trade over the festive period. As Mike Ball's castles deflated (and you can hardly put a bouncy castle in a bowl of water and watch for the bubbles) the 'let down' clients, desperate to appease the marauding gang of furious children, would run to the phone book and quick as a flash Bouncy Castles 4 U would be on hand to save the day. After the fourth time, the police got involved but, by this time, Mike Ball's wife had suffered a nervous breakdown and tried to kill herself. And so on.

I try to feel sympathetic to Mr Ball's plight, but somehow I just can't. Call it compassion fatigue. I find myself looking at the lonely hearts, for solace, if nothing else. Really, how can people describe themselves as, very intelligent, beautiful, sensual, svelte, vivacious, sexy, gorgeous?

Of course they may well be all of these things and more, but to say so themselves? Surely these are things that you may live in hope of being said about you. But then, this is an ad. This is the hard sell. It wouldn't sound very good to say, 'I have been told that I am (see above), but modesty prevents me...' Yeah right. Who said so? Your mum?

What about this one, Leprechaun (48) seeks similar for cycling, philosophy, quizzes and real ale in no particular order. Or this, Culture Vulture seeks Wise Old Bird. I almost consider writing down the number but then remember that I'm neither wise, nor old, even if today I feel about the same age as Methuselah's wife. (That's several centuries younger than Methuselah, naturally.)

Gus is stuck in to the sports section and I envy him his interest. I try to read some leader comment but fail. I turn on the radio to hear the last few bars of the theme music of *Desert Island Discs*. Too late, we've missed it. I will just have to content myself with my own version of this game as I wait for the kettle to boil again. *Desert Island Dicks,* same format as *Discs* but men instead of music. It's just as problematic as the latter, but inversely so. In the case of *Desert Island Discs* you have to whittle away endlessly at the 27,549 pieces of music that you could not possibly live without, whereas with *Dicks* you scrape the barrel, wracking your brains to think of eight men that you could put up with till you were rescued by the WRENS. Obviously they'd be chosen for their individual merits, but the one you'd keep above all the rest would be a good all-rounder. Despite the obvious drawback, Haden has been coming out on top for a while. What could be better? The complete works of Shakespeare, Haden and I. How happy we'd be, Tarzan and Jane meet the bard. And after a couple of months, I'm quite sure he'd be willing to disregard the small matter of my sex.

I'm bored. It's drizzling outside. I need a change of scene. I ask Gus if he'd like a walk in Richmond Park, then lunch in a pub somewhere. His ears prick up, as do Badric's.

The inhabitants of South West London that are not heading in the same direction as us are queuing for the carwash. I have observed this phenomenon for a while now. Every carwash has men, and it does seem to be men, sitting in their cars reading the papers as they edge towards the big nylon rollers, or the jet wash, if you feel like getting a bit more interactive. The Church of England needs to wake up. In this time-pressured age, it would do well to integrate carwashes into their more than half-empty naves. Instead of a token, you could get communion, then have the sermon piped into your car before it emerged, forgiven and as shiny and new as if it had been dipped in the River Jordan. Their wives may well be found on the other side of the six lane highway in the garden centre, satisfying the incontrollable urge to fill a half-price terracotta pot with John Innes No2, which doesn't sound very pleasant come to think of it, and stuff it full of all things bright and beautiful.

If used to the Highlands, Richmond Park is no big deal. But it is for Badric and me. Badric starts to make a strange, howling noise as we approach as if his inner wolf had just been woken from sleep, and he hangs his head out of the window with what look like tears of joy coming out of his nose.

We bounce over the potholes in the car park and find a space between two of the hundred or so jeeps, 4x4s, off-roaders, SUVs, or whatever you care to call them. They are disgorging their contents – superbuggies, mountain bikes, kites, picnic baskets, rugs, extra jackets, golfing umbrellas, shooting sticks, rifles (not really), dogs and children. Yes the Barbour Brigade is out in force, the green wellies are on, the Driza Bone hats firmly on heads. The dog leads clink in the breeze like masts at Cowes Week. I need to get as far away from this lot as possible. I'm half expecting to see Fiona come striding towards me to give me another slap.

We walk up to the highest point, to the hollow oak into which Badric and I can fit, but not Gus. It must be the best part of a millennium old. I like to come and sit here. I recommend a hollow tree for comfort every time. Badric sits with me, very quiet and respectful as if he too knows what a rare thing it is to find himself sitting inside a tree, but if he sees a dog go past, he'll leap out, making the un-suspecting dog-walker jump out of their skin.

It's from this high point, I inform my cousin, as David had informed me, that Henry VIII stood to watch for the rocket launched from the Tower of London, to signal that Anne Boleyn's head had been chopped off and he could now go ahead and marry Jane Seymour. Charming.

Badric skedaddles through the trees. He's gone up a gear, that retriever's snout is working overtime. Inklings of spring are all around. This walk is doing me good. Despite my crotchety mood, leaden limbs, bust that feels about the size of Dolly Parton's and the dull sickish headache which will persist until that hormonal switch gets flicked, I'm feeling better already.

14

The pineapple

I rejoice for approximately thirty seconds. When are they going to invent a painkiller that works quickly? The digestive system is useless for the quick fix. That's why people smoke dope instead of eating it. Of course, it can be eaten, but you have to employ some forward planning. Remember the folly of saying to your student boyfriend at four o'clock, 'Hey, let's eat some of that hash cake we got in Amsterdam!' forgetting that you are due to meet his parents for the first time at seven-thirty.

If I'd set my alarm for half past one and taken a pre-emptive painkiller, I wouldn't be awake now at three-thirty facing an hour's wait for the two I've just taken to work. There are times when the pain is so bad that I can see myself putting a tourniquet round my arm and pulling it tight with my teeth as I mainline the contents of a capsule or three. The woman who played Angel in Wives told me that when she was doing a job in Spain, she was lying on the beach talking to a model when she complained of a headache. The Spaniard took a gigantic pill out of her handbag and handed it to her. When she tried to break it in half the model started laughing and indicated that it should be stuffed up her bum. Common practice apparently. Kicks in a lot faster. Debbie (Angel) said, 'Thanks love, but no thanks.'

I remember when I 'started'. Mum cried a bit, then told me it was a wonderful thing because it meant that I was a woman and that I could one day have a child that would bring me as much joy as I had her. YE-UCK! But at least she didn't throw a party for the occasion. To mark the occasion of Shelley's menarche, Carla planned a wonderful do, you know, to dispel the negativity that surrounds periods, because they are marvellous things really. Shelley stormed off and didn't speak to Carla for a fortnight. Anyway, a period party might make you think you were in for a real treat every month, instead some painful, visceral glimpse of a fragile and fearsome mortality, that you, yes you, woman, are responsible for, wonderful, hardly, awesome, perhaps; but as for it putting you in the mood to party ... no. You're just as likely to put on a pair of miniscule white shorts and head out to the beach for a game of vollcyball.

I toss and turn and try to read, give up, then try to sleep again. I feel as if I am being trawled, as if something is being torn out at the roots. I think about David. I wish I'd let him say his piece, God knows I'd waited long enough for him to explain why quick as a flash, he'd gone off the whole idea; why what we were doing was wrong all of a sudden. If I had the energy, I'd go up to the attic and search for clues. In the film version of my life I would stumble upon a diary, which would reveal that his wife had six months to live. In the real life version I am more likely to stumble upon the ladder and break a bone.

The day I met David I was looking for a present for mum and dad's wedding anniversary. I was relatively rich at the time; the money for the pasta sauce ad had just come through. We were a few months into *Wives* and I suppose I wanted to show them that I was doing well. When not filming I was spending a lot of time wandering around. Wandering around accompanied by a droning interior monologue bemoaning the fact that fate could have dangled Haden before me like that, and then had a good laugh at my expense. The flat I was sharing in Streatham was getting claustrophobic. We were all getting on each other's nerves. Things had never been the same since we came back from a month's tour of my home turf, Scotland, taking Brecht's *Caucasian Chalk Circle* to church halls and sports centres for a pittance. I'd loved it. It was such a relief to get away from Gobshite and the ubiquitous pasta sauce ad.

Brecht's alienation effect involves the actors appearing in whatever they happen to be wearing: tracksuit, jeans, leggings. The theory being that this enables the audience to remain objective and not to be swayed by emotional attachment to someone's sorry rags. I got the distinct impression that our audiences felt a little bit short-changed and the local reviews confirmed it. But our little theatre group, for all its high ideals and tiny subsidy, was dying a death and when Jenny told me that I'd got Shiraz, I was happy. My comrades weren't. Never has the pop of a champagne cork fallen so flat. It was for this reason that I was more than half-living in Battersea, house-sitting for a friend of a friend. Nina was nannying next door at the time. We didn't really make friends till she stormed out of the house one day in a rage. I never quite understood what had happened, but it was clear that she needed some comfort, and that she wouldn't be going back.

Anyway, that particular day, I decided to go down to Lots Road and get them something really nice for the house. Something old. Everyone values something old, something with the patina of time etched upon its surface, just as long as it's not a female human. As I'm browsing, gazing into cabinets of trinkets and constantly having to remind myself of my mission, steering myself in the direction of small clocks and crystal decanters, I looked up and into the face of a man.

'Can I help you?'

'Oh, er, actually I'm just looking.' For some reason I blushed scarlet.

He helped me choose a mahogany barometer, slim, with a small mend at the top, which he assured me made it a very good deal. I walked back to the house with it under my arm, terrified of damaging it, even though he'd swathed it in bubble-wrap and tape. I stopped in Cremorne Gardens and realised that I was already thinking of an excuse to go back, as I looked across the river to St. Mary's church, little knowing that it was to be the scene of my undoing. Or the undoing of my shirt buttons in the very near future.

My phone is ringing. Shit, what time is it? Ten fifteen, my clock glares at me, accusingly. David?

'Hello.'

'Hi, darling, are you OK? You sound a bit croaky!'

Damn, it's Jenny. Clear the throat, sound frightfully business-like.

'Oh hello, Jenny. Just a bit of a cold, nothing serious. How are you?' Grovel, grovel.

'Well done darling, you're pencilled for the job!'

The job? God yes, the job.

'Great!' Trying to sound hyper-keen.

'I'll keep you posted, you're one in ten, fingers crossed!'

I am a one in ten ... nobody knows it but I'm always there, a statistical reminder of a world that doesn't care...

I put on my dressing gown and go downstairs to find a note from Gus telling me that he's gone to a meeting in town and that it looks like the London office want him down for the week. Would it be OK to hang around?

I hear the loo flush upstairs. Ferdie's in. We need to talk. My conscience is bothering me. I take a cup of coffee upstairs, have a shower and dress. First things first, Badric's sitting in the hall, concentrating with all his might on the front door.

It's a nice morning. Things are looking up. It's a new week, David's gone, which must be for the best, rules of existence or not, and I'm a one in ten. Not bad for elevenses.

Spring is in the air, and with something resembling renewed vigour (on my part) Badric and I strike out in the direction of the café. Giacomo or no Giacomo, I am going to celebrate this superb new status of mine with a large breakfast. Ruff Guy and Mush are up ahead with another guy I've never seen before. Badric struts towards Mush with his tail in the air when, out of a bush charges something that looks like a squat four-legged killing machine. Its owner lunges at it but it dodges him and hurls itself at Badric, felling him like a big cat might a gazelle. Things go into slow motion as I run towards my poor innocent animal, who yelps as this beast sinks his teeth into the scruff of his neck. The guys run over in a cloud of smoke from their breakfast spliff and I yell at the unknown one to get his fucking dog off. He yanks at his collar and Badric tries to get away but somehow the other brute is free again and attaches his vice-like jaws to Badric's backside. By this time I am insane; I kick the dog in the ribs and he drops Badric and turns his head with a 'WHO DARES TO...' look in his eye and turns on me. By this time, Mush, who is known for his somewhat over-fondness of Badric has got involved, distracting the ugly one from the proximity of my shins. Ruff Guy pulls the two dogs apart and I drag Badric away. He is all of a tremble, and whining, blood dripping from his neck and tail region. From a safe distance I turn to look at these 'men' and their 'dogs'. Hell hath no fury etc. I won't repeat what I said, but the answer I got, not from Rough Guy, who looked dazed (nothing unusual in that), but the other one was, 'Piss off bitch!'

It's hard to tell who is more upset, Badric or me, but I

think it's probably me. I go and sit on a bench near the lake, wishing I'd brought my fags. Straw, camel, back. Jesus, poor Badric! If he's not being clouted with a large stick he's being attacked. Does this make me a bad mother?

Rule No. 8: *Feeling any degree of smugness is just asking for trouble.*

I ring the vet. You just don't know where that dog's been.
    'Jameson, yes, that's it,' I say to the receptionist.
    'No problem, just bring Baldrick along straight away.'
    'It's Badric.'
    'Just bring him along.'

We enter the incredibly chic veterinary clinic, blood dripping onto the incredibly chic wooden floor. Badric is sniffing around, quite happy, until the vet calls us in and then he applies the airbrakes. Two frozen-faced people, one with a wild cat in a basket and the other with a rabbit, gaze impassively as I drag him towards the surgery, stubbornly locked in a sitting position. The vet is OK, but never as nice to, or appreciative of your dog as he should be for the money. He's good-looking and wears checked lumberjack-type shirts. Let's face it ... vets are right up there in the ideal male top ten; up there with BBC foreign correspondents and playwrights. I can never quite look him in the eye since the time when I took Badric to see him for what turned out to be a totally natural phenomenon.
    'Sorry, maybe I've wasted your time but his ... (just say it for God's sake) ... his penis was incredibly swollen and sore earlier, I thought maybe he had an infection, or had been stung by a bee...' Penis is just not a word one uses in common parlance, nor is vagina. But you can't say to the vet that his willy looked sore... or his dick, and certainly not his cock. Anyway, he takes a quick look.
    'Do you think it's possible that he could have had an

erection?'

Floor! Open Sesame!

'Oh, I thought...' I thought that when it just appeared now and then looking a bit like a lipstick that was a doggy hard-on. Jesus. There is something beyond blushing. I can't describe it, but I was doing it.

He is given a jab, antibiotics the size of Spanish painkillers and we leave, £55 worse off, Badric with two shaved patches so I can keep the wounds clean.

I need to eat. Not because I am hungry but because I can't have a drink before breakfast, and I need a drink. I buy a sausage roll from the bakery, eat it, then go into the Duke of York for a gin. It's after midday, who cares? Badric lies down, sniffing the warm fragrant air coming from the direction of the kitchen. I ring Carla to tell her the latest. She can't talk, it's busy at the studio, but she'll pass by later. She says she's worried about Shelley. She hadn't heard from her since the gig, and she usually always calls on a Sunday. I say I'll call her on a pretext later.

When I get home Ferdie is on the phone speaking rapid Portuguese. He puts the phone down with a heavy sigh and I ask him what's wrong. He says that his father is ill with heart trouble. He's in hospital.

'I must go home,' he says.

'Yes, of course, you must.'

'Maybe I stay home now.' He looks at me and I wasn't wrong, it's there, in his eyes. As plain as day.

'Ferdie, I'm so sorry, I didn't...'

'I know.'

I go towards him, but he backs away. He covers his face with his hands, mutters something I don't understand, drops his hands and says, 'I'm sorry Rachel, you are busy in your life, this man David, he lives here now, yes?'

'No! He's gone ... I...'

At this moment he notices that Badric looks like something from the dolls hospital, his bare patches and stitches.

'My God, what is happened to poor Badrique?' as he calls him.

I tell the tale, feeling tears coming to my eyes. He puts his arms round me and we hold each other, and blow me down with a feather, do I start to feel rather comfortable or what? The phone rings. Saved by the bell. We pull away.

'Hello?'

'Darling, it's me, sorry I haven't called sooner, Nige's land line's down and I've only just got a signal...' The phone cuts out, and at that moment the doorbell rings. It's Ruff Guy and his mate, minus the dogs.

'Alright Rachel? Ferd?' says Ruff Guy. He knows where I live because now and then he gets smoke for Ferdie.

'I'm really sorry about earlier, love,' says owner of the beast. I'm taken aback. I should have given him a lecture about dangerous dogs, muzzles and the rest, but somehow the man has just managed to redeem himself.

'He's good-natured really,' he's just got a thing about Labradors. Badric pushes his head past my legs and looks up at the visitors, wagging his tail. I show them the bare patches, the teeth marks. The bloke shakes his head, looks really upset and gets his wallet out. He insists on paying for 'the damage' as he calls it and suddenly I am £55 up again. To top that, he hands me a pen and some paper from his wallet and asks me to sign it, telling me that I am 'fucking great as Shiraz.'

I go back inside. Ferdie asks if he can use my computer to book a flight. I say, 'Sure,' and think better of following him up the stairs. I think we're both feeling just a tad vulnerable at the moment.

Rule No. 9: *There's always a perfect time for making matters worse.*

I tidy up a bit, sweep the floor and plump up the cushions on the sofa. Gus's stuff is in a pile beside it. When Ferdie is gone, under normal circumstances, this would mean I'd have the place to myself. How wonderful that would be! Even for one night! I'm starting to feel slightly out of control. My inner wee wifey needs to wash the kitchen floor and do some serious de-dog-hairing or else she'll start demanding Valium. I see that Ferdie's been shopping. The fruit bowl is brimming. I bloody hope he's not thinking of leaving me with that little lot! He comes down the stairs. There's a flight to Rio tonight. He says he must ring Carla, and *Danse*. He says that, of course, he'll only stay for a week or so. *Danse* is still touring, he's not going to miss it. Anyway, he says, his mother will drive him crazy. He makes his calls, then goes back upstairs to pack, shouting down to me that he has replaced my pineapple.

My pineapple? He means the pineapple. Let me explain. The week before last I was on a serious health kick. It could be that this helped sustain me through last week. You know what it's like at the beginning of the year. I was shopping at the organic shop. It's wonderful. All you have to do is go in there and you feel better. As if you're making a contribution to the future – yours, the farmers', the birds', the bees', the whole lot, even if the dent in your finances threatens your mortgage payment. You waft around the shop that smells of fruit-sugar and spice and all things aroma-therapeutic, the taped whale song soothing your very soul as you fill your trolley with quality goodness, thinking to yourself, 'hang the expense' because this is a political act. This is retail therapy on a deep level; you are now a green consumer. Or will be by the time you've ingested all that veg.

At the checkout, the girl that radiates health and serenity says, 'You do know that this pineapple costs ten quid?'

'Ten quid? You're joking!' I say, as I fill my shopping bag, yes, shopping bag; you cannot ask for fifteen plastic bags in this sort of place without getting some pretty bad vibes.

'Yeah. Shall I leave it?'

There's a queue behind me. Someone taps me on the shoulder.

'Excuse me, but weren't you in *EastEnders* recently?'

'No.'

'I'm sure I've seen you on telly...'

The checkout girl scrutinises my face. 'I know ... you're in *Chefs' Wives* aren't you! I hope you're not going to waste this lot!'

The rest of the queue is having a good look.

'Yes, that's right,' I smile, politely, not acknowledging her hilarious chuck-up joke. The girl is still waiting for my decision on the pineapple. Someone says, 'Go on, you can afford it!' I look at the man who said this. What the hell does he know?! Now I'm in a quandary. Do I, celebrity style, keep it, or do I, normal person style, say, 'You must be bloody joking!' Instead I say, 'What's going to happen to it if I don't buy it?'

'Oh,' says the girl, 'it'll get thrown out eventually.'

'What?' I want to ask if she'll take my mobile number and ring me when this time comes. 'Why don't you just reduce it?'

'Well, it is Fairtrade...'

(i.e. the picker got 5p instead of 4p, and see that one over there covered in ants? He can take it home for their tea.)

'I'll take it,' I say. What the hell. Sixty quid, seventy quid what bloody difference does it make. The queue is stunned into silence.

'Any cashback?' Cashback? Do I look as if I'm made of money?

I get the thing home, and place it in the fruit bowl, a magnificent symbol of a world gone mad. At least it can rot in a loving home. This cannot be what the man from Del Monte means when he says, 'Yes!'

Mutiny on the Pineapple Plantation
By R.L.Jameson

Cut to the man from Del Monte, his
face that of a tragedian as he sees
one of his premium pineapples being
kicked around by his workforce as they
take their two minute break, the dusty
topsoil blowing away from where another
1,000 acres of irreplaceable rainforest
(pardon my geography), has just been
cleared to make room for yet another
pineapple plantation. He falls to
his knees, reaches for the pineapple,
holds it to his breast, and looking
heavenwards, cries out, 'NO!' Even the
parrots fall silent as he looks around
at his boys, those ingrates that he has
saved, feeling the boundaries of his
world dissolve. Where did he stop and
the pineapple begin? And the canning
plant, the slices in syrup, the chunks,
the juice, the ready-made Pina Colada
– what did it all mean? His precious
pineapple! He holds it aloft with his
arms outstretched as if offering a
sacrifice to the Gods. For now it needed
a new destiny, bruised as it was, it
was never going to get past quality
control. Yes, now that poor fruit needed
a new destiny; it could no longer
expect to fulfil its birthright, to rot
in a wheelie bin in London SW11. As he
stands up, feeling certainty return, as
proud as a pineapple in a panama hat,
the silence is split by the sound of a

```
gunshot, and he falls to the ground,
dead. The pineapple pickers throw back
their heads and whoop. The plan worked.
```

And there it sat, beautiful, silent; the most expensive pine-apple in the world. Every time I saw it I felt guilty. Every time I saw it I was in a hurry. Every time I saw it I wanted to pick it up and kiss it. I started to love it. I didn't like to leave it.

'Badric! Guard that pineapple with your life!'

Then one day I came home and it was gone. Just like that, the foliage in a jam jar filled with water, supported on a scaffold of sharpened matchsticks. Ferdie had left a note.

> *Hiya Rachel, I eated your pineapple. Sorry. I*
> *get you another one. It was the best I ever had!*
> *Ferdinand x*

No! I don't want another one! I don't want some substan-dard 'in', 'un' or is it 'non'-organic unfairtrade pineapple from Asda I want... But it was gone. And I feel pride in my grief, like a mother, that it was good. The best.

15

Shelley

I offer to drive Ferdie to Heathrow, then remember that Carla is coming round, that I said I'd ring Shelley and that Gus doesn't have any keys. I cross the street and knock on Miss Jackson's door. She's still got her set from when she was my domestic servant. The 'trickle-down' effect in action. It trickles down till the source dries up, which it did. There's no reply.

I ask Ferdie for his set and ring Teresa's bell.

'Who is it?'

'It's me, Rachel. I just wondered if I could leave these keys with you and if you wouldn't mind my cousin picking them up when he gets back from work?'

There's a pause. That's gratitude for you.

'Oh, OK. ' She opens the door and sticks her head out. She looks dreadful; pale with dark shadows under her eyes and as she holds out her hand for the keys I see a deep bruise on her wrist. I retract the gratitude thought.

'Everything OK?'

'Yes, thanks. Sorry I'm a bit busy. Tell Gus I'll be in all evening.'

Tell Gus I'll be in all evening? Very chummy I'm sure. Must have been that night on the armchair when he was on the sofa. He looked comatose, but maybe he wasn't.

126

'Thanks Teresa.' That woman is weird.

I ring Shelley. Life has provided me with the perfect excuse.

'Hi Shel, how are you? Good. I was wondering if you'd walk Badric later? I'm taking Ferdie to the airport. Yeah, his dad's not well. Yeah, must be if he's going home ... anyway, spoken to your mum recently? I couldn't get through to her earlier (lies, damn lies) ... Shelley? What's the matter? Hey, don't cry, listen, wait here after you walk the boy and we'll have a chat when I get back OK? My cousin might be in but he's OK, OK? ' I tell her about Badric's earlier trauma, to keep him on the lead and to give any evil-eyed beast a wide berth.

Better ring Carla.

'Hi babe, yeah, I just spoke to her. You're right, she's upset about something, but she's OK. She's going to do dog duty for me later and then we'll have a chat. Yeah, don't worry, I'll let you know. I'll ring you when she goes... I'm taking Ferd to the airport. I know. Listen, guess what happened to Badric...'

Then Gus. I tell him to get keys from next door if Shelley isn't there, and that he can have Ferdie's room; there are clean sheets in the chest in my room. Talk about organisational skills. I'm wasting my time. I should be running a multi-national.

Ferdie, that paragon of cool, is ready. Packed, and as calm as if a long-haul flight were just a stroll round the park. Compare and contrast this with myself on the rare occasion that I find myself about to be catapulted across the globe. Not for Ferdie the sitting on a suitcase after repacking it three times in a neurotic frenzy, or the checking to see if my passport had leapt out of my handbag and run away since the last time I checked, two short minutes ago. No, he is calmly preparing a tuna fish salad, saying that he doesn't want to eat any of the 'rubbish food' at the airport. The airport is the sort of place that justifies the eating of 'rubbish food' in my opinion, washed down with plenty of rubbish wine. I'm not going to meet my maker sensibly hydrated and on a salad. Oh no. When that plane nose-dives into the ocean I'll be glad that I'd thrown caution to the wind. It is salutary to bear in mind that there were people on the *Titanic* who waved away the dessert trolley.

He offers me some and we eat in silence. The issue of the one-off, or should that be two-off is not raised. I think it's a 'life's too short' moment. I tell him not to forget to take some of that fruit, (please) just in case of a delay.

As we're leaving the phone rings.

'Ah, that's better!' It's David. 'I'm out of the valley now, it's a much better line.'

'Sorry David, I'm just on my way out. I'll ring you later.'

There's a silence dominated by what is it? Exasperation I think. Oh well, treat 'em mean an' all that.

Ferdie talks about his dad on the way. He's only sixty, drives a cab in Rio, which is just as bad as London. They'd moved into town when the farm he worked on burnt down. He never really got used to it. Never even really found his way round Rio. Got stressed out. Missed the country, missed his dogs, which couldn't cope in the hot apartment block so they were given to his brother who didn't treat them right. His mum worked in a home for disabled people and his brother was a waster. He and his big sister had always loved to dance, and his dad had some bongos and used to play them as he sat on the balcony, which his mum tried to make into as much of a garden as she could. She said the noise irritated her, that's why he had to sit out there. You could hardly hear it above the sound of the city, and he used to watch his dad, as he'd sit drumming out a rhythm with his fingers with his eyes closed, a beer at his feet and a cigarillo in his mouth. His mum worried all the time, always nagging at his brother, telling his sister that she was dressed like a whore, till she moved away and now she's got two kids and a new baby. She's OK, but really, she was the better dancer. She should have had a career, but now she just dances in the front room, or when friends come round. He's looking forward to seeing her. She's called Rosa, he hasn't seen the new baby, he's got some money for her and he'll try and take her out one night. He said his dad was a 'hard man' who wanted him to get a proper job and I get the feeling that there was not a great deal of love lost between them.

'Yeah,' he says, 'I could not live like this. No way.'

'But they must be proud of you now,' I say.

He shrugs. 'My mother she worries, wants me to go home, get married. I take a video of *Danse* for them.'

The flight's on time. Ferdie tells me not to wait. He wants to go through and buy a few things for his mum. We hug and I feel terribly upset; it happens at airports. I absorb all the tearful goodbyes that have ever been made, as they hang in the atmosphere like emotional humidity. On the way home I think about David. I should have rung him by now, but I'm enjoying punishing him. Horrible but true.

No sign of Gus when I get in, but Shelley's there. Badric comes over, then goes back to his girlfriend. She tells me that Nina called and could I give her a ring? I say I'll do that later. I can see that she's been crying a lot, her eyes are swollen and red. She said she had a nice walk, and that she'd bought Badric a tin of Pedigree Chum as a treat, because of what happened to him earlier. The tin is beside him at Shelley's feet. He looks at me with guilt in his eye. He knows I don't approve of junk food, for him, at least. But I tell her she was right to spoil him today. I check his bites, find some cotton wool, and she holds him as I clean them with the pink stuff from the vet's. He seems to have forgotten all about it, or had at least until I started poking at them.

I ask her if she'd like a drink at the pub. I text Gus and tell him to join us, then regret it when I see Shelley's face. I text him again and tell him we need an hour or so.

I needn't have worried, because he neither turned up nor got back to me. I finally wring out of Shelley the fact she took half an E and was still really off her head after the gig, and that she ended up in bed with her best friend's boyfriend. Her best friend found out (she didn't say how) and won't speak to her. She tried to speak to the offending bloke, but he just laughed and said it was her fault for flirting with him, that she was asking for it, and that he'd told Nika, (the friend) that she'd been after him for ages behind her back. She said that it was horrible, that she never meant it to go that far, but by the time it had gone quite far, she couldn't say no. He'd said that she couldn't do that then change her mind...

'What are you saying, Shel? That he raped you? Because if he did...'

'No, God no, he didn't hurt me, he just...'

'He just ignored you when you told him to stop?'

'Yeah, but he was ... you know...' Her eyes are filling up again.

I know what she's trying to say. That he was in her already, that she felt responsible, that he seemed to want it so badly, that she wished she'd worn more clothing, that she was scared.

'He said I'd led him on.'

'Babe, there's never an excuse...'

She butts in, 'I was up for it at first ... it's not a big deal is it?'

'Well, it's a big deal for you now, isn't it? Well, as long as he was careful, you can try and put it behind you. Nika should get rid of him.'

'That's the thing,' she sniffed, 'I was on the pill but I came off it cos I thought it was making me fat. I think I'll be OK, maybe it lasts for a while.'

Oh dear. If Carla could hear this she'd ... I don't know. Talk about feminist issues. I go to the bar to get her another drink and a packet of crisps. Let's see. This is Monday evening; there's 72 hours to avert the worst. I put this to her and she nods. 'Please, please Rachel. Please don't tell Mum!' I promise not to, but say that her mum would understand... 'Pleeease!' What can I say? I feel uneasy, as if Carla, with her intuitive powers, is listening in on some psychic extension.

I ring the doctor's surgery, find out where there's a late night-chemist that doles out the morning after pill, and leave my wine so I can drive again. Shelley seems calmer now, relieved that a grown-up has stepped in and made it all right.

Off we go to procure some anti-baby gear. At the chemist in Balham, Shelley behaves like a schoolgirl in trouble, head bowed, as she confesses to the kindly Asian pharmacist that no, it didn't happen because of a broken condom. He shakes his head and sighs as he hands the packet over, telling her that she must look after herself because, 'Boys will be boys.' He gives her a glass of water and she takes one pill, and he tells me to make sure she takes the other one in twelve hours' time.

'Shel, why don't you stay over tonight?' I say, seeing relative peace and quiet heading for the horizon, its possessions in a spotted handkerchief on the end of a stick.

'Really?' she says, perking up.

When we get home, I run her a bath, sprinkle it liberally with lavender oil and encourage her to have a good long soak, i.e., give me enough time to ring Carla and Nina.

I decide to ring Nina first. While she's eulogising Adrian, the perfect man, I can think about what I'm going to tell Carla.

'Hi Nina, it's me! What?' The perfect man has dumped her. 'Why?' She'd like to come over. 'Er, well I've got ... Is tomorrow any good? Oh right, babysitting, well, OK then.

131

You don't have to, but...'

But yes, *spaghetti polonaise*, as we call it, might be just the thing. Have to feed my juvenile charge after all.

Here goes.

'Hi babe, yeah, she's here! Fine, bit upset, argument with her mate Nika. I told her she could stay over. Is that OK? Yeah, I'll get her to ring you after the bath. DA? Where is it? Oh yeah, I know... what's it for? A tabloid? Yeah, definitely ... tomorrow would be better for me... Don't worry, leave it tonight if you're knackered, I'll see you tomorrow for walkies anyway. Well if you want to see her ... Nina's coming over, she says it's all over with her and Adrian. Dunno. Find out later I suppose. Hey, did I tell you about Badric?'

I call up to Shelley to ring her mum when she's finished and that no, I didn't say anything. I say I'm going to get a few things from the shop and head down to FoodEtc for some wine, milk and fags. Ben's in there, buying a bottle of vodka, king sized-rizlas and sixty Marlborough Lights.

'Hi Ben.' He looks up from his wallet.

'Oh hi, Rachel, don't suppose you fancy some company?'

Jesus. It never rains but it chucks it down.

'Em, I'm having a bit of a girls' night but...'

'Great! I could do with one of those!'

I'm just a girl who can't say no, tra-la... Please refer to **Rule No. 5**. I owe Ben anyway. He helped me make some of my less minimalist decisions in the house. His idea of fun is choosing fixtures and fittings. You know the type; I redecorate therefore Iquea.

On the way back Ben tells me that Steve popped home once to get some clothes, looking positively radiant, and took with him his (Ben's) favourite jacket, just to add insult to injury.

'Oh, poor you,' I say, looking over at Miss Jackson's house, noticing the distinct lack of curtain twitching with a vague sense of unease.

We get in and Ben goes straight to the kitchen, pours himself a large Vodka and tips it down his throat. Shelley comes down the stairs in an old Kaftan type thing of mine. Her hair is wet and down to the middle of her back and she looks like something out of a Sunday magazine article about East being the new West.

'God! Who are you!' coos Ben, 'You're absolutely gorgeous!'

Shelley goes all shy, and I tell him it's Carla's daughter, and that he has met her on several occasions in the park.

'Well ditch the trackies, darling. That dress is to die for.'

She asks if she can have a drink, but I tell her discreetly that it might make her feel sick, then relent and give her the nearest thing to an alcopop as I can manage, some red wine mixed with some flat lemonade that is lurking in the fridge.

The doorbell rings and I let Nina in. Badric goes mad. He, like most males, goes potty over Nina. She enters like a Polish whirlwind, if there is such a thing, and goes straight to the kitchen, demands wine, and unpacks the groceries, laying into an onion with venom.

'My mother says it is best to eat when you are angry!' she says, brandishing the knife like one possessed.

'Really?' Ben slurs, 'My mum just gets pissed.' So it's genetic then, I think, watching as he pours himself another large one.

Shelley is rummaging through the stack of videos, and I feel useless. I know – I'll lay the table. What a quaint, curious exercise.

'Ben, are you staying for some food?' Nina flashes me an angry glance, the cleft in her forehead appearing like a ravine, then disappearing as she relents.

'Great! Yeah!' he says, his enthusiasm bordering on hysteria. He's definitely spent too many nights in on his own recently.

Enter stage right, the front door, Gus and oh-God-not-you-again, Teresa.

'Hey guys, ye didnae have tae go to aw this trouble!' Says Gus, looking around. Badric's overjoyed now, with a knowing 'the more, the merrier' look in his eye. The merrier, the more chances of scraps. He is glued to the kitchen floor, watching Nina's every move.

'I need more mince if these people are eating!' snaps Nina, wiping what I hope are onion tears from her eyes.

'I'll go,' I mutter, half-heartedly.

'No, I'll go,' says Gus. 'Anybody want anything else?'

Just a teleporter to take me to a quiet riverside near Limerick.

I tell my guests that I have a call to make. I go upstairs and find a pile of crumpled soggy tissues on my bed. Poor Shelley. Could be that this is not the best place for her to be tonight. I put off the best till last, like dessert, and first check my email. Spam, Spam, Spam, Spam, a couple of would-be internet date enquiries, which I delete without further investigation, and one from Juliet, another ex-*Wives*, my friend from up North, meaning Dalston.

Hi Rach,
Thought I'd indulge in the luxury of sending an email in the five minutes of time to myself between yelling and feeding. Come up and see us soon, would love to speak to someone who isn't in a nappy! Any work?
Take care,
Jules x

I'll just skip over that one for now. Next, Haden.

Hello darling!
House full of men eh? Am I invited? I'm due back Wed 9am, don't suppose you fancy a trip to Heathrow just to remind yourself how the other half live?
Haden xx

134

I reply, and instead of saying, 'Ever heard of public transport?' I tell him I'll be there and that he's lucky because I've just decided to give up acting and get the Knowledge instead. Right. Now for David. Typical, 'The Vodafone you are calling may be switched off. Please try later.'

'Hey,' asks Nina when I come back down into the throng, 'did you hear about Giacomo? Slipped on some olive oil and cracked his head open. He's in the Chelsea and Westminster!'

> **Rule No. 10:** *A broken heart is preferable to a broken head.*

Nina detests Giacomo. I'm not altogether sure why. Giacomo told me that he took her out for a drink once and that she didn't stop talking all night. She said the same, and that if Italy was so superior in every way then how come there were so many Italians in London? He said that she was pissed off because he didn't fall madly in love with her. Whatever.

Gus gets back with the mince, and soon the meal is on the table. I ring Carla and tell her that we are about to eat. She says that as long as Shelley is OK, she'll leave it for now. I feel relieved.

Nina smokes two cigarettes in a row while the rest of us start, exhales her last drag through her nostrils and proceeds to tell us all about Adrian. He has dumped her in favour of someone distinctly more eligible than a Polish nanny-cum-cleaner. This woman has got a house that she inherited in Chelsea, but doesn't live there, preferring to live in her camper van somewhere in Cornwall. Her name is Bella Stravinsky, she's twenty-eight and is a marine biologist doing a doctorate on some virus that is threatening the seal population. She's been all over the world doing this sort of thing. She's tall, slim, with long straw-blonde hair and lives in a wetsuit. She's written a book about her time spent as a member of a pod of dolphins, and since she's loaded and the house is paid for, all proceeds of the book are going to marine conservation; oh, and the charity she's set up to give children who've had limbs blown off by landmines the chance to have a swim with that dolphin that hangs out in a bay off Ireland somewhere. A sort of AquaDiana. Teresa and I exchange glances. Sometimes there is just no comfort to be given.

'I think I read about that dolphin. Isn't he the one with the permanent hard-on?' slurs Ben. God, the papers. They can't leave it alone for a minute can they?

'No, just when she's around.' Nina finishes by adding that she had a two page spread about her in *You Magazine*, and is sponsored by a wetsuit company. She lives on the money she gets for modelling this rubber gear, but doesn't take it at all seriously. Well who would?

Dolphins with erections, limbless children, wetsuits, landmines... Is it just me, or does anyone else feel as though they're in a Buñuel film?

'Sounds like ye're in competition wi' a fuckin' mermaid, darlin'!' says Gus. Ben says she sounds fab, then, 'God, sorry Nina!' adding that he bets she can't make pasta like this. Nina says it's OK. Anyway Ms Stravinsky's a vegan, naturally, and that will get on Adrian's nerves eventually. And as for him, well, all he was interested in was 'making love to her bottom'. And she doesn't mean 'front bottom...' Oh please, 'front bottom', don't get me started on that one. Everyone roars with laughter. I consider asking whether once the pubic hair was dispensed with he suggested anal bleaching; the very latest thing, a sort of bum equivalent of tooth whitening, but we are eating.

'What's wrong with that?' asks Ben. Gus and Teresa offer to clear up, and disappear into the kitchen together. When they reappear, Gus asks me if it's OK to smoke weed in front of Shelley and I say, 'I suppose so.' Well

136

I don't bloody know, do I? Shelley asks if it's OK to put the telly on. I say, 'of course,' and sit down next to her. She rests against me. I like this aunty feeling. Let's see if there's something educational on the box to remind us all that there is more to life than our dysfunctional and by and large hopeless attempts at relationships. Boys in the room; flick past the itch cream ad for 'the intimate feminine area'. Allow us some dignity for God's sake! The intimate feminine area? Sounds like one of those hideous communal changing rooms in Top Shop that blighted my youth.

And would you believe it, it's another makeover show, this time posturing as something a little more serious. Women who have had liposuction are suing. They didn't get the results they were hoping for. They had their brains sucked out instead. Instead of the firm belly, thigh or backside they were promised, they'd been left with something that looked like a half-deflated balloon. Now they had to have yet more surgery to remove these unwanted festoons of sagging skin, and hankered after that good honest fat with heartbreaking hindsight. Shame it went to waste. I see a gap in the market.

> *Ladies! Liposuction. Is it the right option for you? FatBank.com. is here to help! For just £14,999.99 we can bring you peace of mind, storing your excess fat in our special repository in Bexley Heath for up to ten years, should you ever want it back. Discreet and hygienic.*

> *'It was marvellous to think that it was my own fat that helped tighten my intimate feminine area. After three children, my husband is happy again! A big thank-you to FatBank.com'*
> *Moira, Llandudno*

Or even,

> *'It was marvellous to think that it was my own fat
> that helped enlarge my penis. After three children,
> my wife is happy again! A big thank-you to
> Fatbank.com'*
> *Tom, Llandudno*

Yes, when you decide that you can no longer live without
that all new fashionable Afro-bottom, you can simply have
some of your very own adipose tissue relocated. Then
when you ask your friend, 'Does my bum look big in this?'
you can scrutinise their faces to see if they are lying when
they say 'Yes! It does! Honest!' Or maybe you could make a
charitable donation to some poor thin-lipped creature in
desperate need, or bequeath the lot to the starving in Africa. Why share the food when they could have the fat? Can
you imagine how satisfying it would be to think of your
fat pulling some walking skeleton back from the brink
of extinction? Huge tankers crossing the oceans (and for
God's sake make sure the boats are double-hulled), with
WorldFatBank.com emblazoned down the sides, Bob
Geldof on the telly, slamming his fist on the table, urging
us to give what we can, even if it's only a pound. Or a kilo.
Deposits could be made at any GPs surgery. It would become as routine as giving blood. I can see the 'Do something amazing today!' car stickers already.

'My thighs, at the back, they are very fat,' says Nina
sadly.

'That Adrian fella didn't mind, did he?' says Gus. Teresa
laughs a little too loudly at this observation.

'What's so funny?' Nina spits at her, 'No one's perfect!'

'Except you, darling,' says Ben to Shelley, who announces that she's tired. I tell her to go up to my room.
She says goodnight to everyone and heads up the stairs,
the mature adult conversation is obviously too much for

her. Everyone goes 'Aahh', as she passes as if she's the girl from Impanema. Talking of which, I suddenly think of Ferdie, up there somewhere, drinking plenty of water and stretching at regular intervals.

It's the ads. Mascara. I can't believe that we haven't yet exhausted the possibilities of the stuff. Let's face it, you put it on and if it gets wet it runs, and if life hasn't removed it for you during the course of the day then it ends up on your pillow, and any left behind conspires with the bathroom mirror the next morning to make you look even more ghoulish than you would do without it. Come on advertisers! We modern women need a better reason to buy than 'tear proof', for Christ's sake! We're not babydolls! We wear combat trousers! We need mascara in which to place our trust when on a G8 demo. What about 'teargas proof'? Or a mascara than can stand up to a blast from a water cannon?

Riot by FaxMactor. Fight for it!

Ben says he's going to head off. Nina gets up and says she has to be up at six, so she'll go too. I need a walk, so I call Badric and get my jacket. Ben weaves his way down the pavement and turns down his road, after giving Nina and me an enormous hug in turn, thanking us for a 'fab' evening.

'Teresa is a strange woman, She doesn't say a lot does she?'

'No, I think she's got some problems at home.'

'Ttt, men!' says Nina looking down.

'Hey, come on, angry. Remember?'

'Yes, angry, angry!' she says straightening up. She asks about David and I tell her that he has gone.

'Good riddance!' she says and I concur feebly.

'Alone again, both of us.'

'Yep, alone again.' Wishful bloody thinking.

I go to the park gate, squeeze in and break into a run, down the Prince of Wales Drive side of the lake with Badric diving in and out of the shrubs, and stop at the Barbara Hepworth. I run my hand over the cold, textured surface of 'Single Form', one side bulging like a belly, a porthole in the top through which I can see the moon. Objective, impervious, it'll still be standing when Badric's Island lies in ruins, this beautiful bronze standing stone.

Why oh why did I say that Gus could have Ferdie's room? I think as I prepare the sofa. I go upstairs and look in at Shelley. She's sleeping. While in the bathroom I hear noises. Blimey! Gus can snore! Then I realise that this is a duet, and those are not snores. Bloody hell, Gus and Teresa are bonking in Ferdie's bed! Thank God Shelley's asleep. I creep back downstairs and Badric and I sit out in the garden for a while. I smoke the half a spliff that I find in the ashtray, go in, set the alarm on my phone for seven-thirty so that Shelley can take the other pill, and text David.

Hope ur OK. Miss u xx

I press send and off it goes, the little envelope on my screen disappearing into the ether. Damn, damn, damn! What the hell did I do that for? Come back little text message! I didn't mean to say that!

16

My millennium memories

I listen to the news on the radio to try and inject a bit of reality into the evening. The words wash over me as I lie on the sofa in the semi-darkness. A car zooms past, bass booming. An alarm eventually stops. A siren screams on Albert Bridge Road, and a helicopter chops its descent into the heliport, not far from Swan Wharf. The sound of the voices is by contrast calming, reassuring. I don't really hear what they're saying, but that doesn't seem to matter. It suggests that there is some sanity to be found, that there is someone, somewhere, who knows what the hell is going on; that there are people who do not live in London, who live in Gloucestershire and York, North Wales or the Isle of Skye; people who read books and revive country crafts; people who don't watch telly and have never heard of Trinny and Susannah; people who go to the theatre and in the summer listen to the Proms every night on Radio 3; people with good relationships, happy marriages, children who don't look like dollies or junior members of the National Front.

David listens to Radio 3. I know this because I was there. That fortnight we spent together the first year, with baby Badric, the last of the litter. Fiona was elsewhere, with family, so David slept on *Swan* with me. My New Life for the New Millennium. A few years late maybe, but so what? I was living it. It all seemed so symbolic, as I lit the stove with the piles of old newspapers, bills and insurance policies that David was prone to horde, but was throwing out to make some cupboard space for me. Papers that distracted me from the task, Millennium papers going on and on about it; The Millennium kitchen; the Millennium garden; my Millennium moment; my first major mistake of the Millennium; how to be a New Millennium Man; a Millennium Mum; sexual mores for a sizzling New Millennium; Millennium menu makeover; 2,000 thousand free tickets to the Millennium Dome for the first 2,000 people to ring this number.

One afternoon turned into two nights, then into a week, followed by a few days of wandering around in a daze, then back, this time with a suitcase. The house-sitting stint was done. I couldn't face going back to the flat in Streatham. Alan, one of the guys in the theatre group, who I'd had a bit of a fling with on the Brecht tour was always hanging around. Not hanging around me in particular, just there, one of the gang. The gang that told me that *Wives* was a total sell-out, like they'd have turned it down. Anyway, there was no contest with David's little cabin, the scent of the honeysuckle growing by the gangplank wafting in on the breeze. I wanted to have my bath when the tide was high, the water sloshing back and forth, and to sway about in the little galley, hanging onto the pots and pans when the Harbour Master went past, Badric wobbling around on his rubbery-puppy sea legs, watching the spiders that came out at night to mend their webs, little filigree curtains, one on each porthole, broken at high tide, when the Canada Geese stuck their necks through for bread, making Badric give his first ever bark, taking himself by surprise.

I was happy. In a telly-less, ad-less, soap-less world of books I hadn't read, prints I'd never seen and music I'd never heard, till the nights when he did go home. But, I'd say to myself, and to Badric who took his place in the bed, that it would all be worth it in the end, because he was sorting things out. These things took time. Poor Fiona, I'd think, as I'd fall asleep, the water with its particular living smell slapping against *Swan's* steel hull, cocooned. That's when I wasn't wondering what he saw in me, what a Z-list celeb, starring in a daft soap on the back of a stupid pasta sauce ad that he hadn't even seen, could possibly have to offer him. Jealousy eating away at me like rust.

'Here is her picture: let me see: I think,
If I had such a tire, this face of mine
Were full as lovely as is this of hers:
And yet the painter (photographer) *flatter'd her a little,*
Unless I flatter with myself too much.
Her hair is auburn, mine is perfect yellow:
('Perfect Yellow' by Cloreal, because you're worth it)
If that be all the difference in his love,
I'll get me such a coloured periwig,' (For when I'm not filming)

My mobile beeps, bringing me back to reality.

1 message received. DAVID MOB.
Miss you too. Wish you were here. Dxx

Love knocks me sideways like a freak wave.

I'm woken by a clatter on the stairs. It's still dark, Teresa is half-way down, dressed, and has just dropped one of her high heels.
    'Shit! Sorry, Rachel. I didn't mean to wake you.'
    Oh, don't mind me. I just own this madhouse.
    'What time is it?' I groan, rubbing my eyes and really annoyed. I was having a good dream. I was on a beach

143

somewhere.

'About 6,' she says, voice lowered, 'I didn't mean to ... I didn't mean to fall asleep, I must get home...'

'Oh, right, bye then,' I say, turning over.

'Rachel, sorry about this, but, don't say anything to Mark, will you?'

I raise my head and shake it. I'm turning into a walking confessional. She sneaks out. It would be very interesting to be a fly on the wall next door. I'm surprised someone hasn't genetically modified a housefly, a webcam in place of those googly eyes.

Right, a bit of time before the alarm, which of course spells no more sanity-inducing sleep. Oh well, six hours will have to do. If Mrs Thatcher could function on five, then surely I can manage bugger all on six.

In fact it's quite pleasant. The early bird I am I flutter about listening to the serious matters on the radio, make some coffee, eat one of Ferdie's bananas, have a shower and creep into my room to get some clothes. Shelley doesn't stir. I shower and dress, tidy up a bit and dispose of enough dog-hair to stuff a cushion. I feed said fluff-dispenser then take him out.

The park is busy. I realise that, for many, this time of day is not the crack of dawn. It's not an achievement for these people and their dogs. And it has to be said, it has a particular magic. It feels fresh, the birds sing as they go about their business, and there is altogether a different class of dog walker at large. This could be a sweeping generalisation, but I do think that your dog is less likely to be savaged and you are less likely to be sworn at before nine o'clock in the morning.

Badric is ready to go at any time of the day or night. He is, you could say, a thoroughly good chap. He wouldn't know a bad mood if it barked at him. He is mono-moodular, permanently positive, never-endingly nice, and this morning as I watch him in the early morning, his coat gleaming in the sunlight, I feel once more that if the NHS prescribed puppies instead of Prozac, the world would be a happier place. I go up the squirrel run, past crocus corner, and resolve to visit Miss Jackson later.

There's something going on over by the Peace Pagoda. As happens of a morning the marble steps are infested with people running up and down, which could be mistaken for some new form of worship, which it is really; self-worship. Don't get me wrong, there are definitely worse habits, but anyone would think the pagoda had been put there as some sort of aesthetically pleasing piece of outdoor gym equipment. Not sure what Buddha would have to say about it.

I take a cup of tea up to Shelley and wake her. She takes the pill and goes back to sleep. I go back downstairs and continue to give my wee-wifey free rein. Now what can I do? I know. People from Miss Jackson's generation don't lie around in bed all day. They get up early and have pots of tea with tea cosies on them, and a rack of white toast cut diagonally and spread with marge and Golden Shred. They listen to Radio 2 and open their letters with a letter opener. They, unlike us, know when they've got it good.

I ring her doorbell. Badric sits down resolutely. He's not going anywhere until he's had his biscuit. But I do not hear Terry Wogan or smell toast. I knock a couple of times then bend down and call through the letterbox.

'Miss Jackson, are you there?' No reply. There's no way Miss Jackson would have gone anywhere without letting the entire street know. I try again, louder this time.

'MISS JACKSON! IT'S ME, RACHEL, ARE YOU IN THERE?'

Nothing. But hang on, there is a noise, a sort of, 'Hhhe...'

'Help!' Oh no, quick! Think...

'Hang on Miss Jackson, I'll be back in a minute!' I rush home, pulling Badric with me, and through to the kitchen. I rummage furiously in the drawer designated 'stuff'. There's a set of her keys in here somewhere... Come on, come on, where are they?

'Stop it Badric, for God's sake!' He's leaping up because for him, when I rush about, it means it's a funny game.

'What's up?' It's Gus, dressed only in his boxers. 'Sleep OK down here then?'

I know that he's actually asking me whether or not a) I heard them at it or b) Teresa managed to sneak out unseen. I tell him what's happening and he says, 'Aw no!' He bounds up the stairs and comes back down dressed by which time I, against all the odds, have found the keys. As we cross the road, Teresa comes out of her front door and clip-clops towards her car, her hair wet, looking remarkably well, in fact. Must be the magic of Gus, I suppose. They make a show of being casual to each other, which seems pretty pointless, since she knows that I know and so on.

Miss Jackson is lying at the foot of her stairs, her right leg sticking out at a nasty angle. She moans. 'Hhhe ... Hello dear, I think I must have fallen asleep.'

'I think you must have fallen down the stairs.'

'Have I, dear? Oh my.'

I ring the ambulance and go upstairs to get some blankets. It's bloody cold in here. Miss Jackson's bedroom is like the 'before' shot in a makeover show. Everything seems to be brown; the carpet and the bedspread; the air itself has a brown tinge. There's a picture of the Sacred Heart above her bed and that's about it, apart from the big brown wardrobe. I know that if I opened this wardrobe it would smell of mothballs. I also know that it would fit into the back of a Volvo and make a lovely cabinet for a home entertainment system in Tennessee. I take the eiderdown off the bed and hurry back down and put it over her.

I look at her face. In the year since she stopped working, she has really aged. I'm not sure how old she is, but this last year age seems to have caught up with her, as if by working you keep ahead of it, but when you stop to catch your breath it's upon you, all of a sudden, and you can't shake it off. I sit next to her on the hall floor, and the tiles that look so stylish in my house suddenly are just what they are, cold, hard tiles. In fact, the house is just what it is, a pokey two bedroom Victorian terrace, built for people who worked on the riverfront, not a charming, period, bijoux residence that would benefit from the expertise of an interior designer and would sell for a small fortune, being as it is in South Chelsea and close to local amenities. I can see from the junk mail on her mat that the estate agents are hovering like vultures. 'Looking to sell? Do you have a property to let in the SW11 area?' 'FREE valuation of your house! Call this number NOW!'

I hold her hand. I should have visited her more often. Should I feel sorry for her? No husband, no children, or is that what she wanted? She might be gay for all I know. I do know she has a niece called Eleanor who lives in Southend, who pops in when she's in town and that's about it: Josie from the Bingo, the postman, and me. She's told me before that this street has really changed, that everyone used to look out for each other. I wonder how long she's been lying here. I should have ... oh, I don't know. It's not our fault, is it? What with the expectations we have of life and the expectations that life has of us and the noise and the traffic and the affairs and the ... everything. Of course we scurry back into our burrows, close the curtains, screen our calls, phone our mums when we're feeling ill or dutiful and curl up in a little ball. Sometimes.

The ambulance arrives, and pulls up in the disabled bay that Teresa has just vacated. I tell Gus that I'm going to go with her, but the paramedic tells me that I can't go in the back with her because of insurance. I tell her I'll follow in my car.

'Gus, can you make sure Shelley eats something when

147

she wakes up? I'll ring you when I know what's happening, oh, and by the way, Helena rang late last night.'

'What?' Gus's hair almost stands on end.

'Yeah, she's in London! Come down to see you, but don't worry, I told her you were fine, just a bit too busy to come to the phone.'

Now he's doing an impression of a goldfish. I turn the ignition and the car starts first time.

'Only joking!' I say, winding down the window and blowing him a kiss.

'I'll get you for that, so I will!' He's still mouthing insults at me as I drive off.

Miss Jackson has broken her hip, she's a bit dehydrated and in a mess, but apart from that she's OK. She needs an operation straight away to put a pin through the broken bit, and she'll have to go into residential care till she gets better. She'll be walking with a Zimmer frame for a while and won't be able to look after herself. I sit next to her while this is explained. She looks tiny and frail away from her own little world, as vulnerable and frightened as a little girl who's lost her mum in a department store. When the doctor leaves us, she starts to cry. She says she doesn't want to go into a home; she used to work in one and she knows what they're like. I tell her that it will only be for a while, and that she'll be home before she knows it.

'Do you think so, dear?'

'I know so.' I say, feeling my nose grow.

After an eternity a porter comes and wheels her into the lift and up to the ward. I tag along. She is transferred to a bed and again we are left to wait. Old women of varying degrees of decrepitude eye our arrival. Some smile, some say hello, some remain silent, some are sleeping.

'Don't know what they've put me in here with this lot for!'

I say nothing, but know what she means. It's that denial

thing, that 'you've got the wrong person, you see, I'm only twenty four. I know, I know, time has insisted on passing, but not for me, honest, I'm twenty four!' It's like looking at yourself in the bathroom mirror, static. Everything's fine, nothing's changed and then you see yourself on telly or in a photo and you're smiling and you see to your horror that your face crinkles when you smile, just like an adult's. And this isn't about skin, this isn't about laughter lines not being funny, it's about the reality of time, of lifetime, of mortality. The realisation that I'm not going to be remembered as the youngest person to do this or that amazing thing, that at my age mum had a ten-year-old child, and it reminds me that despite being encouraged to make a will when I bought the house, I still haven't, and as for a pension, well... That and the fact that I have now, unbelievably, been smoking for half my life.

The process continues, and they seem to be of the opinion that the sooner they operate the better. Wow! Lucky Miss Jackson. We all know the joke about it taking nine months to get an abortion on the national health. It's not a good joke. I tell her that I'll get some of her things and bring them in. I leave her and step into the corridor and head for the lift. This is an environment engineered for reassurance – clean and breezy, art on the walls, goldfish swimming in their tank, plants reaching for the sky – designed to take your mind off the blood and guts, the dreadful pain and death, the 'procedures' going on all over the place. I look down on it all as I wait for its arrival – the coffee bar, the bustling crowd, pregnant women, the people about to go on anaesthetised journeys into the unknown. It has something of the airport about it. A sign points to a Chapel. They have one of them in the airport too. Obviously the church comes into its own when control is about to be surrendered.

As I head for the coffee bar, I suddenly remember that Giacomo is in here somewhere. Wherever he is I bet he could do with a decent espresso, or even a half-decent one. I go to the huge reception desk and ask where I would find someone with a head injury.

'Name?'

'Er ... Giacomo ... He's Italian...' The woman looks at me wearily.

'Surname?' Surname? This is London, love. We don't do surnames. 'Hang on ...' I wrack my brains. Strangely, I do know, and I remember.

'Giacomo Biagi, that'll be him'

I buy *due espressi* and head back to the lifts. I find the ward and go in. Giacomo is lying stock-still on his bed with a bandaged head, looking like a statue on a mediaeval tomb. It's always surprising to see someone horizontal when you've never seen them so before, however hard they may have tried to bring this about. Intimate somehow. He senses a presence and opens his eyes.

'Ciao bella,' he says, with unexpected, sardonic wit. I tell him I've brought him a coffee, and he points to a straw on the side.

'This is brown sugar!' he grimaces, sucking it tentatively.

'Sorry,' I remember his lecture about its flavour ruining coffee.

I tell him about Miss Jackson.

'So you not just come to see me, eh?' he says, but in a good-natured way. I tell him that I have to come back with some stuff for Miss Jackson.

'Is there anything you need?'

'Yes, one of these nicotine patch. There's money in there,' he says pointing at the locker with his eyes. I tell him we can sort out the money later. He tells me that he's got really bad concussion and that sometimes it can last weeks. He had to have a brain scan and everything. Scary. He's trying to get his brother to stop his mamma coming over. He told her that he had a nice big flat and if she saw his little room, she'd go crazy.

Dick Whittington's got a lot to answer for in my opinion, the Italian version, or Polish, whatever. It's a **Rule No. 6** thing.

I drive home making a mental and I mean mental, list of things to get and do. Nicotine patches, contact Miss Jackson's niece, ring Carla, email Juliet etc., etc. When I get to the door, Gus opens it just as I'm turning my key.

'David's wife is here to see you.'

'Oh ha, ha! Good one, very funny!' But his expression doesn't change and my stomach goes into freefall. My legs carry me indoors and there she is, Fiona; sitting on the sofa.

'I'll leave ye to it,' says Gus. 'I'm off tae work.'

17

Fiona

She stands up.

'Rachel, I know this is a bad time. Your friend told me about your neighbour.'

Yes, you see I'm not a totally wicked person.

'Yes, I'm sorry, I must get in touch with her niece...' I pause, hoping that she will take this to mean that yes, it is a bad time, and disappear. But then there would never be a good time for this particular scene. And if she went, I'd only have to wait for her to come back again. She stands her ground. My mouth is bone dry.

'Do you mind if I wait?'

'David's not here. He's in Ireland.' I immediately regret saying this. He may be hiding from her after all. I then retract my regret. I'm not keeping his bloody secrets for him.

'I know,' she says. And I feel wounded, just like that. Her 'I know', speaks of a conversation, a relationship, of inside knowledge. Silly me, of course, she knows everything. She knows him better than anyone. Is that what knowing someone amounts to? Time spent, time passed? But I knew David from that first evening, or thought I did; knew him as if I'd always known him, as if there could never have been a time when I hadn't. I tell her to wait, and Badric to stay, as I go back out into the cold air and shut the door behind me. I'm shaking. I take some deep breaths then cross the road. My fingers are practically useless, but eventually I'm back inside Miss Jackson's and I go to her phone, next to which is an address book, with a padded, floral cover. I find Eleanor's number easily as it is in her 'Emergencies' list at the front, and dial it. It's an answering machine. I calm my voice and tell her in a matter-of-fact, not-to-worry way what has happened, leave her my numbers and put the phone down. Two seconds later it rings. I nearly jump out of my skin. It's Eleanor.

'Glad I caught you. I was just hoovering!'

I fill her in, and she says she'll go straight to the hospital and then come and stay in her aunt's house for a while. She asks me to wait while she gets a pen, then makes a list of things that Miss Jackson will need, saying she'll pop into M&S on her way, and take in anything she wants from home tomorrow. I thank her, deciding that it would be a cheek to ask her to get some nicotine patches and drop them into Giacomo.

'No, thank *you*, love,' she says.

I need to sit down for a minute. Calm, calm, calm. I remind myself that 'Anxiety is my Friend.' Jules told me this on the set of *Wives* when I was stressing about buying the house, getting panicky. Told me to breathe, that I was just tired, that it was just adrenaline with nowhere to go. Now my life has turned into a soap opera. It's official. Not a day has gone by without a drama since ... since before Granddad's funeral for God's sake. The spotlight will have to move onto someone else's story soon, surely? Even characters in soaps have boring days when nothing happens. That's when you don't see them. That's actually when, in real life, they're having root canal work, their varicose veins removed or even a facelift. Bear that in mind next time your favourite character doesn't show up for an episode.

When I met David, Shiraz had been out of an episode, can't remember why now, something in her life, a week at a health farm perhaps, giving Ricardo ample opportunity to savour the delights of his new gaggle of preposterously attractive foreign waitresses when he wasn't with Mercedes. For David and me it was perfect timing. We had a long weekend together in Somerset and there followed a distinct lack of antique hunting. When I got back, the women on the set said, 'God, look at you! You look well! Either you've had a little eye-job or it's love!' Actually, the clarity of my skin and brightness of my eyes was down to twenty-five litres of cranberry juice, forty gallons of water and no alcohol for four days. That and love, naturally.

Fancy looking years younger? Get Cystitis ... from Men!

Not that I minded, of course. I'd bear anything, anything, at that stage of the game.

There, breathing has resumed some sort of normality. Take the mind for a walk. It works for me. Now, time to face the music. I realise that hunger is rumbling behind the knot in my stomach. A blood sugar crisis is something for panickers to avoid at all costs, but I can hardly ask her to wait while I nip down to FoodEtc for a sandwich. And there's no way I could eat a banana in front of her. Right, turn key in Miss Jackson's lock, cross road, wonder why I hadn't noticed the huge jeep before, and whatever did happen to the Volvo? Turn key in my door, pat my happy dog and in. So far so good. She is not standing there with an unstruck match in her hand. The place is not doused in petrol. She does not appear to be wearing a belt packed with explosives under her strangely outmoded Puffa.

She stands up again. I sit down. She sits down again. Badric pushes his head against my knees.

'Would you like a cup of tea or anything?'

'Actually, I could do with a drink,' she says. Hey! That's

my line! I don't want to muddy the waters by letting her get friendly. We're not going to form a 'victims of David' support group.

'Sorry, I don't think I've got anything...' I look at her, as I go through and put the kettle on anyway. She's forty-two. I know this because David is nine years older than me and she is the same age as him. They went to University together. She is a solicitor. She looks sensible. Nice. You'd be more than happy to have her as your solicitor. You would know that your mortgage negotiations would be safe with her. I feel very scruffy all of a sudden, but in a hip kind of a way in my Parka. Her Puffa is a real one, not a fake from the market like mine. Puffa 'n' Pearls. It's what the Barbour Brigade wear when they want to look a trendy, or when the Barbour's in Harrods getting its annual service. Seriously, your Barbour gets called in for a respray of waxy stuff. I suddenly want to burst into tears, thinking about Fiona deciding what to wear to go and see her husband's young (gorgeous) lover. Or ex-lover, whatever. I can see her at the coat stand, reaching by sheer force of habit for the Barbour, then spotting the black Puffa and thinking to herself, 'Hmm ... this may be better. Shall I leave the arms zipped on, or take them off?' Suddenly she seems pitiful. I'm becoming fixated on the Puffa. I can't see beyond it.

'Would you like to take your jacket off?' I say, pouring hot water into an empty teapot, then stuffing the teabags into the water and scalding my fingers.

'Rachel, I really just wanted to say how sorry I was for ... slapping you, that's all.'

And that was it. No buddy-buddy. No all-American beautiful moment. No revelations. No mud-slinging. Nothing. Just a good old English, mind-your-manners, never-mind-that-you've-wrecked-my-marriage apology. My turn for the goldfish impression.

She leaves, and I tear down to FoodEtc for essential supplies, feeling as if I've just got away with something, got

155

off lightly, I feel high, ever so slightly delirious with relief. Even the man in the shop says hello and smiles. Now my vindication is complete. I remind myself that I am a one in ten and never did get round to that large celebratory breakfast. I know, I'll buy the requisite stuff and a paper, and sit quietly at home for a few hours. A bottle of wine will come in handy. I must ring Carla. I don't feel up to DA tonight. One reason for this, hard as I might try to dismiss it, is that I'm going to find it difficult to look her in the eye when I report once more that Shelley is 'fine'.

Back home there's a note from Shelley on my pillow, thanking me for 'looking after her' and 'would it be OK to come over and watch *Wives* next week?' She's got work to catch up with and had to face Nika sometime. Shelley lives with Nika and another friend up near Clapham Junction in an ex-council flat, in one of those little blocks that break the line of a terrace, built on a bombsite, sticking out like a sore thumb, as if they'd come crashing down to earth unannounced, squashing three innocent century-old houses flat.

I check my email. 'There are no unread mail messages in your inbox'. See if I care. I begin to write to Juliet.

Hi Jules,
Good to hear from you, am pencilled for a car ad,
would love to come up and see you and ...

I've forgotten the baby's name. Something beginning with J ... Is it Josh? Or Jake? Jasper? Jack? Jude? Java? Jehosiphat?

Good to hear from you, am pencilled for a car ad,
would love to come up and see you all soon.

No, put the bit about the job last. You never know, bearing in mind **Rule No 10**, she might think I'm rubbing it in. The cursor hovers over the 'send' button but I don't click.

I can't face Dalston and all that goes with it this week. I'm not a total masochist. I pick up the phone to ring David and it rings in my hand. If it's him, it'll be one of those lovely 'I was just thinking of you... evidently I have magic powers' moments. But it's Gus checking to see if I'm still alive. When I tell him she was merely apologising he bursts out laughing.

'What's so funny about that?'

'Oh come on! You're shagging her husband and she's apologising to you?'

'What, you think I should be apologising to her? I don't think I got off exactly lightly, do you? So you'll be going round to apologise to Mark later I take it?'

'Sorry Rach. I didn't mean to get ye upset. I know you've had a hard time it's just ... a bit mad, that's all.'

Oh, well, that's OK then.

'Anyway I'm cooking tonight! So get yourself hungry hen!'

I can't be bothered with my celebratory fry-up now. I shall have a tomato sandwich and anticipate tonight's culinary extravaganza. Gus is a brilliant cook. So is Uncle Rab. The sort of men who never lift a finger in the kitchen unless it is to surpass themselves.

I ring Carla at work. She's auditioning a female vocalist later, so no walkies, and DA will have to wait till tomorrow, because this woman is really good. She says that she spoke to Shelley, and that she'll see her on Thursday, because it's Michael's birthday so they're going to the cemetery.

I fill her in on the rest: Miss Jackson; Giacomo; Gus and Teresa; the Fag-arties; Nina versus Bella Stravinsky; and last but not least, Fiona.

'Bloody hell!'

'Oh yeah, and did I tell you about Badric?'

'Yes Rach, twice. And Shelley told me too. So did Barry.

In fact he witnessed the whole thing from a distance. It's quite the talk of the park, darling. And what about David?'

'I can't get hold of him.'

'As usual,' she snorts.

'Surprise, surprise!' In walks Gus, followed by cousin Louise, looking full of the joys of spring. She makes a fuss of Badric and gives me a hug. Over the amazing Thai fish curry, she tells us all about Joe, her new bloke and Gus and I, the bitter and twisted, give the union our begrudging best wishes. He's gone to a stag party tonight, well actually it's tomorrow night but it's in Prague. Whatever next? Could be that Holy Joe is just about to blot his copy book, but let's give him the benefit of the doubt.

The phone rings. It isn't David.

'Hi, Rachel, it's Teresa speaking. Could I have a word with Gus?'

'Hang on.'

'It's Teresa,' I mouth. Gus shakes his head and puts his hands out in front of him as if in defence, shaking his head vehemently.

'Sorry, Teresa, he must have just gone out.'

'Oh, I thought I just saw him come in, with a girl.'

'Oh ... must have just missed him then,' I say, cringing. 'I'll tell him you called. Bye.'

'Who was that?' asks Lou.

'Don't ask,' he says, head in hands.

'It's the girl next door,' I say, with an explanatory expression on my face. She gets the gist. 'What happened to the love of your life then?'

We discuss the lucky escape/tragedy at some length, while Gus does something amazing with lemon grass and coconut milk.

'Right,' says Louise, 'after dinner, you are going to ring her and say that you want to give it another go. OK?'

'I dunno ... what di ye think Rach?'

'Don't ask me, for God's sake ... but yeah ... Lou's right. If you still love her, you might as well.'

'Rachel! What do you mean? "You might as well".' Half-hearted or what?' Louise isn't impressed.

'I just don't want Gus to get hurt, that's all.'

'Too bloody late for that!' he mutters, bitterly.

I draw the curtains, in case Teresa feels like spying. I see that the lights are on in Miss Jackson's. We catch up on the family gossip – Dougie has got a job down the road from Auntie Ellie's in a used car place.

'Would you buy a used car from Dougie?' asks Gus.

'I might, because I felt so sorry for him.'

'That's your problem, Rach,' says Louise.

No, just one of them.

Louise is tired. Gus wants to hide. I want to go over and see Eleanor, so the evening draws to an early close. Eleanor is watching telly with a ready-meal on the coffee table. She fills me in; the op is tomorrow. She says she wishes she lived nearby, but there's no way she could afford it. She's told Miss Jackson, or Aunty May, as she calls her, to sell up and come and live near her and the kids, but she won't budge. We agree that we don't blame her. Moving is bad enough, let alone when you're seventy.

Back in the street I see that Teresa is sitting in her car, in the driver's seat this time. Nothing suspicious about that. Her window slides opens as I approach.

'Hi Teresa,' I say, casually. 'Off out?'

'Hello, Rachel. Actually, I thought I'd just wait here for Gus to come back.'

I look at her. This is borderline bunny-boiler behaviour.

'Couldn't I just give him a message? I'm not sure if he's coming back tonight.'

'Oh.'

'Really, Teresa, it's bloody cold tonight. I think you should go in. Look!' by some miracle, Mark is walking up the street, mobile glued to the side of his head as usual, 'there's Mark.'

'Oh no,' she says, with a mixture of boredom and irritation. He looks over, sees me, smiles and waves. Strange. Suddenly she's the weirdo and he's the nice guy. She gets out of the car and greets him, and we all say a neighbourly goodnight as our front doors close on another day.

Inside, Gus is on the phone, nodding and listening intently, as if to a diagnosis. He signals desperately to me to refill his glass and bring him a cigarette and a light. I do this, wave to say I'm going to bed, and leave him to it. Looks like it could be a long one.

18

Haden

Haden's flight is on time. I have just enough time to get a card for Miss Jackson and to seek out a chemist where I buy a box of nicotine patches for Giacomo.

And there he is, Haden, looking around for me, seeing me and waving, giving me a hug. Ricardo and Shiraz forever. He's knackered, glad to be back, bloody freezing and ever so brown. He did meet someone nice over there. Hotel staff of course. Haden and I understand this in one another. Both feeling as we do that we are fraudsters, that we just managed to slip through the net into polite London society. Of course, we can schmooze with the best of them, but it's so tedious, pretending that you are interested in anything other than the free booze.

Haden is more 'out' now than he was back at the beginning of *Wives. Chefs' Wives* depended on the heartthrob factor. Ricardo was as straight as a raging bull, remember. You couldn't have him falling into cleavages left, right and centre knowing that the audience would be saying, 'Yeah right!' It happens with soaps. People suspend disbelief then forget to unsuspend it afterwards.

Anyway, back then we'd go out together, just for a laugh. *Bubbles!* magazine would get into a right lather about it, 'Shiraz and Ricardo out on the town! Could it be love on and off screen?' We'd ring each other with delight when we saw these headlines, resolving to have an argument in the street next time, or be seen out with other people. It was hilarious. We'd go to premiers, club openings, private views. There we'd be, out the back having a laugh with the foreign staff, the other immigrants. They didn't know who we were. They're the sort of people who work nights, who don't watch telly, and aren't interested in the soap stars of a foreign country. Who is? As for us, we were busy trying to beat the world record for how many nights running you could have canapés for your dinner.

'Any feedback from the rerun?' he asks.

'Nope,' I say, I don't think anyone's watching it. Does anyone watch repeats on Sky?'

'Yeah, you'd be surprised.'

'You're right, I would.'

I pull up as near to the Chelsea and Westminster as possible and Haden waits while I tear inside and up to Giacomo's ward with his nicotine fix. A stout woman and a moustachioed man are at his bedside. I interrupt a conversation of rapid Italian. They turn to look at me. I put the paper bag on Giacomo's locker, tell him that I'm double-parked, say hello and goodbye and leave. I hear their conversation resume at full speed and volume and wonder whether that was his mother, and she'd just seen the reality of his bedsit.

My head turns this way and that to read the signs as I speed in what I think is the direction of Miss Jackson's ward. Her bed is empty. I'm told she's gone for her op. I ask a nurse for a pen, get in the way of several busy people doing important things, take the card out of my handbag, scribble 'To dear Miss Jackson, GET WELL SOON! Love from Rachel and Badric xxx', shove it in the envelope, put it on her locker and get out of there as quickly as possible.

'Your mobile rang,' says Haden as I get back into the car, panting. I grope in my handbag. That'll be David, for sure. One missed call. Shit, Jenny. I ring the number, Haden handing me a pen and a piece of paper.

'Oh! Great! Blonde? (So one of them did fancy Shiraz.) No Problem, Monday night? Fine, oh OK, thanks Jenny!' Grovel, grovel.

'What?' says Haden.

'Will you give me a lift to the airport on Monday? I'm off to Cape Town.'

So, the one in ten has turned into the chosen one situation. Plan A is back in action. Thank you, thank you, Sky TV. When I get home after dropping Haden in Stockwell, I see that Jenny has faxed through a load of bumph, including the flight and hotel details. Jenny has not yet fully grasped email and it's potential, says it scares her. Still, we are a fearful lot on the whole. A fearful lot with an absurdly optimistic tendency and a bad memory. We would never have got this far without a bit of all three. Therefore, as I fret about this job and all it entails, I am looking forward to it, all recollections of nightmare shoots deleted. I glance through the rest of the paperwork and burst out laughing. It's for Foyle & Fagherty. Wait till I tell Carla.

I ring mum. Dad picks up the phone, says 'Well you be careful!' then hands me over to mum who is suitably pleased. She asks how Gus is, she sounds happy that he is here, that her brother's child and I get along so well. Everything mum says to me is so heartfelt, so earnest. Her love for me is so palpable that again, I feel that mixture of gratitude, guilt and a yearning to know how that love feels, for myself. I put down the phone and a long sigh exits my chest almost unnoticed, as if my heart has its own voice, its own life, and is completely used to being ignored by me.

As I reheat some of last night's leftovers the phone rings. It's callminder. 'First new message,' says the robot, 'message received today at 11.08am:' 'David speaking, just ringing to see how you are, I'll try again later. Bye.'

Curses! I ring 1471 but to no avail. I try his mobile but am informed that 'The Vodafone you have called is not responding. It may respond if you try again.' As if it's my fault. I'm not doing it right, like a useless lover. I give up. The phone rings again and I pounce.

'Hello?'

'Oh hi, Rach. Hey guess what? Helena's thought about it and we're on again!'

I sleep, I walk, I wait for the phone to ring. I email Ferdie, I ring Eleanor to see how Miss Jackson's op went. It went well. I pace around, I wish I didn't have to do this, but I must, I ring the hairdresser who has set up by himself since *Wives* and make an appointment to go blonde again. I look up Cape Town online, check out the hotel and decide that now is the time for me to read *The Long Walk to Freedom,* which has been sitting on my shelf in mint condition since I don't know when. I position it purposefully on my bedside table, then decide that there is no time like the present and take it downstairs. Just because I am going to South Africa blonde doesn't mean that I have to behave like one.

Gus said he was working late then going out with some of his colleagues and that I could join them for a drink to celebrate my job if I wanted. I decline the offer. It sounded a bit like Teresa-avoidance to me, and it's nice to have the place to myself. Badric and I get comfy on the sofa. I try to read, but sometimes reading is difficult. I have an ideal vision of myself, curled up on an armchair, bathed in the yellow glow of a table lamp illuminating the diminutive print of a page of a classic, Thackeray or perhaps a Russian, Dostoevsky or Tolstoy, three-quarters read in my hand, a Beethoven sonata playing softly in the background, or perhaps some Schubert, and just one glass of good red wine in front of me. No cigarette, of course. There's no place for a cigarette in a fantasy of this calibre.

And if there were, it would reside in a silver box on the mantelpiece and would be, at the very least, a Gitane, one of the twelve left from the twenty I'd bought last Christmas.

But no, sometimes solitude is just not that damn comfortable, and a cup of tea and a Marlboro Light is the dismal reality. They are Gus's from last night, not mine, I'm sick of Marlboro Lights, London's fag of choice. Funny how it happens; at school it was Rothmans. Marlboro Lights are everywhere, it's like, yeah, I'm hard, but I care. I dumped the horse but kept the boots and the hat. When was the last time you saw someone with a packet of reds? Who'd be that brazenly self-destructive these days? Solitude and reading? Since we're in yank mode, let's just say that sometimes it sucks. I reach for the remote.

Sex. Sex. Sex. The less I do it, the more I seem to see of it. According to these women, it's the be all and end all. Their motto is 'I fuck, therefore I am'. Don't get me wrong, I'm not suggesting that we lie there and think of England, or get to our deathbeds without ever having had some decent sex, with man, woman or plastic thing, but really, ten times a week? Five portions of fruit and veg and five orgasms a day or else you are a loser, a weirdo, or just a sad old frump. And if you can't have the real thing inside you, i.e. a penis with a man attached – inconvenient for some it would appear, since you can't slip it in your handbag and whip it out when you're stuck in the traffic, just think of the time you've been wasting on the news/music/audio book/teach yourself Spanish course – then you can get down to your local sex shop like every good liberated woman should, and buy yourself the very latest vibrator. In fact, like your phone, vibrator technology moves on so very quickly that it is easy to be left out in the cold, with a vibrator so shamefully outmoded that you might hide it deep in a knicker drawer, when you should be displaying it on your bedside table with pride. Perhaps, just so you always know where it is, it should be round your neck or slung about your hips, on a trendy strap like your sunglasses. The choice is mind-boggling: bejewelled, every colour of the rainbow, with as many settings as a Magimix, rechargeable like your toothbrush, and so on. No wonder electricity consumption has skyrocketed. What about a carbon neutral eco-vibrator?

> *Just an hour on your windowsill or next to your balcony kitchen-garden our solar charger will give enough power for several decent orgasms, with wind-up option for rainy days! Just £49.99! Hurry while stocks last!*

All those women vibrating on their king-sized beds with their man-sized appetites and tissues to match. Yep, women are getting in touch with their masculine side; it involves a vibrator that can double-up as a strap-on. Imagine what Freud would make of it.

'Ja,' he would say, 'All you vimmen who said Penis Envy vas impossible, vell look! Look around, vhat do you see?'

Yes, look out boys! You might think it's great that now when you snipe, 'She looks like she's gagging for it!' the frenzied female fuck fanatic will rush over to you and say, 'Yes! Yes! I am! I am!' But you better be good, because you're in stiff competition with something that can spin around, throb, vibrate, you name it, it can do it, whilst supplying orgasms the like and number of which you will never, ever, equal. And she can strap it on and fuck you back into the bargain, if you're up for it. Just as well it can't take the rubbish out.

Remember those distant days when it was considered rude to use your phone on the train? Maybe the time will come when women will enjoy a quick orgasm while waiting for a bus, or even between courses at a restaurant. Phones that vibrate, why not the other way round? Why have two gadgets when you can have one. Hurray, now we can be just like blokes. You know, those ones we've been complaining about for all these years, the ones with the one-track minds, who only think about getting their end away? Sorry, but I just do not believe that there can be many women out there, who in all seriousness, without laughing, could strap on a penis. It's the equivalent of a man putting a couple of oranges up his T-shirt. Ridiculous.

Maybe I'm a prude. Rachel Jameson, spinster of this parish. I will live here till I fall down like Miss Jackson. My lonely hearts ad, when I get round to it, will read, 'Prude seeks Square for dull times.'

I turn over. A car ad. The dream these ads sell are worse than the bog standard lie. The shining car on the open road. Where exactly are these open roads? The Moon? Chernobyl? And when exactly are you going to need to 'do' 0-60 in however many seconds? Unless your house happens to be on the hard shoulder of the M1 of course, or if you've just nicked the damn thing from a service station forecourt. Even getaway drivers would be careful not to draw that much attention to themselves. I should know.

It's the pathetic antiquated stereotypes that are so annoying, and it's even more annoying when they try to up-date them. The patronising of the 'good little driver' has given way to crazy lady (sexy-crazy, not crazy-crazy), as she weaves and spins her way around her boyfriend's prize possessions that she's laid out on the (empty, naturally) *piazza*, in front of their glorious *apartimento*. The chiselled visage of the man as he steers his mighty beast down that open road, firm hand grasping the thrusting gear stick, his woman's dress ridden up slightly to reveal her thighs, ever so slightly glistening with sweat as she sits in a semi-swoon of desire at his mastery of machine and as soon as they get to that motel, of her. Now he's the passenger and he's impressed. She can handle a big car, and a big man. They exchange glances, her beautifully mani-cured hand grasping the thrusting gear stick.

I can hardly wait till tomorrow to get the script of my next fine piece of 'work'. To say that I feel uncomfortable about this is an understatement. I've had enough. I know I've said it before but this time I mean it. Shack on Stornoway here I come. Rachel's Rural Retreat for Washed-Up Soap Stars, Penitent Ad Folk and Any Number of Dogs. I text Carla to confirm tonight's DA, and tell her about Foyle & Fagherty. She texts back.

Yes & NO!!!! ☺

Gus appears, slightly the worse for wear, but not in a maudlin way, as he has been of late, but in a joyful, love-sick sort of a way. He wants to ring her.

'No,' I say firmly, 'it's too late.' And you have had too much to drink, I think, wondering whether Gus's alcohol consumption is something I should be concerned about. He asks whether Teresa has called. I say that she hasn't. He seems pleased, but I sense a touch of ego in there somewhere.

It's time. Off I go, into the night, pick up my partners in crime and we head for the end of York Road, just before the roundabout. Carla has described this ad. A woman is pulling up her shirt as if to remove it, and the text screams:

Keep abreast of the News with the new-look Daily Press!

Sounds like a suitable candidate. We pull up nearby. It's fairly quiet tonight.

'Shit! It's gone!' says Carla, turning to us and shrugging. It's not the first time this has happened.

We look up at the replacement. I laugh. It's quite funny.

Cereal Monogamist? (Eat the same thing every morning?) That's for the thickos who don't get it.

Try 'Get Your Oats' by McTavish!

'Hey Mica, give us a bunk up then,' says Carla, 'It's getting on my nerves anyway!'

She gets up on Mica's shoulders, takes her spray can out of her jacket and scrawls, *THIS ADVERT DEGRADES CEREAL!* But she doesn't sign it.

On the way home I tell them about South Africa, which sparks a debate that we're all too tired for. Mica thinks the whole thing is fucking outrageous. I agree, Carla agrees but says that she would love to go, that one day she would go, to Africa, she means.

19

The crème passionelle episode

'Have you lost weight?'

I shrug my shoulders as I sit down on the chair and he shakes my hair out of the towel. I wonder if this is all part of a hairdresser's training. There is no way that a hairdresser would say, in the 'developed' world, at least, 'Have you put on weight?' Can you imagine? There's no way you'd be going back there, however handy with the scissors. In the face of groaning supermarket shelves and endless temptation, the greatest achievement is to resist it all. Isn't that bizarre? You know the one about how hell is a place where you sit before a banquet with a ten foot fork or something, well this is the banquet, but instead of a ten foot fork you've just got to resist it, chuck it away, waste it, throw up — anything, rather than advertise the fact that you are weak-willed, prone to sugarlust. If skinny, you're fabulous, you've won the battle. Your iconic status is reinforced everywhere you look. All those wibbly-wobbly bits are under strict control, never to wibble-wobble again. If you're obese, you're a pariah, a symbol of what we all could be, and would be, without our superior moral fibre.

'No sugar, thanks,' I say, displaying mine.

Andre zips back with a cup of coffee, and a small biscuit wrapped in cellophane, which I fall upon, rip open hungrily and eat for my breakfast, as I wave goodbye to my non-descript, blank-canvas hair. For it was he, Andre, who coined the phrase, way back then. I pick up a magazine. 'Pregnancy cured my anorexia,' it proclaims. Oh right. Remind me to suggest that to the next anorexic thirteen year old I meet. I flick through it and put it down again. I'm saying nothing. I'm not even going to give it the oxygen of publicity. So there. Save to say that it would be a nice surprise, one day, to find a few thumbed copies of the *New Scientist* or *The Economist* lying around. A *National Geographic* from 1988 would be heaven.

I stare at myself in the mirror. Just how do I square a fossil fuel binge to the other side of the world to earn a large sum for doing very little indeed for the very thing I loathe? Sell out, sell out and sell out. That's me. My thoughts turn from one uncomfortable situation to another; i.e. David, as I wait for the bleach to do its thing. I wonder what he's doing. I must speak to him today. I'm playing games. I have to talk to him before I get on that plane. In that it might be my fast track to oblivion, I must try to leave my house in order, as it were. I wonder what he'd say if he saw me blonde again. Not that he said a great deal about it whatever colour or length it was. Therein lies the crux of the matter: that when a man loves you properly, he doesn't give a toss about the shade of your hair, your pouty lips or whatever else that these magazines that keep catching my eye postulate. A couple of pounds here or there, so what? It's the part of you that can't change that he's in love with. Isn't it? Well, it's a nice idea. I might be doing a good impression of someone who has risen above such trivial concerns, but then I'm an actor. Of course it's worse for women, because you know that the time will come when it's battleaxe or nowt, as men glide into the best parts ever penned; while we wither away, they become more distinguished by the minute. If a man dyes his hair, it's just about OK, but not quite. If a woman doesn't, it's not. If a woman is grey, it spells old granny, menopausally challenged, past it. And people don't fancy old grannies, generally speaking. But I'd wanted to go grey with David. Or maybe he could do the going grey bit for me.

Swan's galley led into a living room of sorts, with a wood burning stove, a couple of tatty-in-a-nice-way armchairs and a small table where we'd eat. Afterwards, on summer evenings, if the tide was right we'd put on wellies and walk along the muddy bank, beachcombing; Badric up to his knees in the grey-green sludge and loving it, usually finding nothing other than bits of smoothed coloured glass, rubbish and the odd dead pigeon. Course it couldn't last.

'What's the matter?' I remember it with awful clarity. I was up on deck with Badric, I had the house by then but *Swan* drew me back like a magnet. The truth was I had no feeling for it. I wanted to live on *Swan*. I wanted to live if not on *Swan*, then on a slightly bigger boat, but in the same place, with David. By St Mary's, where Blake married, where Turner painted, where the poor lad was buried after his roasting in that limekiln. How could something with four walls ever compete? It was an affair in itself. The river wasn't just a grey, wet expanse that kept South London in its place, it was the real world. Everything else was a sham, especially my job. When you sleep in a cabin and wake to see a Canada goose peering in at you, you know that an ordinary bedroom is never again going to cut it.

'Darling, I've sold her.'

Not even, 'Darling, I'm thinking about selling...'

'But ... but...' I would have bought her! It would have been easy! 'No,' he said, 'it wouldn't have been easy.' Muttering something about the lease of the mooring, something else about her needing to go into dry dock and have a new steel plate welded on to her hull. I knew about this possibility, and the thought of her going away for a few weeks been bad enough. We'd been pumping the bilges for weeks as if we were sinking.

I could split a piece of driftwood into kindling by then (with gloves on; I had to watch my nails), I could light a stove. I knew about wheelhouses and engine rooms and hatches and gangplanks and ... 'No! Say you've changed your mind!' I pleaded, tears rolling down my cheeks. *Swan* was the biggest part of the jigsaw. I knew that without her there wasn't enough to make a picture, and the fact that he'd made this decision alone tore through me like an alarm call. This wasn't a partnership. Fiona was his partner. Fiona who didn't like it on *Swan*, one of the very few things he ever said about her.

I couldn't help him pack. I stayed away. He kept saying that at least we had the house, my place, but it was never going to be the same. The promise of a future seemed remote, impossible. But I did go to see her off. It was a bleak, grey, cold day, no wind, deathly. David was busy with the gangplank and the electricity cables, the mooring ropes and the gas bottles, the phone line and the plumbing; cutting cords. Badric sniffed around oblivious, while I pulled my coat around me and bit my lip.

I can even remember exactly how David looked that day, pushing his hair back from his face, long legs in his jeans, the jumper that smelt of bilge water and oil, his preoccupation. The tug appeared and the other boat dwellers that were in emerged to see her off. The tug gave a toot and they pulled away, last year's dying honeysuckle tearing and breaking where it had tangled itself round her chains. Then just water as if she'd never been there at all. I watched till she disappeared under the railway bridge and round the bend, off to Eel Pie Island. She may as well have had a pennant on a pole bearing the word, 'Happiness' disappearing with her.

'All done!' trills Andre, holding a mirror to my back that

leaves me none the wiser, other than revealing that I have metamorphosed into Shiraz, 'Are you OK?'

'Yeah, fine,' I say, asking for a receipt and stepping out into the world, all set to Have More Fun.

Back home, I stuff my hair into a baseball cap before I take Badric out. I see Nina in the distance with Thai, so I hurry to join her. She's stressed out; Thai is being a complete brat and her head is splitting, did I have any painkillers on me?

'Shall we chuck him in?' I say, looking out over the water that is glinting in the sunlight, tide going out.

'Yes, good idea!' she says as he starts screaming blue murder. She hands him a rice cake. No wonder he's so miserable.

Up ahead I see Ben. He sees us and waves. I can see that he is bursting with news as he approaches.

'Rachel! Love the hair! We put in a good word for you darling!'

'Oh. Thanks. We?'

It would seem that there is some justice in the world after all. Steve has come back.

'That was quick,' says Nina.

Yes, grovelling and begging apparently, and would you believe it, his new boyfriend, you remember, the boy wonder that was supposed to be Ben's birthday present, did exactly the same thing to Steve, i.e. invited another member (pardon the pun) along to join them for a two-day debauch, you know, with pills, the lot. Except it wasn't even Steve's birthday, which was better and worse at the same time. And Steve couldn't handle it. Simple as that. Suddenly knew how Ben felt and had the strong urge to come home and spend cosy evenings flicking through Interiors magazine with his one and only. Bless.

'Wowee! Would ye look at you?' says Gus when he gets

home. 'You look gorgeous! We are going oot tonight!'

As it happens, he has something to celebrate. Apart from being on speaking terms with Helena, he's just been promoted. Anyway, this is his last night. He's going home tomorrow, getting the sleeper after work. He's glad, he's had enough of London, it's been fun, but ... Helena, you know.

'OK.' Why not? After all, London lies just outside my front door. London with its million cultural opportunities, theatres, galleries, clubs. But as we all know, for some time now, staying in has been the new going out. I have a shower and dress while Gus has a bath, singing at the top of his voice. I check my email, no news from Ferdie yet. I email Juliet, and tell her that I have a job. Hopefully that should put her off for a while longer. I ring David's mobile.

'Hello, hello?'

'He-he-he-he-lo-lo-lo-lo...' Then it cuts out. Fuck this fucking useless technology! Come on, come on! How come we can keep contact with someone in space and not speak to someone in Ireland? I could have written to him by now for God's sake! We are ready to go out when the doorbell rings. I open it to see Shelley and Nika on my doorstep. Friends again, so it would seem.

'Hi Shel, Nika. How are you?'

'Fine thanks,' says Shelley. 'Your hair looks lovely! We've come to watch *Wives*. Mum said you said it would be OK.' Did she? Did I? Gus calls out, 'Who is it?' I tell him that who what and the wherefore and he says 'Great, we can go out afterwards!'

'We went to the cemetery today,' says Shelley.

Bugger. I forgot.

'How's your mum?' I say nodding, as if I hadn't.

'OK.' Conversation over. I must ring Carla.

I have no desire whatsoever to watch *Wives*, but 'I'm just a girl who...' who really needs some assertiveness training.

But even then Shelley would manage to soften my heart. Gus asks when it starts. Shelley says, 'Ten minutes,' so he rushes off to the shop for supplies, coming back with a bottle of champagne. The girls giggle as it spills over the tops of their glasses and I join in.

It's strange to see myself look so different (last week) and now so similar, what with my going out clothes on and newly blonde hair. We settle down to the *crème passionelle* episode.

Ricardo's new restaurant is doing superbly well. Jean-Pierre's restaurant is yesterday's news. Mercedes likes her man to be on top. Ricardo is now that man. Shiraz also likes her man to be on top, and has the advantage of knowing all Ricardo's little secrets, like the fact that his father was, in fact, a lorry driver from Alicante and not the hero of the Spanish Civil war who went on to become a lion tamer, still giving women children till shortly before his death. Ricardo's new dessert has had a full page spread in *The Foodie* magazine. His *crème passionelle* is said to be inspired by a woman's body.

'Huh, that'll be Mercedes' body, the fat cow! And it's only a bloody low-carb trifle rearranged!' scoffs Shiraz, as she and Isobel stare balefully at the image of a split fig in shaped panna cotta drizzled with a passion fruit and pomegranate coulis.

Gus snorts with laughter. 'Go on Rach, say that again!' The girls giggle as Gus fills up our glasses.

'Shut up!' I say, 'come on Gus – let's go,' I plead. 'Shel, you don't mind, do you?'

'No,' they both shake their heads. I get the feeling I'm inhibiting them somehow. They're embarrassed to engage with something, which by my presence, is rendered even more fake. Strange. Let them swoon over Haden and Bob (Jean-Pierre) on their own. Gus tells them to finish the bottle and Badric is cordially invited to sit between them on the sofa.

'Have you got your key, Shel?'

'Yeah,' she calls out, 'Don't worry.'

Gus manages the unmanageable, hailing a black cab in my very street. See, sometimes it is good to live on a hump-free rat-run. As I'm closing the front door I hear the phone ring and David's voice on the answering machine. 'Sorry about that, I'm at Nige's now, but you're not at home.'

LEAVE THE NUMBER DAVID YOU IDIOT!! I think, as I rush towards the phone, 'I'll try you later.' Click. My mobile, he'll ring my mobile. Gus is shouting for me to get a move on as I charge up the stairs, grab the mobile and see that it is dead. It doesn't even have enough power to turn itself on and tell me that it is dead.

'Shel, if a man rings, get his number will you?'

In Soho Gus looks around.

'Is this it?'

'What?' My feet are hurting already.

'The be all and end all?'

'Depends what you're into I suppose. C'mon, decide. It's freezing.'

'Chinese?'

'Fine.'

Typical West End Friday, we eat, we fight through the mass of people, the souvenir sellers, the salsa dancers, the pan-pipe players and the drunks on Leicester Square, cross Trafalgar Square and aim for Whitehall, get as far as I can before my feet became bloodied stumps, near, but not near enough to the bus stop.

'Fourth time!' calls Gus as a gang of girls shout, 'Shiraz, where's Zsa-Zsa?!' 'Gus, let's get a cab.'

'How does that feel, Rach?'

'Painful.'

'No, I mean getting recognised.'

'Depends on what you get recognised for I suppose.

177

For *Chefs' Wives* it's ... ridiculous, embarrassing.'

We ask the cabbie to drop us at the garage so we can get some fags. Gus stumbles, I hobble towards my door.

'Carry me please, Gus.'

Drunk people will. We're giggling as he staggers towards my gate. Two fingers separate the slats of next door's Venetian blind. Teresa's eye is at the gap.

'Hurry up for Christ's sake!' says Gus, as I take my keys out of my itsy-bitsy handbag.

We get in and Badric performs his canine dance of greeting around us. I feel bloated. Gus is clutching his stomach as well, and collapses on the sofa, as I let Badric out the back and check the answering machine. Two messages. First one's from Teresa. 'Hello, this is a message for Gus, it's Teresa speaking. Why are you avoiding me? I think you owe me an explanation! Give me a ring on my mobile, soon!'

'Bloody hell! She's rung my mobile about ten times today.'

'Just tell her it was a one-off, that you were on the rebound, but that it was fantastic and you'll never forget it, or something. For my sake if nothing else. You can't go home without talking to her. She'll pester me forever and in the end I'll have to give her your address.'

'OK, OK. But not tonight.'

Next it's Carla's voice, and she is definitely not happy. 'I've just had a very interesting chat with Shelley. What the hell d'you think you're doing, sorting out my daughter's life without telling me? I want to talk about this, tomorrow, not tonight, I'm going to bed. Oh, and tell your pisshead cousin not to ply young girls with drink if he can help it.'

'Your pisshead cousin? Charming! She sounds bloody furious! What have you done?' I tell him the reason why Shelley was here the other night, and he tells me that Carla's just being a mum, which is quite generous considering the 'pisshead'. I suddenly feel very tired. He comes

178

over and puts his arms around me.

'What about a nightcap, since we're both in trouble?'

I might even miss him tomorrow.

20

The holy grail

Carla and I are to meet in the café in the park. She isn't working till later. She wants to sort this out. I'm starting to feel a bit pissed off with her. She's being very righteous and I'm supposed to be apologetic. I don't think so. What would she have expected me to do?

It's a bright morning so we sit outside. I ask the numb-skull who is struggling with the concept of the possibility of some real milk for my coffee instead of two cartonettes of Milac Maid synthesised vegetable fat and lard or what-ever the hell it is, how Giacomo is doing. He shrugs and looks blank. I look at him. I want to yell,

'HE'S YOUR COLLEAGUE FOR GOD'S SAKE!' But I don't think even that would register.

Carla has got her sunglasses on, which puts me at a dis-tinct disadvantage.

'Like your hair,' she says sarcastically.

'Thought you would,' I say sarcastically. 'How was yes-terday?'

She turns her head towards the middle of the lake.

'Oh, you know. It was a nice day though, sunny. We just sat there talking to Michael for a bit, tidied up, did a bit of weeding. Put some flowers down. Wished mum was around, the usual.'

Carla's mum has gone home to Jamaica. Carla's happy for her but misses her badly.

She says that it was obvious that Shelley was upset about something, but that she was too busy thinking about Michael.

'I even thought she was upset about him! I just feel a fool apart from anything else.'

'What else could I have done? She's an adult, she told me something in confidence, I had no choice. If I'd said that we'd have to speak to you, she might have run off. We didn't have that much time.'

'But, Rachel, you didn't have to tell her that you were telling me! You could have just let me know.'

'No I couldn't.'

'Why not?'

'Because she asked me not to.'

'And when did you start getting so high-minded?'

'Excuse me?'

'Come on Rach. You're not exactly Miss Integrity are you?'

'What's that supposed to mean?'

Tears slide out from beneath her glasses. 'I know. Sorry. I just... Oh I don't know. Yesterday, thinking about Michael and everything, I suppose I was upset to start with. I think I was jealous, I know that sounds mad. I was jealous that she felt she could talk to you and not me,' she sighs.

'Yeah but, you're her mum! Could you have talked to your mum?'

'God no! But I've tried to do things differently, but...' She pauses, takes a tissue out of her pocket and wipes her nose, 'I've gone wrong somewhere. I mean, look at her, she's a wannabe clone, just like the rest of them.'

'No she isn't, Carla, she's lovely. But of course she wants to be like her mates. It's normal.'

'I just miss her. I love my place, you know I do, God knows what I'd do without Jessie, it's just ... I don't want to cling to my daughter just because I'm lonely. I'm pathetic aren't I?'

'Babe, you are the least pathetic person that I know.'

'Hey, d'you fancy trying speed dating?' she says, brightening, 'Or are you too famous at the moment?'

Later that day I have a brainwave. For immediate pecuniary and other reasons, including ones relating to self-esteem, despite the glam blonde look, I am shopping in Arding & Hobbs rather than Peter Jones and thinking about Carla, when she sends me a text.

Thanx 4 earlier. Sorry ☺ xx

I'm going to go online when I get home and check out the hotel in Cape Town again. She can come with me. I feel excited at the thought. I'm pretty sure she'll go for it. What is plastic for after all? It can be her birthday and Christmas present for the next decade or so.

I'm here to get a few things for going away. It's starting to become a reality. On the rare occasion that I go away, Carla looks after Badric. Hopefully, this time, that won't be possible. Shelley is the obvious choice. She can stay at my house and look after Jessie and Badric there.

I've already been to the bookshop and bought a Cape Town guidebook. There probably won't be any time for tourism, still, it's nice to know what you might have seen as you exist in the bubble of a shoot for three days. I keep an eye on the time. My car (OK, I confess. I drove the less than a mile to Clapham Junction), is in the Asda car park. After all, two hours of free parking is worth driving any short distance for in London, but I do feel obliged to buy something big and heavy to justify the journey, thus making a mockery of the free parking, but it's the principle of the thing. Whatever the thing is.

A new swimming costume is not big and heavy, but for

what it is, it's ridiculously expensive. Still, it wouldn't do to turn up at the pool in my old Speedo that's beginning to decompose like a dead butterfly's wing. Perhaps some new underwear too, while I'm at it. As I peruse the bras, which is an extremely trying exercise, as they insist on displaying these things on small plastic hangers that like nothing better than to become attached to the one next to them, whilst somehow managing to shed their bra, which instantly ties itself in a knot, which you try to sort out on your hands and knees, which is where you have to be anyway, as you crane your neck trying to find the Holy Grail, i.e., a bra your size, or the size you were the last time that you allowed yourself to be measured by a matronly woman who's 'seen it all before'. One such matronly woman comes to my rescue, sorting out tangled bras, hooks caught in lace and pointing me in the right direction as if born to it. Her bust is positively mountainous, as if this might make her a highly qualified expert in the field.

'Need any help, dear?' she says.

'No, just looking,' I say, as if you'd just look at bras for the sake of it. Of course, I could be doing research for an article exploring the reasons why, when everything else has become practical and snappy – Velcro and idiot-proof plastic fasteners superseding the shoelace or buckle – the bra has adamantly refused to throw off its lacy Victorian charm. Apparently, there are fifty or so bits of material that make up one of these things. Fifty or so bits of material, a couple of bits of wire and a yard of lace, two or three hooks, six or nine eyes, and some more rings and fiddly little buckle-like arrangements. Maybe their expense is justified after all. Of course there is such a thing as a sports bra, a sort of one-piece thing that squashes you flat, which is not really the sort of support you want, and some plainish ones, if you don't relish the glamour look, but I'll wager that there will not be one of these in your size in stock. And even if the nice lady rings through to Allders in Croydon, there won't be one there either.

'Sorry, dear. There doesn't appear to be a bra for you anywhere on the entire planet. Try Venus.'

I read somewhere that women are choosing to wear bras one size too small, giving them a miraculous cleavage, but maybe they just gave up looking, the risk to their health a small price to pay for the time saved.

I've had enough of bras so I head for pants, joining two other women who are rummaging in the 'sale' mini-skip. I decide to go for a lucky dip, but no, miniscule and pink with a puppy on the front saying 'down boy' is not my style at all. Try again, no, nor is a white pair the size of mainland Europe, nor something that was a doily in a former life. Reminds me of some pants David brought me back from a trip to New York, flimsy and frilly, from Victoria's Secret. What, I wonder, is Victoria's secret? That she just faked it? That really, she thinks this stuff is ridiculous? That she's only with him for the presents? Could it be that beneath the lace she's actually flesh and blood? 'At the sight of the vulva the devil himself flees', was it Freud who said that? Of course the devil would be a raving misogynist wouldn't he? Oh, I can't be bothered with this. A three-pack of black knickers with minimum lacy adornment will have to do.

I watch some young girls admiring the Miracle Bras and the like. They hardly look old enough to wear a bra. In the name of research I go over to the 'trainer bra' section and at first assume that they must be in the process of relocating it, till I realise that these black satin and lace things are 'trainer bras', size 30AA, etc. Bloody hell! My first bra was nothing like this! Not sure what's meant by 'training' or 'trainer' bra anyway. Maybe to train you to get used to wearing something under your T-shirt? Or to train you to get used to the intense embarrassment of your dad noticing? Or maybe to train boys to undo them, so they have become skilled in their removal when the time comes that there is something underneath worth the effort involved. But I'm making light of something sinister. Some of these bras are actually padded. I can also see little teeny-weeny bikinis, two little waterproof triangles to cover up nothing. Isn't it bad enough that we have to puzzle over sex for the rest of our lives? Why draw attention to it sooner than necessary? And as for pump-up bras ... well, really. Maybe I should get one, to wear on the plane; a sort of belt and braces thing for the plummet into the sea. Woman found alive thanks to extra buoyancy from inflatable bra! Just don't embrace anyone too enthusiastically in a pump-up bra, or the result might be akin to sitting on a vertical Whoopee cushion.

I wait in the queue at the check out to pay for my purchases. The woman in front of me is in an agony of deliberation: this or that nightie, the maroon matching set or the cream? My blood pressure is beginning to rise. A £4 ticket in the Asda car park looms. She rushes over to the nightie stand and grabs a black one, then changes it again for dark blue. She must have a new bloke or something, but that's no excuse. Come on, love! It's not exactly *Sophie's Choice*, get on with it! As her card takes ages and ages to go through she turns to me and scrutinises my face, her eyeballs scanning from side to side. She can't place me. She says nothing.

My turn at last. The woman asks me if I'd like to try on the swimming costume. I have no wish to do this. I know that it will be more or less OK, but to try it on under the fluorescent strip of the changing room would be unnecessarily masochistic. When it comes to my body, I like to try to remember to feel thankful that it is in working order and respect its right to a bit of privacy. And after all, familiarity breeds contempt.

I ring Jenny to say that I've got the fax, and to mention, ever so casually, that it just so happens that a friend of mine is going to Cape Town at the same time for a mini-break, as you do. I apologise for ringing on Saturday, hearing her annoyance. Well, she didn't have to pick up, did she? In fact, I was hoping that she wouldn't.

'That'll be nice for you, darling. Just make sure to get your beauty sleep, won't you?'

I check the flight details and availability online. Plenty of room. Good. I ring Carla.

'Hi babe, what are you up to next week?'

She says that there's nothing happening, in fact it's a quiet one, since the studio is getting a makeover, and they can't rehearse. Lien's got tonsillitis, so he says, and it's not the same without Ferdie, so 'Don't worry, course I'll have Badric. Listen, I'm serious about the speed dating.'

'How about coming with me?'

'Yeah, right.'

'Seriously.'

'Seriously?'

'Seriously!'

'But...'

In a flash she is round and we infect the dogs with our excitement. They tuck their bottoms underneath themselves and tear round and round the front room, claws a-clatter. I tell her that she can protest about the money for fifteen minutes max, then never mention it again, reminding her that the trip is being paid for by our secret enemy after all, and that my plastic is a mere interim solution. I get the flight and the room organised while she rings Shelley on her mobile, goes into the bathroom to speak to her, then comes back smiling, handing me the phone.

'Hi Rachel, listen, I'm really sorry that I told mum ... I'm so happy that she's not cross with you anymore.'

'So am I, she's scary!'

'Shut up!' says Carla, dancing around.

Later, without Gus and the rest of the crowd, the house

feels calm. I put on the radio while I consider the eating options. I feel good. It's a relief to be alone. When I first moved in I used to rattle around like a pea in a pod, jumping at noises whilst waiting for David to appear, going into a sort of suspended animation when he wasn't there. But I got over it, or got used to it. The less I nagged him about when things would change, the less it seemed to matter. It's not reality. It's better than reality. No domestic drudgery for me, no headaches and no hassle. Once, twice a week and hundreds of texts in between, never mentioned, as if there was an affair within the affair, another dimension to it, more honest, more loving, better acknowledged.

Once a month or so, it felt dire, but that's pretty good going in the general scheme of things. Those were the days when we'd split up. I would suddenly see the wrongness of it and pronounce pompously that I could no longer be a party to such dishonourable behaviour, the lies and deceit. How could he? Didn't I deserve more? 'It's over!' If I said it once, I said it a hundred times; all or nothing. That's what I wanted. Maybe it was hormonal, this vision of David and I sitting round a table with a brood. I don't know. I learnt, if I didn't know already, that understanding yourself is every bit as difficult, if not more so, than understanding someone else, as I found myself ringing his mobile, or wandering into the shop, swinging back into mistress mode, undeterred.

Of course, my mood of the moment may be putting a rosey tint on this state of affairs, but the more I thought about it, the more I questioned whether cosy domesticity was all it was cracked up to be, the more I watched my friends, in their long-term relationships, descend into bickering, boredom and blame. Who wants to be an 'other-half'? Not me. As they got married and pregnant, I saw nothing but time and space and equity in my house expanding into infinity. I could travel the world. I could carry on drinking and smoking with impunity. I could buy my Stornoway retreat and raise my skirts (not that I ever wear a skirt, let alone more than one) for whomever I pleased. I could drink whisky for breakfast, or become nocturnal, and people would wonder, call me mad and pity me, but that would only be because they were jealous.

I open a bottle of wine and raise my glass to freedom, solitude, time, Foyle and Fagherty, the light shining through my wine, and to the moment, while it lasts.

21

A quiet night in

I have an email from Geoff. I'd forgotten all about him.

> Hi Rachel,
> Saw you on telly the other night. You were great!!!!
> Cant believe what happened on our date!!! Im really
> sorry! (Hope your dog is Ok) I'd love to buy you dinner
> sometime to make it up to you, because we were
> getting on really well up til then!
> Speak soon I hope,
> Geoff xx

Whoops, deleted. Then one from Juliet congratulating me on the ad and telling me that I'd better come and see them when I get back. She says she can't believe how thin she was on *Wives* and that now she is a 'lard arse'. That's babies for you, she writes.

That's all it takes for the toast of two minutes ago to become the opposite of a celebration. Well, I can't avoid it forever. It's been brewing for a couple of weeks anyhow, since he reappeared. It would be great if, with a brush of the hands, it was done with and I'd never think about it again, but it doesn't work like that. Things don't really ever go away, they're always there, it's just that you don't think about them so often.

We were having a weekend away, being on again, after yet another break. I'd been in the house for a while and *Wives* was going on and on like an after-dinner speech. We stayed in a hotel we'd stayed in before, ate what we'd eaten before, but it wasn't the same. I'd seen this mood before, the elusive David, impossible to pin down, tuning in and out like bad reception. Still, I didn't quiz him. But when I woke in the night he and Badric weren't there. I got up, went over to the window and looked out. Badric was busy, nose to the ground, and David was sitting on one of the garden benches, hipflask in hand, staring into space. I switched on the bedside light and he looked up at me, and in the split second before he waved and got up, I saw something in his eye that turned my insides to jelly. I knew what he was going to say. And that, unlike me, he'd mean it.

Dad always used to laugh at mum and me, the way we always knew whodunit. Films end, the lights come up, there's nothing you can do about it.

'Don't say it,' I said when he dropped me off.

'Darling I'm so sor...'

When you don't get what you want, the best thing to do is pretend that you didn't want it in the first place, like that good job. Or when you get what you didn't want, the best thing to do is pretend that you did, like a naff Christmas present. After all, I knew it had to happen. If he wasn't going to leave her soon, there was no point to it. I was almost being lazy. It was becoming a convenience. I could flirt, I could go out on the town with Haden, I could be one thing, and then another. Both, or all sides of me were covered. But in the back of my mind, a voice was nagging away. 'Tut, tut, tut,' it said, waggling its finger at me, 'Get it together, Madam. End it now before it's too late.' I did try, but I could never sustain it. So I didn't create a scene, or slam the car door. Instead, I went inside and felt a surge of relief that lasted about forty minutes. If that.

Three nights later Alan from the theatre group rang, out of the blue. A blast from the past. See **_Rule No. 9._** The next thing I know I'm waking up beside someone I woke up beside ages ago, with the mother of all hangovers. Alan hadn't changed: still the dope fiend; still writing his screenplay; still on his futon on the floor, in the flat in Streatham, my old flat, he moved in when I moved out. How weird is that? The others had moved on; I was glad. I didn't want any of them to see Shiraz on her knees, unless it was on telly in front of a toilet bowl. Three weeks later Juliet confided in me, in the studio loos, that she was pregnant. She was thrilled, so was Paul, and that I wasn't to tell anyone yet. That morning I'd sat on the edge of the bath with ice for blood as I watched a blue line appear on a white plastic stick, my twenty-day lost weekend over.

Why, why did I do that with Alan? If it hadn't been for that, if I'd been one hundred percent sure it was David's ... Holding the little Predictor magic wand in my shaking hand, I felt as if I was getting what I deserved. This was it. Punishment. You don't get away with it that easily, husband snatcher! Later that day, on set, Haden asked me if I was OK. I said I'd tell him after we'd finished. We went back to his flat and he listened and fed me. I watched him as he cooked. He's a good cook, obviously not quite up to Ricardo's standard, but who is? I admired his ease, his casual Mediterranean way with olives. I thanked the high heavens that he was gay. God, in his wisdom, had given me something I couldn't fuck up.

'Are you sure?' Next it was Carla's sofa, again being fed, this time carrot cake. 'Yes. I just want an end to it. I need to put the whole thing behind me.'

Carla nods, shrugs, tells me it's up to me, not to feel guilty, that it happened, and that if I'm not up for it, then fine.

'But it's a life, might be my only chance.'

'It's not a life. Not yet. It hasn't got a nervous system.'

'You mean it hasn't got a nervous system *yet*. Maybe I'm going to do this because I can't face telling Mum that it's either the child of a married man, or a waster from way back. I don't think I need to tell Alan, and I certainly won't be telling David.' Not till he tells me why he ended it. He never really even explained why he had to sell *Swan*, not really. He needed the money. Why?

I could hear suspicion in Mum's voice when she rang.

'Are you all right pet?' She didn't pry, but I could picture her putting the phone down and going down to the shed to see Dad, telling him that she was worried about me, that she was sure there was something wrong. I could hear him reassuring her, saying that if it was that bad, they'd know about it, that if I wanted them to know, I'd tell them. And she'd sigh and agree, walk back up the garden with her arms folded, knowing in her bones that something was not right with her only child. And that's exactly why I couldn't tell her. She'd wanted more children so much. I didn't fancy telling her I was about to destroy a potential grandchild. I thought of the two of us all those years ago making fairy cakes and eating them, still warm and a bit raw in the middle, as we watched telly, feeling sorry for the *Incredible Hulk*. No, I definitely couldn't tell her.

It's not the sort of thing that you can agonise over for very long, not like buying a house, or deciding where to go on holiday, you don't get a trial, or a cooling off period. No choice is bad, and choice drives you nuts. Trivial decisions you can dilly-dally with for donkey's years. Life or death decisions you have to make quickly, it's ironic really: like whether to jump from a burning building, or hack off your own arm as it pulls you towards a mincing machine. There's no time to debate the issue at length. I suppose the bottom line is you just have to put yourself first, and remember that you had no choice ... or at least felt that at the time, for the rest of your life. It's only delayed contraception. Loads of people do it. There will be other chances. It's no big deal. *Because you're worth it.*

So I booked myself in. I remembered to breathe, reminded myself that anxiety was my friend, and off I went. Carla waited for me and came to stay for a few days, feeding me, walking the dogs. And what did I feel, the foeticidal maniac, despair, regret, guilt? God no. Relief! Pure, blissful, blessed relief! Let the bellies of SW11 swell, but not mine. No Sir-ee.

We were told that *Wives* was dropping in the ratings and it looked like the new series might not happen, and that this one was ending in a couple of months' time. And no job means no money. But, as usual, Carla saved the day. Her new percussion player needed a room. Ferdie moved in, my hair returned to its old colour; my insteps resumed their natural shape; my bank balance resumed its natural state. And with Carla's library of feminist theory for the mind, Gobshite for the body, and Direct Action for the soul, all would be well. The only thing I had in common with Shiraz was a once-weekly, primetime, gnawing ache.

I'd dreaded seeing Juliet's newborn baby. It could, I say could, not should, have been me. Unbearable one minute, the little thing at her breast, making me sick with grief, then quite happy, thank you, as the yelling started and Juliet, exhausted, would say that she really wasn't sure if she was cut out for this lark after all. She'd even make envious remarks about my flat, stretch-mark free stomach. I'd make a joke of it, asking her what she'd prefer, a flat stomach or a baby? We laughed at this, both saying that at that particular moment, we honestly weren't sure. Light-hearted and as free as a bird, I'd get into my car, turn the music up full blast and head off into the night. Maybe I could do it, one day, but not quite yet. And I damn well couldn't do it alone. Hats off to the cuckoo. Hats off to that bloke in Italy who can sort you out with a baby when you're sixty-five. Then I'd wake in the night with an ache far worse than period pain, but which would pass. And in its absence I forgot about it, till the next time.

What else could I do? Go mad? Sit Badric in a pram with a bonnet on his head, and wheel him around cooing at him and dangling a stupid little book over his head like every other person that I saw, everywhere I looked. Haden said that it was all down to hormones, as if I could rationalise it all away. I tried. Actor in minimalist shabby-chic Zone One home, who sometimes feels she might be happier in Carla's garden shed with a baby. Who is also very happy not to have that baby, but who cries at the sight of any birth on the telly, even a rat's; who can't stand the sound of screaming kids; who finds more and more that apple cores, pips and seeds of any variety get chucked into the garden rather than into the bin. Is this normal? I wonder. Is there anyone who's had an abortion that feels resolved about it? About anything? Cleopatra knew resolve. Called for an asp and that was that.

> *'My resolution's placed, and I have nothing*
> *Of woman in me; now from head to foot*
> *I am marble-constant, now the fleeting moon*
> *No planet is of mine.'*

The phone rings. It is him, master of my destiny, methinks, with more than a hint of bitterness.

'At last!' he says. He's caught me at a bad moment. I'm not feeling gooey now. I'm feeling scorned.

'What?'

'You're so hard to get hold of these days!' He's happy to hear my voice, living in a fool's paradise prompted by a lovey-dovey text message.

'Your wife came to see me.'

There is a pause, then he says, 'Yes, I know, she wanted to apologise.'

This could be my cue to blow my top. The nerve has been touched. It's that him-and-her thing again, like they'd cooked up a little apology between themselves. It makes me the last to know, and it fucking annoys me. To be fair, she may have told him after the event, but why are they talking at all? If it's really over this time, then why? Surely that's what you pay solicitors for? But then she is a solicitor, and of course they've got plenty to talk about. I say nothing; just breathe poison down the line from the dark well of accumulated hurts turned to venom.

'I'm coming over next week. Looks like I might be able to avoid bankruptcy after all!'

'Oh. Congratulations,' I say, with as little enthusiasm as possible.

'Could we celebrate?'

'We? Oh, you mean you and me?' God, I'm a bitch.

Silence followed by a sigh then, 'I'll only be over for a day or two, Tuesday probably.' Pang! Goes my heart, 'I'm helping Nige rebuild the barn. It's doing me good, giving me some time...'

'Sorry, I won't be here. I'm doing a job in Cape Town.' I try to sound smug and successful, but my fury is fizzling out. I'm not going to see him for ages now.

'Oh, that sounds exciting.'

We talk about nothing for as long as it is possible so to do, and then say goodbye. He said he had a lot to tell me, but not over the phone.

'Blimey, sounds serious. You're not dying are you?'

He laughs.

'Only for want of you.'

And that is unusual for David. That's the sort of thing he'd usually save for texts.

I struggle up the stairs with the ladder. Don't think for a minute that I'd forgotten the stuff in the attic. I just needed the place to myself to look into this matter further.

Anyway, even if I do find a diary, I don't absolutely have to read it, do I?

It's been a while since I've been up here. It's a strange place. It's almost like sliding back the door of a tomb. The place itself seems surprised by the light, as if it has disturbed someone, something. Dusty, warm, still air reeking of memories. Attic smell, quite distinct from cellar smell, and garage smell, all of which I like: the extremes of houses, unadorned by plasterboard and frou-frou, revealing the bones of a building. A repository for ghosts. I fumble around for the light switch, then pull myself up and inside. I tell Badric to go to his basket before he knocks the ladder over, but he stays put, wagging his tail, looking up at me from the landing with that concerned expression on his face that he assumes when I do something outside the general scheme of things, like lying on the floor or swimming alongside him in the sea.

Over there sits my boxed childhood. My schoolbooks, some toys, a hockey stick and a tennis racket in a press, even the pictures I painted. A plastic bag with the programmes of plays I was in, once upon a time, an envelope of certificates, the staging posts of my life. My old *Complete Works of Shakespeare* is up here, I could have sworn it was in my bedroom, but there it is, 'The Eileen Adams prize for Speech and Drama', a decorous paper slip stuck to the first page, 'Rachel Jameson.' It seems like yesterday; that sure-fire feeling of destiny. Ha, ha.

But it's David's stuff I'm interested in tonight. There it is, all piled up. Stolen goods? The great antiques heist? What? I crawl over, careful to put my weight on the joists, and take down the first box of about fifteen or so. Loads. This could be more revealing than necessary. What if they're full of pickled body parts? David the serial killer; mistress after mistress disposed of and deposited in the next victim's attic, or guns, knives, cocaine...

I tear the tape off the first one, and open it, my head

held back slightly in case it blows my head off. Hang on, I recognise this; it's a pencil drawing in a chipped back frame, Old Battersea Bridge ... and this ... that little tortoiseshell box that reminded me of a horrible story about Hemingway turning a giant turtle onto his back, and leaving it where it lay, its paddles paddling hopelessly at the air, after an argument with a lover or a wife, I can't remember which. Then a copy of *London Walks* dated 1893, and more and more, and the next box, cups, saucers, all mismatched, some chipped, the plate I hated with foxes being chased round its circumference by hounds ... a note, from me, telling him when I'd be back. Another one, a shopping list. 'Asses' milk for Rachel, wine, puppy food, loo paper, coal.' And a 'to do' list in my writing: 'pamper self, wait for David.' Minus the furniture, what seems like the complete contents of *Swan*, slotting into the shapes they'd carved into my brain like chess pieces into a moulded box.

I could go on. I could even confess to more than a tad of sentimentality as I fingered these things, wiping hardened dust from a hand mirror, not dust from my attic, but dust from *Swan*, particles of suspended time, forensic would confirm it. It was our dust, his and mine. It's romantic but my inner sleuth is exploring motive. Maybe he just had to hide it from her, maybe she found it and threw it all out on the street, or maybe he just never got round to sorting it out and taking half of it to the dump, just like my stuff; something to sort out one day never. Sniffing, I realise that this evening has, so far, amounted to a complete emotional overview of my entire life. Jesus, I must be some sort of masochist. Give me junk TV, quick! And junk food to go with it. But first, without further delay, a large drink and a cigarette.

Back on the landing, Badric greets me as if I'd just got back from Timbuktu. The phone rings.

'Hello? You're joking! Really? No, it's not that, it's just a bit, well, sudden. When's the happy day? Yeah, that sounds sensible ... Helena's idea? Good. Yeah, course I am. Wow! Just so long as you know that you've crossed the floor of the house ... it means you're a traitor! Who am I going to moan with now? Of course I'm happy for you! Well I'll see you there then. Shall I bring Teresa? Hey, did you speak to her? Gus! A text? Well, I suppose it's better than nothing.'

Well, well. Gus proposed to Helena right there and then on the platform of Glasgow Central, and she said 'Yes.' Pretty romantic really. Incredible how sobering a drunken bonk with the wrong person can be. Now he'll have to face that, 'Do I have to fess up to something I did when we were on an official break?' dilemma. Tempting as if can be to get into that truth and reconciliation mood, some things are best taken to the grave: Not just abortions, affairs and big things like that, but lots of things, lots of little crimes and misdemeanours.

There's a knock at the door. No! Not tonight! Please. I so wanted tonight to be the exception to the rule. (**Rule No. 5** that is.) It'll be bloody Teresa I suppose. But it's Eleanor.

'Sorry to disturb you, Rachel, I tried ringing but...'

'Hi, what's wrong? Come in!'

She comes in and Badric promptly sticks his nose up her skirt.

'Is it Miss Jackson?' I hope she hasn't had a stroke or something.

'No, no, she's fine. It's just that there's a girl out there...' She starts whispering as if someone might hear, 'I think she's drunk. She's sitting in her car in her underwear. It's ever so cold. I just wondered if you knew her, or whether we should do something?'

Oh for fuck's sake. Let her freeze to death and do us all a favour.

'That'll be Teresa from next door. I think she's got a few

personal problems at the moment.' Exacerbated by my errant cousin from across the border, I'll be bound. 'I'll have a word with her, don't worry. How's Miss Jackson anyway?'

I'm pleased to hear that she is fine, that 'would you believe it', a lady has just been admitted to her ward that she used to work with twenty years ago, and that, in fact, she seems happier than she's been for a while.

'It's the company, see?' she says, 'She'll miss it if she ever comes home again.'

I tell her that I'm going away next week, but that I'll make sure to visit her before I go.

'She'd like that. She's always boasting about you to the old girls on the ward, and the nurses, how you've been on the telly. You should hear her, you could almost be the daughter she never had!'

The daughter she never had. I catch a glimpse of myself looking something like Miss Jackson, shrinking and fading in a hospital bed thinking about the daughter I'd never had. Oh please! Drop it! Yeah, thinking about the daughter I'm so bloody glad I never had, as I look back on my glittering career and string of relationships with fascinating men who have since been recognised amongst the greatest minds of the twenty-first century, befitting a woman of my status, my portrait next to Ellen Terry's in the National Portrait Gallery.

Eleanor pulls her cardigan around her and watches as I tap on the windscreen. Sure enough, there's Teresa, in her bra and pants, not even a matching set, for shame! Her head is lolling slightly as she looks up at me. She winds down her window.

'Hello, Rachel. Thanks for telling me Gus was leaving,' she slurs.

'Who?' asks Eleanor, in a loud whisper. I loud-whisper back, 'My cousin, it doesn't matter, you go in. I'll get her home.'

'Teresa, I'll be back in a minute, OK? ' She looks at me blankly. I go back inside and get my dressing gown.

'Come on, put this on.' She opens the door and gets out. Eleanor has pulled back the net curtain to watch, her face pressed close to the window, a hand to her furrowed brow like a sailor scanning the horizon. Teresa wobbles as I help her into the dressing gown. I reach in for the keys on the dashboard, lock the car and support her until we are standing between my gate and hers.

'Your hair looks nice,' she says, stroking it at the back. I shrug off her hand. 'I'll open your door, shall I?' I say hopefully.

'No, no, I can't go in there!' she says with more than a hint of amateur dramatics.

'Why not?'

'Mark's in a bad mood,' she whimpers, starting to cry.

'Teresa, does he hit you, or what?'

'I don't want to talk about it. I'll just go back to the car.'

I'm tempted to tell her she's being completely ridiculous but I resist. I get her inside. To my surprise she reaches down and pats Badric.

'You're really quite nice for a dog, d'you know that?'

So much for my quiet night. I'm starving, and she's in my bath. The pizza is half an hour overdue and I'm wondering how Badric would fancy living in South Africa. I put her in Ferdie's bed, which might not be such a good idea, since it was the scene of the crime with Gus. How I wish I hadn't asked him to strip the bed, I think to my irritated-beyond-belief self, as I wrestle with a clean duvet cover. But don't worry; I can manage it, because I am female.

She's sobered up slightly when she comes through, just as I finish the bed-making.

'Need any help?' she says, unconvincingly, as I plump up madam's pillows. 'Thanks again Rachel,' she adds, 'You've been really good to me recently,' and with that hurls herself into my arms, and presses herself against me.

'I really like you, Rachel.' I try to disengage but she squeezes me tighter.

'Thanks, but I'm just doing what anyone...' Blimey, I'd never have guessed she was so strong; her arms are like a vice. Must ask Gus if he noticed, then again, he's a big lad himself...

'No I mean, *really* like you.'

It takes a moment for this to sink in. When it does I leap out of her grasp like a cricket. She laughs.

'God, Rachel. Don't be scared!'

'I'm not scared! I'm...' Actually, come to think of it, I am scared. Scared that I'm going to commit murder if that pizza doesn't... And by the grace of God, it does. A loud knock at the door and I am saved.

'YOUR HELMET! TAKE YOUR HELMET OFF! SHUT UP BADRIC!'

Jesus wept. Some people never learn.

I put the box down, go upstairs, stick my head round Ferdie's door and see, to my relief, that she has crashed out. I wish there was a lock on that door. I go downstairs and eat my pizza, Badric happily wolfing chunks of crust. I would dearly love to go down to the river, but I can't leave that madwoman alone. I feel like ringing Gus and telling him that he's not the only attractive person around, but think better of it. No doubt he and Helena are gazing at one another in some bloody candlelit bistro, the bastards. Honestly, what is Teresa like? I hadn't anticipated that little turn of events. I need to put a stop to this. It's getting beyond a joke.

I have been the object of an attempted seduction by a woman before, at a party of one of the writers of *Wives*. A cocaine fuelled revel full of luvvies, where it was difficult not to slip into character, as it seemed to be a shining example of life imitating art, if you can call *Wives* art, the atmosphere being similarly thick with back-biting, gossip and the coveting of other people's bank balances and the rest. It was in a sumptuous house in West Kensington, and I found myself upstairs with a woman called Tikka, as in Chicken Tikka Masala. We were looking for a loo, and found a bedroom with en suite facilities. Tikka was holding an open bottle of champagne, saying between swigs that she always just grabbed a whole one rather than wait for someone to appear with a tray full of half-filled glasses. I think I'd managed to drink at least one already in the conventional way, but nevertheless accepted her offer of a mouthful or two.

'Not with Haden tonight?' she inquired, eyebrows raised.

'No, he's got 'flu,' I said, suddenly feeling the urge to lie down on the bed. I closed my eyes and tried to enjoy the sensation of being horribly drunk, with a champagne headache approaching like a black cloud. I think I must have either lost consciousness or dozed off, because the next thing I knew, I woke up to find Tikka, bare-breasted, and in the process of undressing me. Into my drunken mind wove the life list, the '1,000 things to do before I die' list, which has, at about number 570 or thereabouts, 'Have sex with person of own sex.' The opportunity appeared to have arisen to strike this one off, so I allowed this creature to have her wicked way for a while, as I lay there with my head now beginning to throb, but which so far was registering no protest. In fact, I realised that sex was sex whomever you were doing it with, drawing the line at zoophilia, and quite a few other 'philiae' for that matter. Anyway, Tikka and I didn't get too far into the proceedings before I quipped something about the fact I kept expecting there to be a penis ... to which she cooed, 'Oh how romantic, a pianist...'

'No, I said penis!'

For some reason, this put her off her stride, and I got a fit of the giggles, and that was the end of the matter, although she did ring me for a while. Bisexuality eh? Well, it may double the chances of a date, but personally I'm glad that only half the world can do my head in.

I let Badric out the back and send satisfying clouds of smoke into the night air, before I head upstairs. I check my email before getting into bed. Ferdie's dad has died. Heart attack, a big one while he was having his op. At least he got to see him before he died. He hopes Badric and I are OK; that his mother is very upset, that he thinks he must come home for good. Of course, he'll come back first. Would it be OK to bring a friend? Her name is Tania, another dancer, a friend of Rosa's who he hasn't seen in a long time...

I reply to him straight away, try to say how sorry I am, and that, of course, to bring Tania. I write something else along the lines of 'I feel bad about the night we sp ...' in several different permutations, but delete each one and eventually give up. After all, he could have broached the subject but didn't.

I go to sleep thinking about Ferdie's dad, about life without Ferdie and whether to get another lodger or go solo again. After the last couple of weeks the prospect is very appealing, but could I afford it? Then think again about his dad, of how he didn't make it back to the hacienda or whatever. Mum and dad have always talked about going home, more seriously of late. But Mum says she likes being near me. So many problems, diasporas; the urge to see over the horizon, to get away; to find, forget, or try to, loved ones all over the place.

22

Fame

I wake Teresa at eight o'clock, by knocking loudly on her door, and saying that I have to go out soon, i.e., 'Get lost.' Half an hour later she comes downstairs, in my dressing gown and holding her head. I give her some Alka-Seltzer and watch her wince at every noise. Oh dear. You know it's a real bad one when even the noise of two Alka-Seltzers dissolving is excruciating.

'Look, Teresa, I'm glad I've been able to help, but I really think...' She puts her hand over her mouth and darts into the loo. I hear her being sick, which makes me want to be sick. After a few minutes she emerges, green about the gills. I begin again.

'I don't know what's been going on at home, but...' She puts her hands up to her temples and shakes her head at me, pleading for mercy. I acquiesce. She asks if she could borrow a coat, and I lend her an old pair of socks and my full-length fake fur job that I wouldn't mind never seeing again, just in case I don't, and off she goes, a walking fantasy; woman dressed only in underwear under a furry black coat. Without the recent vomiting, naturally.

The sun is shining. I put on my tracksuit. Badric is standing square, wagging his tail in an absent-minded sort of a way, as he does when he is waiting for me. He's very good about it, all things considered. He has learnt not to get over-excited until he smells the lipstick that resides on a little shelf under the mirror on the hall. That usually means going out, although sometimes it doesn't, and sometimes I go out without giving the lipstick signal at all, just to confuse matters. But when I speak the immortal word, 'walkies!' he throws himself into a tap dance tarantella on the tiles. I rescue two overripe fruits from the bowl and off we go.

It occurs to me that I should call Nina and see how she's feeling about Adrian. Nina doesn't hang about — in fact her relationships usually dovetail neatly into one another. She told me that men are like jobs, you don't leave one till you are one hundred percent sure that you have got another one to go to. I'll give her a ring later. After all, in a couple of days' time I will have to say goodbye to my dog, which becomes less and less bearable the longer I know him. This, therefore, is what we parents call 'quality time.'

It's early, but not that early. And what with the sunshine the park is brimming with the usual Sunday mob.

> *People flocked there in their thousands. To the point that the Government had to intervene, such was the sheer number of riff-raff.*

My blonde barnet might as well be a beacon. I'm just through the gate when Ruff Guy's mate, the one with the killer dog, runs, yes runs, over to me and says that he saw *Wives* the other night and that he told the whole pub about his dog (who has a muzzle on and looks furious about it) biting my dog. This, I realise, amounts to a claim to fame for this man. I smile politely and make to walk on.

'On your own are you?' he says, 'I'll walk wiv you.'

I thank him, but say that Badric's a bit frightened. Luckily, Badric is doing his Ridgeback impression, so the man is convinced.

205

'Another time then!'

I pretend not to hear, and consider going home for my hat when I see Ali, up ahead. He's seen me.

'Ay, Miss, you're a star again, good, eh? I tell my boys that you eat my kebabs so they must be good eh? Next time you get yours for free!' Great. Suits me. Who needs a table at The Ivy anyway? I break into a jog, head up the squirrel run, past crocus corner and out by the pagoda. Some of the step freaks give me a second glance but I might be starting to get paranoid now. I head for The Meadow, Battersea Park's little nature reserve, where the most commonly spotted creature is the lone man, although I did once see a couple of newts in the pond. I wend my way round the woodland path and there, with his back to me stands Barry, binocs pointing skywards.

'Hi, Barry, anything interesting?' Barry jumps and turns to face me. He looks completely blank until Badric comes bounding out from behind a bush.

'Well hello, young lady, and hello to you too Baldrick,' he says, reaching down to pat Badric's head enthusiastically.

'It's Bad...' Oh never mind.

'I didn't recognise you there, young lady!'

Oh Barry, I love you. I walk with him. He tells me about the nuthatch and the green woodpecker. He says there are a fair few of the Greater Spotted, but the green one is a newcomer, there are plenty of them in Richmond and Wimbledon, he says, holding open the gate to let me out of the Meadow. Which is where I should have gone this morning, perhaps, I think, as Ben and Steve appear.

'Hi darling, when are you off?'

'Tomorrow night,' I say, as I am sucked into the Fagarties' force field and away from Barry.

'Coming for a coffee?'

'No, I won't thanks.'

'Go on!'

'Oh ... OK then.'

One buggy, two buggies, three buggies, four buggies. What's the collective noun for buggies, I wonder? A torture of buggies? They are parked three abreast outside the café.

'Bloody kids everywhere!' says Ben. 'Darling, I hope you're not thinking of having any.'

'No, not at the moment.'

'Thank God for the likes of you. All our girlfriends are pregnant or dropping sprogs left right and centre.'

Steve adds, 'Can't see you with a baby anyway, Rachel.'

Oh right. What's that supposed to mean? There's a tap on my arm. A little girl in a pink tracksuit asks for my autograph. She holds out a pen. I scribble, 'To... 'What's your name?'

'Bianca.' I scribble a greeting in her notebook and try not to shove her forcibly out of my way, preferably into the lake. I want to go home. Now.

'Actually guys, I'm going to head off. Things to do, you know.'

'Shame, never mind. Have a great trip!'

With karma in mind I have a little chat with Bianca, who makes it perfectly plain that she has never watched *Wives*. Her mum, on the other hand, looking on shyly and giving me a little wave, obviously has.

I am home for approximately three and a half minutes, and just about to have a shower when there is a knock at the door. I put on my dressing gown, which smells disconcertingly of Teresa and go back downstairs. I'm surprised to see Mark at the door.

'Hello, Rachel, nice night? I see you're just up,' he says, or should I say spits.

I'm taken aback. He's looking at me strangely.

'I think we need to talk, Rachel. May I come in?'

'Well, I was just about to have a shower, but...' He looks

at me as if I've just said that I'm about to do a naked belly dance on the table. I stand back and let him in.

He takes a cigarette out of the box on the arm of the sofa without asking, and starts pacing around. I get a lighter from the kitchen and hand it to him.

'Didn't you think it was all a bit close to home? I mean, our home,' he hisses, coming a little nearer and then stopping abruptly, scenting the air like a dog. 'My God, you even smell of her!' He flings himself down on the sofa and puts his head in his hands. 'I must say, you two have got a nerve! Her walking in wearing your bloody coat, and now this!'

'Mark, Mark, hang on a minute, I hope you're not suggesting that Teresa and I...'

'Oh come on Rachel! She's been sneaking in and out of here for days now! She more or less told me she had something going on next door! Well, come on, do tell. Is it love?'

Oh dear, I'm feeling a strange mixture of outrage and extreme amusement.

'Mark! Are you saying that you think Teresa and I are having some sort of scene? Are you serious?'

He looks up at me, his hands falling from head to cheek, pulling down his lower eyelids, now like a bloodhound. God, he looks dreadful.

'Would you like a coffee?'

'No I don't want a fucking coffee. I want my wife back!'

I resist the urge to say, 'Tea then?'

'Look Mark, she's been round here a few times recently, but only because she was locked out or whatever, I can assure you that you've got nothing to worry about ... with me, I mean.'

'Well who then? Where's that lodger of yours anyway? Or was it that other bloke that's been hanging around?'

I wonder if he means David or Gus. If he ever finds out about Gus, I'm going to plead total ignorance.

'I don't know, and it's really nothing to do with me.' I sit down on the armchair. He gets up and starts pacing again.

'What am I going to do? I don't know her anymore. She's so unhappy, I can't reach her. She hates me.' He doesn't really address this to me. It would have been quite an impressive display if he was acting, which he's not, I remind myself. In which case it's just real life. Shame. As he's leaving, he says he likes my hair. I thank him, lean against the front door for a minute, breathe out, experience a paroxysm of mirth, then take off the dressing gown, stuff it into the washing machine and walk up the stairs, naked and blonde; a regular femme fatale.

Later on, I decide to go and visit Miss Jackson and Giacomo. I ring Nina's mobile on the way but it's turned off. Carla keeps sending me funny texts.

R u sure they let blicks into this hotel?
Underprivileged single mum jets off to Cape Town
courtesy of blonde soap star!

Miss Jackson doesn't recognise me at first, but when she does she calls out to the ward. 'See, everyone! Here she is!' They all look over, wave, clap (oh, please) and smile, dentures giving some of these smiles a sinister looking monotoothed perfection. They really should age dentures a bit, black a few of them out, chip them, soak them in some tea, anything. Clean shiny ones make old people look like old movie stars who've run out of money just before the face job. I notice these things, you see. It comes from years (not years as in years and years, just a couple of years), of scrutinising my own face on telly, of noticing when make-up got it a bit wrong. That's my excuse anyway.

I sit on the bed and chat about South Africa, about Badric and about the hospital food, and so on. She seems remarkably unconcerned about the prospect of residential care or anything else for that matter. I get the feeling that, after years of keeping things together and looking after herself, she's just divested herself of all responsibility, shaken off the shackles of the day-to-day and doesn't give a damn.

'Where's that nice man of yours dear?'

'Oh, you mean David,' I say, feeling myself blushing.

'David. Yes, that's him. What a nice man. He said hello to me you know...'

'He's in Ireland,' I say.

'He'll be back,' she says nodding sagely.

I say goodbye to Mystic Miss Jackson and head for Giacomo's ward. I am more than a little surprised to see Nina in the chair by his bed.

'Nina! Hi! I was going to call you later.'

'Hello, darling,' she says, and there's a little silence when we all look a little bit embarrassed. Nina's embarrassed because she hates Giacomo, or so she keeps saying. Giacomo's embarrassed because he hates Nina, or so he keeps saying, and is supposed to only have eyes for me, and I'm embarrassed because ... they are.

'Hi Rachel. Thanks for coming, and hey, thank you for the nicotine patch!' says Giacomo, with a slightly OTT chirrup about his voice.

'Hi, how's your head?'

'Much better thanks. They say there is no permanent damage, although I may go mad any time.' He shrugs, mouth turned down, palms to the heavens, Italian style. 'Who knows?' We all laugh. I tell them my gossip about my neighbour. Cruel isn't it? Having a good laugh at someone else's expense. Cruel, but funny.

'I told you that woman was strange,' says Nina.

'I don't think she's strange Nina, I think she's unhappy.'

Actually, she is strange. She doesn't like dogs.

'Oh come on, Rachel, it is strange to sleep with your cousin one minute and try to sleep with you the next.' Put that way, I suppose it is strange. Not strange as in strange that anyone would want to sleep with me, or strange as in a very old-fashioned way of looking at bisexuality, aka the new fashion for, 'if it's human, it's a possibility.'

'Isn't it, Giacomo?' Giacomo looks at each of us in turn.

'Donta ask me!' He gives another of his shrugs.

After listening to some tales of Thai and the modern parents I say I'd better get going. Nina says she has to go too. I offer to give her a lift back but she says that she's meeting her friend Mira at South Ken. I ask her what she thinks about the stuff in the attic. She says he still loves me; it's obvious.

'Nice of you to visit your arch enemy like that, Nina,' I have to say it.

'Yes,' she says.

'What's going on?'

'Oh, nothing really.' It's all in the 'really'. It's the opposite of 'actually', suggesting something is beginning rather than ending, as in her saying about Adrian that it was 'going well, actually.'

'I had a drink with him before he slipped over.'

'Oh, you never mentioned it.'

'Well, I suppose I had Adrian on my mind. I went up to Northcote Road with him. There's so many Italians round there, I like it. I'm going to learn Italian. Giacomo and his friends say they'll help. Maybe I could go and live there. Giacomo says he might be going home soon. Said he could get me a job no problem.'

'Oh.' Giacomo, Nina, Ferdie, it's like rats leaving a sinking ship. I feel left out. I want to go and live in Italy! If Carla goes to live in Jamaica that's it; I'm leaving. Maybe Haden will go back to Greece and Miss Jackson up sticks and head for Honolulu. Don't leave me here with Teresa! Someone stay, please!

When I get home I have a message from Haden. 'Still on

for tonight? Give me a ring when you get in.' I'd forgotten, but yes, great. Sunday night out with a film star and off to Cape Town Monday night, darling. Just another normal day in the ever so normal life of R. L. Jameson, spinster of this parish.

It's like old times, being out with Haden. He regales me with stories of the filming, the waiting staff (the one in particular), the seafood and the endless litres of wine, and I tell him about what's been going on and he pulls all the right faces in all the right places. A woman at the next table nudges her friend and they suspend their spaghetti-sucking to have a good look, nod at each other, raise their eyebrows and continue. See that? That's fame, that is.

23

Fear of flying

Whether scared of flying or not, there's that moment of mighty thrust that can't fail to impress as you're tipped back in your chair and, in my case with sweat prickling at my palms, I shut my eyes, wait for my ears to start popping and pray.

Four years ago I went on holiday with Lou to Italy, and in that happy hiatus when the plane was going along horizontally, the seat belt lights came on and we were advised to return to our seats, if taking a stroll or whatever. Nothing unusual in this, just a spot of turbulence, a bit of weather; just another opportunity for me to reacquaint myself with the Lord, and fold my arms across my soon-to-be-turbulent bosom, when suddenly the oxygen masks came tumbling down, and we are instructed to tug it to release the flow, place over our nose and mouth and 'breathe normally'. Yeah right.

Lou and I stare at each other over our masks, gripping each other's hands so tightly that our nails dig in, as the plane went into a dive. Down, down, down. People were moaning behind their masks, Lou was crying and I was just hoping to God that it wasn't going to hurt too much, and wondering when the slide show of my life would begin when the winged chariot levelled out and we were flying along flat again, distinctly nearer the ground, but flying, definitely flying along.

I'll spare you the details of the queues for the toilets, the state of the toilets, the smell of used sick bags and the like, save to say that after a prolonged, shocked silence, broken only by sobs, there ensued a small mutiny, whereby one smoker lit up, and every other smoker followed suit, and probably several non and ex-smokers too. The trolley dolly gave up trying to stop people after one bloke stood up, grabbed him by the tie and told him, in no uncertain terms, what he could do with his rules and regulations. Everyone became slightly hysterical, demanding free drinks and explanations, reassurances, tissues, to speak to the pilot, to speak to anyone who could say that living to see Naples Airport was more than just wishful thinking. People were on their feet, there was a sort of Dunkirk spirit thing going on, friendships were forged, support groups started, the word 'damages' bandied about. People may well have had life-affirming sex in the loos, for all I know. Lou bought a bottle of Whisky from duty free, which we glugged like water as we listened to the captain's explanation of a 'sudden loss of cabin pressure' which meant that he had to descend to a point at which we could breathe by ourselves; nothing serious then. Remember that. There's not much oxygen, so if it happens to you, try not to gasp, pant, panic and hyperventilate. Be calm about your plane dropping like a stone. Relax and breathe normally.

On this occasion I'm in business class because I'm worth it. Carla, unfortunately, is in economy. Before the stewardess pulls the curtain to shield us from *hoi polloi*, we give each other a little wave. She taps her watch and grins at me, reminding me that we are swapping seats at half time, if awake. I sit back in my comfortable chair and stretch out, safe in the knowledge that Carla will sleep through half time, and I won't. And the comfortable chair should be the insomniac's prerogative. Anyway, someone's got to keep their wits about them, in the event of a sudden loss of cabin pressure, or worse. It would only be tempting fate to nod off for a second. I am going to use all my underdeveloped psychic powers to keep this plane in the air. And let's not forget **_Rule No. 3_**.

An air hostess walks up and down looking to her right and left, greeting us with a blast of her perfume, and what you could call a charm offensive. Really, nails that long must be a positive handicap. I hope she's not going to be let anywhere near the inflatable safety chute in the event of an emergency.

I can't help it, I feel it starting, the sweat on my palms, the heartbeat quickening. I remind myself that 'anxiety is my friend' as the giant metal tube separates itself from the earth and tears into the night sky. Up, up, up. Then there's that bloody great turn, one wing dipping down, London lying twinkling beneath like somewhere I really, really want to be, where my dear dog is expecting my key in the door any moment.

Ping! The lights are on. I breathe out and manically rearrange my stuff. I check for the umpteenth time that important stuff is where it ought to be. My stuff I mean, although I do like to check every now and again that the fuselage is complete with wings. Now where's my drink? Business class is good. You have that drink pretty quickly. For some reason when airborne I always have a Bloody Mary, and I know I'm not alone in this. I think it's the visceral, dramatic quality of it that seems so appropriate. It doesn't taste the same with your feet on the ground somehow. In the same way that Ricard is great in France, and Campari in Italy just dandy, but both absolutely rank down the Duke of York.

I watch the map on the screen in front of me as the plane edges its way into European airspace, and slip into a pre-prandial reverie about the ruler of my heart, sitting

215

in front of Nige's fire, or in the pub, Guinness in hand, watching an Irish jig danced by a flame-haired Celt flashing her emerald eyes, as an advert would have it. It occurs to me that playing hard to get, or my rather feeble attempt at it, might backfire. I toy with my chicken Kiev, eat my chocolate mousse and drink wine with the gratitude of the condemned man. I try to doze, read, watch a movie, play a game, do the crossword in the in-flight magazine, all the while spaying my face with Evian in a nod to hydration as I order a nightcap. I remember work, consider the importance of first appearances, spray more water on my face, order water to go with it and do the right thing, i.e., pour it down my throat as if I were walking across rather than flying over the Sahara desert, all the while remembering neurotically to rotate my ankles and stretch my legs. It must be half time by now. I get up and head for the toilet with my toothbrush and pull back the curtain to see how hoi polloi are doing. There's Carla. She's cool, arms folded, she looks slightly cross in her slumber and I resist the urge to go and make her crosser, slipping back into business class.

> *EXTRA! EXTRA! READ ALL ABOUT IT! WOMAN*
> *FALLS ASLEEP ON PLANE!*
> *Rachel Jameson, 32, actress, crippled by fear of*
> *flying since a sudden loss of cabin pressure whilst*
> *heading for a Neapolitan holiday, fell asleep on*
> *a plane heading for Cape Town. She slept over*
> *approximately two-thirds of the African continent,*
> *oblivious to 30,000ft of nothing between it and*
> *herself. On waking, the talons that held out a*
> *cup of coffee and a lemon-scented hot towel*
> *were suddenly beneficent, she marvelled at the*
> *shadows of clouds that she could see on the sandy*
> *motherland below, swallowed two painkillers,*
> *sprayed her face with the last of her Evian, and*

smiled as she queued for the loo, as if she too now possessed secret knowledge, was an initiate. A member of the alternative Mile High Club, for those who have a headache and just want to sleep.

Carla looks totally unscathed by the journey. We are standing in the queue to show our passports in the monocultural anonymity of arrivals. On the other side and are besieged by people offering taxi rides and bag-carrying services when above the crowd I see a sign saying 'Jameson, Table Bay' held aloft by a white arm.

'Look,' I say to Carla, who says she needs coffee, now. I promise her coffee the minute we get to the hotel. She pouts, grumpy on purpose, and we are headed for one of those episodes when the slightest thing becomes ridiculously funny. The guy introduces himself as Ross and tells us that he's my driver. He looks at a bit of paper and says he's just got one person down. I tell him that my friend needs a lift too and he shrugs and says, 'OK.' He stops chewing momentarily. As he's loading the car with our bags, Carla whispers to me that he's bound to be able to get us some weed. I remind her that this is work for one of us.

It's all so very unceremonious; arrival in a new land. This is when you need dramatic film score, the camera panning round in a broad sweep as first impressions bombard your retina, preconceptions meeting realities to the crashing of cymbals before the music segues seamlessly into the South African National Anthem, thick with struggle, pride and victory. That's why we need films, I suppose. A nice potted experience all wrapped up in a couple of hours. Ross holds a packet out to us over his shoulder.

'Want some?'

'What is it?' I ask.

'Biltong.'

'What's that?' I ask again.

'It's a snack food,' he says. I can't see into the packet, but being one to graciously accept the hospitality of another land, I reach into the packet and pull out something reddish brown, flat and smelly. I put it back in.

'No thanks. I'm fine. It's a bit early in the day for...' I look at Carla. She raises her eyebrows, and mouths 'Shmackos?' Because that's what it looked like. And if you haven't got a dog, for your information a Shmacko is a chewy reward made by a dog food giant. This sends us into another fit of barely suppressible giggles. This hilarity fades as we drive on. I notice that there are a lot of shiny people carriers here too, overtaking old bangers and trucks with black guys sitting out the back. It's a big sky, groups of trees with tall canopies casting stark shadows on to the hot land. On both sides of the road, we are passing what looks like a shantytown; a corrugated iron sprawl behind a fence, before a vast flatness with mountains in the distance. Washing is drying outside some of the huts, and I see a couple of skinny dogs, and some kids kicking a ball in the dust. Carla and I exchange glances.

Soon we pull up outside the hotel, the ocean is a startling blue on the other side of the road. A powerful wind rattles the flagpoles, whipping the flags into ribbons. Ross hands me an itinerary and an A4 envelope containing my challenge and, still chewing on a bit of leather, says that he'll pick me up at seven tomorrow morning and gives me his mobile number. 'Just in case I need anything,' he says, with a wink. We step into the cool glitz of the hotel.

'This must be what he meant by *The Long Walk To Freedom*, says Carla as we walk down endless miles of corridor in search of our room.

'Sshhh!' I'm now in serious danger of wetting myself.

'Must have put us right at the back because I's black.'

In fact, we have a room with a view. We look out over

the harbour with Table Mountain as a backdrop; a towering mass of rock with the pointy bit sliced off.

'Wow,' we say, opening the window, only to force it shut again against the gale. Fishing boats, big ones, boats that carry freight, all sorts of things maritime for which a short time on the Thames and a smattering of relevant vocabulary is insufficient. An old red building stands out like a pillar box, a colonial look-out, or lighthouse, dwarfed in stature by the surrounding twentieth century success stories. Seals roll over in the water, undeterred by the rainbow slicks of engine oil on the surface, round the corner a hundred naked clanking masts on serious yachts for serious yachties.

We shower and change and go down to the bar by the pool. The pink sunbathers peer over their Harry Potters as we walk in. Maybe the fact that we are scruffy makes us look really important, like we're so rich we don't give a damn.

'They must think I'm bloody Whoopee Goldberg,' says Carla.

Here, we're sheltered from the wind, from everything in fact. Haden would be proud of us, because we gravitate immediately towards the staff. When we get chatting and Carla tells them that she's a drummer in a jazz funk band (not famous, yet), we get great service, even a few free drinks. They say that a lot of actors come here (I'm boring), but not so many musicians. It's amazing how quickly you can get weed if you're with a muso.

'C'mon,' says Carla, draining the last drop of her coffee, 'let's go and lose some Rand.'

The hotel is connected to an extremely plush air-conditioned shopping centre selling all the same crap you can get anywhere in the world. We browse in and out of shops selling classy and not so classy ethnic gifts, having discovered that we are absolutely loaded, filthy rich with our couple of hundred quid's worth of Rand.

'This place is horrible. Let's go into town.'

'Hang on, can't we just relax for a bit?'

'Come on, Rach, I've got to make the most of you today, haven't I?'

Carla heads for a record shop. I want to sit down near the market, have a beer and a fag and look through the stuff that Ross gave me. I have to apply myself to it at some point before my overloaded brain shuts down completely.

'OK,' she agrees and we head for a bar. I'm the only white face in there. It's not an everyday experience this, but if you're up for it, there's a shop called 'Dub Vendor' in Clapham Junction where it can be replicated without subjecting yourself to the torture of a night flight. We take our beers and sit outside.

'D'you think I should ring Shelley and just check that...'

'No, Rach. Everything will be OK and if it isn't she'll ring us. Relax!'

I flick through the call sheet, glance at the storyboard, and the script – if you could call it that. Well, that'll do for now. I should be able to hold my one line in my head after a night's sleep. It's the usual bollocks anyway. I can't take it in, really, but feel pretty confident that I'll be able to have another look in the morning and approach it with the calm professionalism for which I am renowned. As if.

Carla takes the guidebook out and turns to the bit about the town centre. She tells me that she has planned a little itinerary for herself: Robben Island, Cape Point, up the mountain. Huh. We walk through the market. Stalls are laid out with beaded necklaces and key rings. Large wooden giraffes stand tethered to lamp posts as if they might bolt, printed fabrics hang next to ANC flags and Nelson Mandela T-shirts. It's colourful, full of contrast in the bright light and shadows on the cobbled square. Carla says that you can get all this stuff everywhere, according to the guidebook. It's a depressing thought, that there's a factory somewhere churning it out. Same as the West-End-on-Sea shopping mall really, except there the mark-up's even bigger.

We head up the main drag passing three, four or five half-dead looking people holding begging bowls; past the Cultural History Museum, one-time slave lodge, now with the National Gallery flanking a leafy pedestrian avenue. The park is bordered with exotica and overgrown houseplants. We stand outside the building where Nelson Mandela made his inaugural speech in '89 before heading back to our luxury cocoon.

Later, we wander round the Victoria and Alfred Waterfront.

'Did they get it wrong or what?'

'Alfred's one of her sons,' says Carla, nose in the guidebook again.

'Just as well, since they obviously got it wrong.'

We choose one from the glut of restaurants. Apart from in America, I've never had so much food set down before me in my life. Rich food too, not the health conscious, lean, stylish demi-plate that you get in London these days, but a veritable feast oozing with butter and cream, and an entire loaf of garlic bread, each.

'Jesus, I'll never eat all this.' But I do.

We waddle back to the hotel bar. It's full of white diners in evening wear, women with not a hair out of place and diamonds glittering at their throats.

'Bling bloody bling,' says Carla, ordering a Bailey's and a large single malt for me. She gets a text from Shelley saying everything is fine. A text message from South West London in seconds. A half empty bottle of mineral water left on the next table. A woman walking for half a day for water. Maybe I'm just naïve, maybe I never quite got over my theatre group days, but I just don't buy it; that this is the only way forward, that it's just the way it is. Suddenly,

Granddad comes to mind, wouldn't even buy his council house, didn't believe in it. Once again, as I sit there, swilling my whisky round my glass, I am overcome with the conviction that I am in the wrong job, in the wrong life, that this is a farce and that if I don't change my life soon I ... I don't know what I'll do. Or what I'll do if I do change my life. And whether there is any way to live that could be the right way to live. I'm an actor in a car ad. Where's my *fcuking hypocrite* T-shirt?

Back in our room, we peruse the TV stations, try to find something that doesn't pertain in some way to America, give up, muck about in our room like teenagers and giggle ourselves to sleep.

24

Shoot

Despite some serious indigestion in the night, I wake to my alarm's beeping feeling pretty good. Carla opens her eyes, turns over in her bed, gives me a wave and goes back to sleep.

Ross is waiting outside the hotel. As I approach he gets out and opens the car door for me. From my seat in the back I can see him chewing on biltong. We go through town and out to a leafy suburb. This is to be unit base; an empty car park midway between the city and the open space. Ross pulls up by the portakabins, springs out and opens the door for me. A runner pops out of one with a clipboard, says 'Morning Miss Jameson', brightly, and points me in the direction of make-up and asking what I'd like for breakfast. I'm not hungry in the slightest. Last night's meal is stubbornly refusing to budge. I feel bloated, and when I sit down in front of the mirror I see that my English winter nose is glowing with the after-effects of yesterday's walkabout in the sun. I order coffee and juice and just the one piece of toast, saying a firm 'no' to the full English (for God's sake) and gaze at myself in despair. The costume designer puts her head round the door and says hello, and that she'll see me in a minute. My hair is washed and wrapped in a towel. My coffee and juice sit before me tantalisingly. Every time I reach for them I am in the way of the girl who is transforming me into something less like a red-nosed reindeer. My hair is then dried and put up in a bun. I am given a pair of glasses and by the time I come away from make-up, the blank canvas has been transformed into something quite unrecognisable; a female from a parallel universe. City girl, chic in a grey suit, skirt a little tighter than practical, white shirt a little lower cut than necessary, heels the likes of which I haven't worn for some time, other than my night out with Gus, which wasn't all that long ago, the blisters that were healing nicely remind me. I am Barbie, office edition; subtle fake eyelashes fluttering behind my sexy glasses. Barbie hot. And I mean 'hot' as in hot, sweat pricking at my armpits ominously. Oh well, business women do sweat, I suppose, even cool ones. I direct the little battery operated fan that make-up gave me to stop the lot from sliding off my face altogether to my underarms, then up to my face, then back to my armpits again. I dive thankfully into the car with Ross, who heads back into town for the city shoot.

I look down at myself and consider that the female version of the suit is loathsome and ridiculous. Anything that requires a woman to encase the bottom half of her body in nylon more fragile than a fairy's wing, which, even if the temperature isn't 40 degrees in the shade, is a bad idea, cotton bits in the right places or not. You can't sit there and just be good at your job. No, that would be too easy for a woman, evidently. You have to sit there and be good at your job and look like Lois Lane. But at least we don't have to wear a tie. What a generous concession! Nothing to do with the fact that the boss would be deprived of a glimpse of a cleavage or two to keep his morale boosted after a tricky meeting. Get the men in skirts now! Or tighten up those crotch areas so us working women can see what they might have to offer, and give us all a laugh while you're at it. If women need protection from the worst ex-

224

cesses of testosterone than surely trousers are the obvious choice. If men need to be kept cool for biological reasons then skirts would seem the most appropriate thing. Anyway, men look great in kilts, and the attendant feeling of vulnerability might prove to be illuminating, you never know.

With these and a million more thoughts I look out of the window, as the car is filled one moment with brilliant light, then blue dimness as we drive through shadows. We seem to be going back in the direction of the hotel, past the Aquarium again, but then head round and up into the main street, where Carla and I were yesterday. We turn to the right of the market square and into a street which has been cordoned off for the filming, bought for the day, the set, under brightly painted balconies that look generally foreign. It could be the South America of your imagination, maybe Spain, anywhere really where the sun shines, where people drive cars, where there is traffic. More cars than I've seen elsewhere in town are jammed into this street for the shoot. Ross pulls up by a sort of glorified tent and I go in, fan on again. The director strides across to greet me, hand outstretched. I recognise him from the casting.

'Rachel! Max! Great to see you again! Having a good time? Fabulous, isn't it?' He waves his arm in the direction of everything and nothing in particular.

'Yes, great,' I say, suddenly needing the loo badly and anxious to pull up my tights as they are about three inches from where they should be and starting to chafe at my sweating thighs. A make-up person directs me to the loos, to my relief, but unfortunately on pulling up my tights my freshly sharpened nails go right through them and a ladder runs down my leg. I point this out to the girl, trying to be unapologetic, to be haughty, starry, you know. She seems quite glad to have something to do and hurries off, then reappears with a powder puff, touches up the artwork, smooths my hair, directs a hairdryer under my arms, hands me some Xtra Xtra Xtra Dry antiperspirant, so strong it could clog the pores of the proverbial pig, catches the new pair of tights that the panting runner throws to her and hands them to me. I put them on carefully and we're ready.

Max puts his hot heavy arm around me and takes me over to where my besuited other half is sitting.

'Rachel, this is Dean, Dean, Rachel.'

'Hi.'

'Hi.'

'You don't remember me, do you?'

I look at him; black guy, London accent, a bit older than me, nice face.

'Um...'

'*Pasta Perfecto?* The grinning idiot stacking the shelves as you deliberate over the *carbonara* or the *arrabiata?*'

'Oh my God! Was that you? What happened to your locks? Bloody hell! That's so funny!'

'Come on, they're calling us.'

Dean's already been here for a day. He's done the mockup stressed-out drive through the city yesterday, now it's time to meet me. I am to come out of the office, jacket slung over my shoulder, let my hair down with a shampoo ad style toss, and run. Yes, run, in these shoes, and in this heat, to the shiny metallic charger where sits my hero. I'm sorry, but I can't say any more about this, except for that it took not one, not two, but several thousand takes, resprays of Xtra Dry, re-powder-puffing, re-hair doing, three fresh shirts, another pair of tights, one slightly sprained ankle and several new blisters till Max was satisfied. And all the while I wished that I were wearing a better bra. This sprint towards my lover's vehicle is presumably to portray my inner wild, free nature; my black lover the face of the fantastic, just, multi-cultural world in which we live, with a subliminal grunt to my primal desires, or something. Anyway it's all Dean and I can do not to crack up. We have to stay serious and quiet because he's wired to the guy on the cans, and if we say 'Get on with it, for God's sake,' or 'that man's a pillock,' it might not go down too well.

It is done. I've managed at last to get into the car. I've said my bit, which is 'Get me out of here!' into his cunningly disguised mike as we kiss in greeting. But of course I'm saying it in a post-post-modern, ironic sort of way, in a 'Look at us, we've beaten the game!' sort of a way, we've seen all the movies, heard all the lines. 'Get me out of here!' It could just have easily have been, 'Beam me up Scottie.' Same vibe. Dean then drives the ten or so yards through the tooting, honking, simulated traffic jam as I kick back in my seat and gaze at the unfettered blue of the sky (actually, I am gazing at the helicopter that is doing the oh-so-necessary aerial shot) studiously ignoring the camera on the bonnet.

'Don't you think it's outrageous to get a black guy from North London? Couldn't they have got someone from here?'

'Carla, it's an English director, it's his company. He can do whatever he wants. We're only here for the weather and because it's cheap. Anyway, why not get a white woman from here to do my bit? But then we wouldn't be sitting here having this lovely cocktail would we?'

Carla raises an eyebrow. 'You sound as if you're going to say something about the way of the world any minute.'

'Well it is, isn't it? Put up, shut up or have the guts to do something else.'

'Hey, that bad, is it?'

'Yeah, I can't keep doing this, then easing my conscience by trashing the odd billboard. It's pathetic.'

'Fun though.'

'True.'

'So the director wants to take you out for a drink? Are you going, or what? I thought the casting couch scene happened before getting the job?'

'Very funny. No, I told him I was meeting a friend.'

'Why didn't you just say no?'

'Well, that wouldn't be ... politic, would it? Anyway, Dean's coming over to compare hotels. What's up?' Carla is looking cross.

'I didn't come all this way to hang out with some guy from Willesden.'

'How d'you know he's from Willesden? North London's quite a big place, so I'm told.'

By about ten I'm starting to feel like a gooseberry. Dean and Carla are surprised, in the midst of the Cape Town Waterfront, to have run into another person who saw Mark Murphy at the Jazz Café. When Dean goes to the loo Carla goes all coy.

'Told you you'd like him.'

'Yeah, he's OK, I suppose.'

'Carla Williamson, the only black man you are supposed to be thinking about today is Nelson Mandela. Not some guy from Willesden.'

Carla has been to Robben Island today.

'Highbury, actually.'

'Ooh, swapped addresses already? Look out, he's coming back.'

'Shall we get another bottle?' he says, smiling.

'Sorry guys, I'm going to leave you to it, I'm knackered.'

'Aw,' they say, with a touching attempt at sincerity.

'Hi Shel, it's me, Rachel. How's everything?' I take a sip of whisky. In South Africa you can raid the mini-bar with impunity thanks to the exchange rate, 'Thanks, yeah, fine, she's ... she's in the bath. I wanted to speak to Badric really ... Shel, just put the phone next to his ear...' I cluck into the phone. She tells me he's wagging his tail. 'Anything exciting? A letter? What's the postmark? Well try... Oh, never mind. Thanks ever so much, Shel. Yeah, I'll tell her, bye.'

Right, here goes. 'The Vodafone you are calling may be switched off. Please try later.'

I give up. The wind has dropped slightly, I open the window and blow smoke into the night. I'm in my huge, white towelling dressing gown, having spent over an hour in my huge white tiled bathroom, littering it with little bubble bath empties. The city twinkles and the water is still and black. Lovers are strolling around, hand in hand, and I can hear music in the distance.

'What time is it?'

'God, sorry Rach ... about two I think...'

I sit up. Carla has just come in and tripped over one of my shoes. I put on my bedside light. 'Well?'

'Well what?' Her eyes are all a-bling. She throws herself onto her bed, rolls over, and stares at the ceiling.

'Rachel, he is seriously nice. Sorry, I think I'm a bit pissed. Hey, let's have a smoke out the window. No one's going to catch us at this time of night!' She looks at me. 'Please Masser!'

25

That's a wrap

The next morning I leave her sleeping again and head down to find Ross. He sees me approaching and makes moves to open the car door for me.

'Thanks.' He grins and we set off back to base.

'Have you been to England, Ross?'

'Me?'

'Yeah.' Who else?

'No.'

'Is it good living here?'

'It's OK, but pricey.'

'Have things changed a lot?'

'Couldn't tell ya.'

I give up. Ross is very young, and nice smile or not would seem to be a natural dullard. He also needs his jaw for chewing.

'Morning Miss Jameson!' Same routine, but this time my hair is all wild and free, and my legs are given a fake tan.

We drive out along the giant coastline. Huge masses of rock rise above flat land where houses nestle, overlooking huge curved stretches of beach cradling the brilliant blue ocean. It's impressive; the Southern Ocean, with its ghosts of ships, its bloody history, the Cape of Good Hope. Then up into a leafy suburb, past black women on the roadside with bundles of sticks; past huge neo-Georgian mansions behind walls and barbed wire; past the odd remaining seventeenth century farm building, now a winery.

All I have to do for now is sit there and look pretty while Dean drives from this shady green bit out to a beach. I get in beside him after my re-dabbing, puffing and spraying is done with.

'Tired?' I inquire innocently.

We're instructed to talk as we drive along. Just the occasional word or two as you would exchange with a lover as you escape triumphant from the confines of the city.

'Nice night then?'

'Yes, thanks.'

I look across at him, still acting of course and see that the expression that he has assumed is perfect for this ad; it's that sort of smug, reeking of romance perma-smile with a closed mouth but one that fills the eyes with a sort of earnest, faraway look mixed with the strong possibility that a new lover is only a day's work away.

'Think I saw you in *Paramedics* not so long ago.'

'Yeah. Haven't had many tellies recently. Keep getting theatre.'

'Lucky you.'

'Yeah, but I'm skint. What about you? That chef's thing finished a while back, didn't it?'

I tell him about the rerun, about Gobshite keeping body and soul together and we have a brief moan.

'So you've known Carla for a while then?'

We get to the beach. Max isn't happy with the weather. Above us is a cloud the size of a cotton wool ball. He sends up a special rocket to disperse it. Well, I wouldn't put it past him. This is where I am to escape the confines of my clothes to become 'woman in a white shirt that only

231

just covers her bum'; you know the one. Dean loses just his jacket, tie and shoes (not filmed). I undress (filmed): skirt first, then shoes and tights, as you do ... not. Off we stroll, hand in hand towards the sea, Dean with a picnic hamper swinging by his side.

I understand that this advert is not about getting away completely. Because we wouldn't want that, would we? We wouldn't want to desert the city, to go home to that boring small town. But, courtesy of this cool, zippy, modest, yet not too modest car with its dash of *spirito* and *voom*, you can have it all! A bit of both. The best of both worlds. Of black and of white. Hurrah for Datsui! They know us better than we know ourselves. They knew even before we did that coming with a picnic basket as standard would make our lives complete: our dutiful office lives now punctuated with a soul food sandwich on a blanket on a beach in the sun; our work/life balance now as perfect as that of the gull that flies past obligingly at just the right moment. Marvellous.

Dean and I are directed to run about a bit, jump for joy (I can see the edit of this in my head already, me being spun around by Dean, hair flying about, head back, you know, having a whale of a time on a Tuesday lunch hour), when, talking of which, someone shouts, 'Look!'

A mighty tail fin is rising out of the water. It's not close, but it's there; the splayed V-sign, static for a long moment like *Titanic* before the plunge. And it's gone. The leviathan, swallowed by the sea, never to be seen again, by us at least. We all stand silently for a while. A long shot of us all would show a scattering of humbled folk, dwarfed by the colossal coastline; ants stopped dead in their tracks by the sight of something awesome.

There's a sort of solidarity on set afterwards. We go again on the jumping for joy shot. I get a round of applause from the crew for appearing so demented. The last shot is of us paddling in the bloody freezing sea, and me turning to Dean and saying something meaningful and serious.

'Like you're proposing to him or something', says Max with a hey, c'mon guys, think radical grin. 'Or something about the whale!'

We look into each other's eyes, 'What a plonker,' I say, smiling sweetly.

'The new *Libero* from Datsui. A taste of freedom'

Just a taste mind.

Dean said he heard it was going to be 'Free at last', but someone ruled that it was a bit much.

'Too bloody right it's a bit much!' tuts Carla. We're having an aperitif by the pool and I'm looking at the postcards that she's bought of Cape Point, her outing of the day. It looks amazing; sharp chunks of land tailing off into the ocean like an unfinished line, white sandy coves, the ultramarine water, the veldt, the protea, strange with their feather-like petals, clumps of South African daisies, Cape marigolds and springbok grazing in the distance. At least I know what I'm missing. Carla asks me which one I think her mum would like. I point to the one of the protea.

'Anyway, that's what adverts do, isn't it? Live off bigger ideas like fleas. It's Hollywood in miniature. Keeping you in a state of constant desire ... and when is Dean coming over?'

'God, soon! I better go and get ready!'

The evening air is cooling dramatically, but I decide to have another swim. The pool is warm, if small. I lie on my back and watch the frayed palm tree sway against the darkening sky. Here I am, safe in the knowledge that a several of mortgage payments are mine, even if the money does take an eternity to come through. What I should be doing is taking the opportunity of being here to hire a Land Rover (old style, rough and ready) and heading up-country, making an audio diary for Radio 4 as I go. On

Woman's Hour, Jenni Murray would be unable to conceal her admiration for the woman, who, having realised that she was selling her soul to the devil, headed off to do something really good without further delay, instead of jetting back to London with the rest of the parasites. Yes, five years later she returned (her dog was shipped out to be with her) having set up small theatre groups all over South Africa, transposing Brecht onto the current situation as she went. Theatre, Truth, Reconciliation. Janet Suzman and she had formed an unbreakable bond. 'I had to do something, Jenni. It was as simple as that.' To change or not to change the world is just another choice. People do it all the time. I swim a length of the small pool underwater and come up to see Dean and Carla, shiny, happy people ready for a night out.

'Very impressive,' says Dean. Carla chucks me my towel as I clamber out.

'Listen Rach,' she whispers into my ear. 'Don't worry if I don't get back, yeah?'

'Just text me so I don't worry. OK?'

'And as for you, deserting me!' Dean grins. He's told the director that he's got a dodgy stomach and won't be joining the rest of us for our wrap drinky and dinner.

'Watch out for Max!' he says, pointedly.

I am squashed up next to Max at the restaurant. It's a noisy place so no one can hear a word anyone's saying. His thigh is pushing against mine, which is making my other thigh push against Nick's, the Art Director. I've had too much to drink before my food. This is all part of the job as far as I'm concerned. I just have to bear it. Our group has little in common other than the fact that we are human, involved in this advert, live in London, and have seen a whale together. OK, so we have quite a lot in common. But it doesn't seem to help. Max seems in a hurry to wrap this up as well, and I'm glad.

However, Max has other plans, and having all said our goodnights to each other he steers me in the direction of the hotel bar.

'I think I'll head off too, thanks. It's been a great evening and I'm glad the shoot...'

'I'll walk you to your room.'

'No need, honestly.'

Three miles of carpet later Max is holding my hands as I look at the floor rehearsing my next line. I open my mouth to say the very original, 'Goodnight then,' when his wet lips slam against mine and his hot hands begin to frisk me. I push him away.

'Let's plunder your mini-bar,' he says, grabbing me again. I wriggle out of his clutches. My phone beeps in my pocket. God bless Carla.

'I need to make a call. Goodnight Max.'

'I'll see you in London then!'

Carla is not coming back. She's at Dean's hotel and says it's much nicer than ours.

In the morning, I wonder if I've got time to catch an early boat out to Robben Island before we leave. I look up the boat times. No chance. I don the my giant bathrobe and head down to the pool. I look around. Oh no ... there's Max, sitting in front of a full English. He is sawing at a sausage with the edge of his fork as he holds his phone to his ear with his other hand. His female-in-a-swimming-costume antenna draws his eyes from his sausage to me and he raises his eyebrows and smiles in mid-sentence, holding up his fork and giving me a sort of sausage salute. He beckons for me to join him, but I look away at that precise moment on purpose so he might think I didn't notice. I place my towel on a sun lounger, order some juice and dive in, feeling Max's eyes on my back. I swim up and down, up and down waiting for him to go. But he doesn't. He just waits there like a heron stalking an eel in Chelsea

Creek. I give in and get out. He has directed my coffee and juice to his table.

'It's quite stressful trying to relax, isn't it?' he says, without a trace of irony.

Max is wearing indecently small swimming trunks, flip-flops and that's it. He's proud of his physique, obviously. But the slight dimpling of flesh around his midriff betrays the fact that he is holding his stomach in. Sad really. I pull my towel around me and put my sunglasses on. I look round to see Dean and Carla walk in. Dean has his bags with him.

'Dean! Hi! How's the tum today?' says Max, 'And you are?' he smiles at Carla as they approach.

'Much better thanks. This is Carla, a friend of ... ours,' says Dean, shrugging his shoulders at me. Why is this so awkward I wonder? Dean, Carla and I are all looking, or feeling shifty, like naughty kids. Max isn't that much older than us, but somehow he's on the other side of the fence. He belongs here, in a hotel like this. He likes it in this hotel. Max's phone rings again and he excuses himself and gets up, pacing up and down the poolside as if he owned the place.

'Sorry to disturb your nice breakfast,' says Carla.

'Shut up! Actually, your text saved me last night. I'll tell you later.' Dean goes to the bar for a menu.

'You're taking things nice and slowly, then,' I say.

'We just talked all night, honest.'

'Yeah right.'

'Yeah right!'

Carla looks lovely. There's something ineffably feminine about her today, resulting from having been close to a man for a night. If that's not too politically incorrect a thing to say. If so, I apologise to all gay women and men strongly in touch with their feminine side. Look, it's a straight woman thing, OK? That's still allowed isn't it? I watch her eyes follow Dean. She tells me that they took a cable car up the Mountain last night and it was incredible.

For Max, four is obviously a crowd. He drains his tea from his cup and wishes us a good journey home. He's staying on for a break. He bends down and kisses me on the cheek, adding that it would be great if we could hook up when he's back 'in town' as if London lay just over the hill.

We sit there for a while, eating massive pastries.

Dean waits for us, as we go up to pack and change. The rest of our time is spent buying overpriced ethnic-nackery, as much wine as we can carry, some boxed protea for Mum and for Miss Jackson, a purple denim jacket made in China from a trendy boutique for Shelley, and several packets of biltong for Badric and Jessie.

Dean sits in the front with Ross, Carla and I in the back, as we take one last look back at the hotel. Goodbye to the swagged curtains, the marble, the tacky fake gilding on the flashy mirror frames, the gigantic floral displays and the hundreds of staff. As I'm gazing at the tin huts again Carla reaches for my hand and squeezes it. I squeeze back. She looks out her window and I look out of mine. Dean puts his fingertips over his shoulder and wiggles them at her, and she holds them for a minute.

26

The letter

Whoever said, 'It's better to travel than to arrive,' hadn't spent an hour queuing to land at Heathrow, home laid out like toy town below, seeing Battersea Power Station's chimneys once, twice, three times, the green space of the park looking more like an island than ever.

Home. My eyes travel happily around the landscape of my room. It's a bright morning. The reflective surfaces in the kitchen glitter; even indoors there's an air of spring about it.

Badric is ecstatic. He has eaten an entire packet of biltong without chewing, performed the canine version of *Riverdance,* brought me not one, two, but three of my shoes, a cushion and his lead, all of which he has promptly dropped, finding that he couldn't give me gifts and slobber all over me at the same time. I vow never to leave him again.

I'm knackered and dying for a bath. I make myself a cup of tea, go upstairs, turn on the taps and go back downstairs. I open my bag, stuff clothes into the machine and have a look at the pile of post. There's a note from Shelley on the top saying that 'Jack Omo' rang. She'd picked up because she thought it might be us. Jack who? Oh right, Giacomo. She adds that I was great in *Wives* last night and that she hoped I didn't mind but Nika stayed over too.

I flick through the bills and junk, the renewal notice for Badric's insurance, and then there it is: David's handwriting. Well, it had to be, didn't it? I stare at it for a while, with a slightly elevated heart rate. Whatever it is that he's been trying to tell me is in this letter. I can feel it. I hunt in my handbag for a cigarette, and walk slowly upstairs to my room with it still unopened in my hand, go into the steamy bathroom and turn off the taps. I've got a bad feeling about this. I put out my fag under the cold tap in the sink, and place it upright on its filter, a sepia swirl of poison seeping onto the white enamel.

An hour later I am lying in my bed having rung the number he gave me. A voice told me that he'd be back in a while and would ring me. I'm rehearsing my story. It's my turn now. But would discretion in this case be the better part of valour? Truth and Reconciliation or Economy with the Truth and Reconciliation? I stare at the phone.

> *O phone,*
> *Where think'st thou he is now? Stands he, or sits he?*
> *Or does he walk? or is he on Nige's bike?*
> *O happy bike, to bear the weight of David!*

Badric is sleeping soundly next to me, dead to the world as if he'd been waiting up for me since I left. I envy him. I roll over and pick up the letter again.

> *Darling Rachel,*
> *I'm sitting at the window of Nige's top room where*
> *I am camping. It's raining outside, and bloody cold,*
> *but not unpleasant. We've made some progress*
> *on the barn – he and Jean plan to make it into a*

*holiday let. You'd love it. Nige has been good to me,
I won't bore you with the details, but financially
he has saved my bacon; the least I can do is give
him some manpower (don't laugh). I'll be over in a
fortnight or so. Have been getting around on Nige's
bike, so one way or the other I'm getting fit, which is
something!*

*Fiona and I have begun divorce proceedings. It's
as amicable as it could be, and I hope that we can
salvage the best of it. Our friendship, I mean. I'm
writing this because I have given up trying to speak
to you on the phone, and I'm pretty useless at it
anyhow. I know it would be better to tell you all
this face to face but I'm unsure as to how you feel
about seeing me. Anyway, here goes. I hope it goes
some way to explain why I did what I did, why I
couldn't explain at the time, and to show you that
however stupid my behaviour and however much
it hurt you, I never wanted to. You know how I feel
about you. And before you start shaking that head
of yours, YES YOU DO!*

I turn the page and read again the facts of the matter and
wonder how on earth I could have been such an idiot:
that night when I saw him in the little hotel garden, when
I didn't ask for an explanation, when I should have made
him talk. And yet it wasn't to do with me. Fiona was pregnant, he tells me now. He tells me now that four years pre-
viously she'd had an ectopic pregnancy, that they'd been
told it could never happen, that she'd thrown herself into
her career, that they got over it. The support that they'd
given each other had become like a permanent fixture.
They owed it to each other to keep going. Fiona had told
him to go, to make another life, another family, but how
could he? And then I came along. The whole episode had
taken its toll on his business and Fiona had taken a lot

240

of time off work initially. *Swan* had to go. Then Fiona exhausted herself though overwork, got depressed and took more time off. He had to work as much as he could, and me? Well, he thought it best to back off and leave me to that good looking chap I went out with all the time, the other actor in the television series.

Then the impossible happened. Fiona got pregnant again. How could he tell me that? And that's what made him walk away from me. If it hadn't been his duty to stay before, then it was now. Everything seemed to be all right for a while, then Fiona had a late miscarriage. She's getting through it somehow, he writes, but it was the final blow for them. The bankruptcy petition was from the taxman, but Nige bailed him out, and when he and Fiona sell the house (they've just put it on the market) they'll both be OK in that respect. So there it is. He doesn't mention how he feels about the loss of two potential babies. But I still don't know whether I can face telling him about the loss of a possible third.

I feel sick. It's my own stupid fault. If I hadn't delighted in taunting him, telling him Haden and I were going to this or that party ... and the thought of him and her... Anyway, he couldn't exactly come to the parties and nights out could he? And why the hell should I have disclosed something about Haden that Haden himself doesn't choose to disclose? I shouldn't have had to reassure David. Where was my reassurance? When was this magical day when things would be 'sorted out', going to arrive? Why didn't he tell me about Fiona? But why hadn't I quizzed him about their childless state? Fact was, I was happy to believe that Fiona was some sort of cold-hearted bitch. It left the way clear for me, when the day came. And I could have been more careful that night in that little hotel. What the hell did I think I was doing? I held onto him that night. I know I was trying to keep him there in some crazy, desperate way. And then the Alan thing. I suppose David could say that the abortion was all his fault. Because if he'd explained, if he hadn't been jealous, if he'd left Fiona ... if. Even the other night, watching him as he watched the episode of *Wives*, I was still enjoying it, still resolving never to tell him that Haden was gay; playing with his feelings, and Ferdie's too, come to think of it. I'd concocted something to make David feel what I felt when he went home to Fiona. How glibly I put all the blame and responsibility onto her and David, the adulterer, the bad man, Fiona the cold trout who couldn't let go, while I played victim. He should have been honest. A miscarriage isn't anyone's fault. An abortion is though. Round and round and round all this goes in my head. You can't resolve dead babies, you can only get used to the idea. Tell yourself that it was fate. That it was merely a ball of cells, a ball of mine and Alan's cells at that, lost like raindrops into the river. Do I now have to tell Alan as well?

'No, you don't,' says Carla, 'there's no point.'
We're sitting in the park on the bench near the statue of the little brown dog. The small bronze on the plinth, the creature with his well-observed head, one of his ears flopped, the terrier done to death in the laboratories of UCL, back at the beginning of the last century. A monument not only to him, but to unthinking cruelty in the name of progress; bad things done in the pursuit of good things, to the women who rose up in the defence of the poor thing; who did something for what they believed in, and were ridiculed for it. Carla puts a crocus on the plinth and sits back down beside me. My head is thick with tears and tiredness.
'I'm glad that he knows,' she says. 'Poor bloke. Never thought I'd feel sorry for him, but I do.'
Maybe Carla has other reasons for feeling well disposed towards men at the moment.
We break park rules by going into the English Garden,

deemed officially a dog-free zone. An old lady is sitting on a bench with a Yorkshire terrier on her lap. We exchange conspiratorial smiles with a fellow lawbreaker as we walk past the rose bushes. I'd wanted to walk along the river-side, but we'd run into the Fag-Arties, sweating in track suits, getting fit for the spring, they'd said, bouncing along beside us. Ben wanted to hear about the job. I said I had a bug, I'd tell him next time. We'd veered away from them, leaving them to their workout.

I don't know if I felt relieved. When I picked up the phone I told him, all of it, before he could stop me, or interrupt, or before I lost my nerve. Not what he expected in reply to his letter, that's for sure. There was a silence before he said, 'Poor darling.' But I didn't want his bloody sympathy. Yes I did.

'So what happens now?' says Carla.

'We get drunk?'

'I mean you and David. Is he coming over, or what?'

'In a fortnight or so, apparently, God knows. I'd just about convinced myself that I could put the whole thing behind me, you know?'

Mica's in the pub with her man. She tells us that there's a bastard of a billboard near the Bingo Hall if we're up for it, 'Tomorrow maybe?'

'Why not tonight?' I slur.

'Like you're in a state to drive?' says Carla's. My spirits are rallying. Alcohol and activism. I need something to be angry with. A stupid advert selling a stupid dream will do nicely.

In my dream I am driving a large car, I think it is the old Volvo, around Cape Town. I can't see behind me, not because my view is obscured by a crappy Edwardian ward-robe, but because the car has no mirrors. Weird. I wake up with a pit where my stomach should be and an ache where my head should be. So much for my great New Start; like a government slogan, and amounting to about as much. Just the same old same old except worse. Now we all know the facts (apart from the small matter of my little repeat mistake with Ferdie). All is revealed, so there's a great opportunity for another New Start. Problem is, I dealt with the whole situation by having the facts where they were. Now there is even more to deal with and I don't know how it works. Do I want to see David weeping? I don't think so. That's my job. And what next? He comes and lives here? After a year of my getting over it, I'm supposed to undo all that work? I don't know if I can. Yes, I wanted this, but **Rule No. 1** has to be taken into consideration.

I can't shake off this mood, even after coffee and a shower. A horrible feeling is roosting somewhere in my chest. This is not the way I'd expected to feel upon news of his impending divorce. It's hardly the feeling of victory I'd anticipated. No wonder Fiona slapped me when she discovered that he was back here. I suppose it was the easiest option, a bit like trashing a billboard.

I tuck my hair up into my cap, put my sunglasses on despite the greyness of the day and step out in to the morning. I can't believe a week has gone by. I count the days, the nights, as if the world has got it wrong and it can't possibly be Sunday already. Badric is oblivious to my mood, or at least I hope he is. Up ahead I see Barry, sitting on the bench near the Henry Moore, looking out over the lake. He looks as dreadful as I feel.

'Hi Barry.'

He stretches his lips outwards in an attempt at a smile. 'Oh hello young lady, and good morning to you, Baldrick.'

'Is everything OK? '

He sighs deeply and tells me that he had just found a new home for the Black Swan, it had taken him months, but that at last the swannery in Dorset was looking for a male. It was all arranged. They were going to catch him this week and you wouldn't believe it, he disappeared overnight. All the birders were looking for him. Then this morning they found his body, mauled, ripped to bits, by a fox, presumably, up by the side of the small pool at the top of the Victorian cascades.

'Oh my God, Barry. That's terrible!' I sit down beside him and stare out over the lake. The Black Swan. It always used to upset me, especially when I saw it defending the ducklings last summer. It was symbolic, a totem for all loners; the asylum seeker; the refugee; the would-be family man. I don't have any words of comfort for Barry. I could say that at least its suffering was over now, but who am I to say that the bird was suffering? I mean, it might have been perfectly happy. Might have hated it in Dorset. Might have been quite content being single, thank-you very much. I walk on, biting back tears.

All the way round I go, head down, no one noticing, stopping to get a take-away coffee from the café, which reminds me that Giacomo rang. He's not in the café, in fact I don't recognise any of the staff, as if I'd actually been away for a month. People come, people go. People with winning tickets in their pockets get run over by buses the day before the lottery draw.

I sit on the steps of the Pagoda to drink my still boiling hot coffee. Soon I am getting in the way of the would-be Olympians. Why the hell should I move for them? But I do. The coffee is foul anyway. I hold the cup over the railing and pour it into the river. It's the same colour as the water, exactly. I look up at the Buddha, the golden one in his niche, eyes gently closed in blissful meditation.

As I approach my gate Ruff guy and Mush are coming in.

'Wotcher,' he says, 'Won't be seeing much more of us!'

'Oh, really?' I say. Where is to be then, Wandsworth, Brixton or Broadmoor?

'Yep, getting out of this shithole!'

That's no way to talk about Badric's Island! Even on a day like this.

'Yep, just got the dog's papers. Me and the girlfriend are off to Greece. Bought a bit of land when I sold my flat. It's got a house on it, needs finishing but I'll do that. They're desperate for builders out there. Yeah, we're sorted!'

'Oh, good for you.' Even Ruff Guy's got it together. He tells me he bought his council flat just before SW11 went boom.

'Oh fuck, there's Barry,' he says, 'I'm off. I won't be able to keep a straight face. Did you hear about that swan? Wayne's dog mashed him up big time.'

'Wayne's dog? Is that the one that got Badric? What happened to the muzzle?'

'Yeah, dunno.'

'Barry thinks a fox got the swan.'

'Yeah, keep it that way,' he says, touching his nose with his index finger and giving me a conspiratorial grin.

I hesitate for about five seconds, watch as Ruff Guy disappears up the squirrel run and much to Badric's delight, who thought that walkies was over, I turn back and stride in the direction of the Parks Police HQ. If ever there were a job for the P-Force, then this is it. In the microcosm of the park, this is murder, and for me not to report this would be to pervert the course of justice and make me a party to this heinous crime. If I wasn't feeling so upset, if it wasn't so horrible, then I'd be happy to find myself doing something where the moral imperative was clear-cut for a change. The dog is dangerous. It has already mauled Badric. In fact, I should have reported it then and there. It didn't occur to me at the time. I suppose I just wanted to get him to the vet and then when he came round and apologised...

I tie Badric to a post outside, go in and ring the bell on the counter. As I wait, I look around at the maps of the park and the permitted cycle routes, at a missing dog poster and first aid instructions. I feel ready to take back all the bad things I ever said about the Parks Police. I ring the bell again. And again.

Five minutes later I'm walking home. Things didn't go exactly to plan.

'And your name is?'

'Look, it doesn't matter what my name is, what matters is that there's a dangerous dog at large. It could be a child next.' Thai, even.

'Dog's name?'

'Badric.' He starts to write something down.

'Sorry, did you say Baldrick?'

'No, sorry, I misunderstood, that's my dog. I don't know what the dangerous one's called.'

PPC Plod sighs wearily and crosses out what he's written.

'Shall we start again, Miss?'

'The dog's owner then, his name?'

'Wayne.'

'Wayne who?'

'Sorry, I don't know his surname.' I don't even know his dog's name.

'Description?'

'Well ... he looks a bit like a bull terrier cross.'

'I meant the owner.'

'I meant the owner ... and the dog. They both look like, well you know, people look like their dogs.' The man shakes his head slowly but doesn't look up. 'They hang around with...' Ruff Guy. 'Sorry, I don't know his name or address either but he calls his dog Mush.' I should know his name, in that he comes round sometimes with smoke for Ferdie, but I'm hardly going to tell him that.

'No, I wasn't witness to the attack. Well, I was when he bit my dog. No, I didn't report it at the time because ... I'm sorry, I'm just trying to...'

'I'll make a note of it. There's not a lot we can do if people don't report attacks at the time.'

So it's my fault that the swan is dead. I untie Badric and head for home.

There's is no food in the house. When I open the fridge, Badric comes over and we stare into the abyss together. There's a packet of Shelley's Pop Tarts on the side with one left. I put it in the toaster. Boiling hot jam between two bits of cardboard just doesn't do it for me, but Badric seems to enjoy it. I'll have to go to the shops, there's nothing else for it. And not to that rip-off merchant at the bottom of the road, that place is for emergencies only from now on. I disguise myself again and set off, stoically.

There are some roads in London that would appear to be cursed. Falcon Road, which leads from Battersea Park Road to the Junction, is one of these. When you leave behind the delicatessen and the sofa shop, the slick things for slick interiors shop and the whacky things for whacky interiors shop, the phone shop that used to be a very pretty public loo, with stained glass in the door frames and old mirrors and turn into Falcon Road, things change. The sky goes dark, the hairs on the back of your neck go up, your spine tingles and an otherworldly chill enters the car. There are a couple of shops, a hairdresser and a place selling fast food in a bucket that have stood the test of time, but in three years most shops have changed five times, falling victim to the curse. Maybe there's something about it in Battersea, then and now, about the black day that God deemed Falcon Road forever forsaken. I suppose someone loves it here but not me.

I park my car in the Asda car park and head across the road to the organic shop. Positive, that's what I'm being. I go in and stride straight past the pineapples, not giving them a second glance. I want to see whether my mood can cope with a barrage of aromatherapy and the sight of all this health. Mind, body, spirit. If I attended to each of these properly I could transcend unhappiness forever. There's a hell of a lot to have to learn first, by the look of the burgeoning books section. But once learnt, I'll be Buddha-like in my approach. Traumas and trouble will be like water off a duck's back. Essentially, I'll feel nothing whatsoever except bliss. Everyone else will marvel, or hate me. But I won't care; I'll be so detached. I'll have risen above it. Obviously I'll have to stop caring about anything first, I would imagine that would be the stumbling block. If I rid myself of desire, does that also mean ridding myself of the desire to do anything decent? If I was up for the acceptance of suffering, then why buy organic? Why not let the world and all those in it having a shit time just go to hell in a handcart?

I pay for my stuff and step outside. It's cold and starting to rain. I decide to get some flowers for the house, to cheer things up a bit. I walk down past Dub Vendor, glance inside and wait at the crossing. A lot of people look as miserable as hell. I think about South Africa, about the tin huts, about one man's sadness being someone else's wildest dream. It's not them and us, just us, lucky or not.

Everyone's in cheap, and not so cheap sportswear, heading for MacDonald's, smoking fags. It's a uniform, the colour and quality denoting rank. I'm the same, my tracksuit as grey as the day and doing me no favours. Little girls everywhere in mini-sportswear, pink, with 'Cute' in silver lettering. Nasty gold jewellery all over the place. I don't get it; this worship of the fucking awful. We're living in a crapocracy.

I buy some flowers and head back to Asda. As I'm heading for the exit I see Eleanor coming out with her shopping. I call over and offer to give her a lift. She accepts happily, chats all the way home, then insists that I eat with her. I accept her invitation with as much grace as I can muster. She eats early, about half-five, she tells me, and to bring the dog too. Since all I have ingested so far is coffee and a mouthful of Pop Tart, it suits me fine. I'm hungry, despite feeling bloated and fat after my jaunt to sub-Saharan Africa, as you do.

Before long we are sitting in front of a Bernard Matthews turkey breast, oven chips, peas, bread and butter and a pot of tea. Eleanor tells me how much she's enjoyed being here. Miss Jackson is doing fine and it looks like there's a place for her in the home down the road, just until she's back on her feet. I say that, of course, I'll keep an eye on the place and go and see her, remembering the battered box of protea in my hallway. I tell Eleanor about the wonderful time I had in Cape Town and she is all agog, telling me how she envies us young women, with our glamorous lives and lovely houses, doing whatever we want.

'And no kiddies getting under your feet!'

27

A spot of bother

There's a message from David when I get in, ringing to see how I was and to say that he's trying to re-arrange things so he can get over sooner. I hear him struggle silently, trying to say something that would be the answering machine equivalent of a 2,000 word essay. He gives up. The next message is from Carla to say that we are on for later. Oh, and she hopes I'm feeling OK about things today.

I open a bottle of wine and pour myself a glass. It's only seven o'clock; hours to kill. I put the telly on, then turn it off at the sight of an unfeasibly thin mumsy, hands on hipsters, hair all messy, exasperated, but still infinitely joyful, as her little hero tramps mud through the kitchen in his filthy miniature football kit, sweaty hunk of a dad following suit. Not to worry. It's such a pleasure that she's happy to mop it again with *EzyPezyLemonSquezy* or whatever the hell it is. Either that or she'll plunge the kitchen knife into her ungrateful spouse's back.

I hear the noise of a black cab outside. I pull the curtain aside. David, it must be. No, two people ... it's Ferdie! With ... what was her name again?

I open the front door.

'Hiya Rachel! Hey, blondie!' Ferdie puts down his bag

and gives me a hug. 'Tania,' he says, 'this is Rachel.'

Tania comes forward and puts out her hand. She has thick dark hair cut into a bob, pale skin, nice eyes and dimples.

'Come in!' Didn't know you were coming today. '

'I emailed you yesterday.' I realise I haven't checked my email since I got back. Ferdie says something to Tania in Portuguese and then tells me that they're going upstairs to wash and change.

I hear them chattering away in his room. I go into mine to look at my email. One from Juliet, saying she hoped the job went well and inviting me up for dinner next week. A friend of Paul's is staying. Oh-oh, it's a fix-up. Ferdie's, telling me when he'd be back, with Tania. Lou, just to say hi, and to make a date for me to meet Joe. Geoff has sent his last email again, 'In case I didn't get it.' One from Carla, from Cape Point, with a picture of the deep blue sea and the jagged rocks saying, 'Wish you were here!' And one from Jenny, saying that she finally got her email organised and just to say that everyone was really pleased with the shoot, well done!

I go downstairs. Ferdie follows. I tell him I'm so sorry about his Dad.

'It is life. I show Tania London, and then I go. I have told *Danse.*'

'Carla's sorry to be losing you. So am I!'

'Come to Brazil, both of you. And you? Why blonde hair?' Tania joins us and I tell them about the job. He translates where she doesn't follow. Tania is a dancer too, and teaches dance. Ferdie says that he may teach too when he gets back. Yeah, let's all be teachers! He says that his cousin has a band, so he'll still play percussion.

'But not on the balcony,' he says, joking bravely.

Tania wants to know why Badric has a couple of still visible bald patches. Ferdie explains. I tell them that the dog killed a swan.

'This dog is ... a villain!' says Ferdie. I laugh at his pro-
nunciation, vil-lain, as in leafy lane. 'Why is that funny?'

'It's just the word ... no reason.'

'Heroes and vil-lains,' he says, 'Badrique is the hero!'

Badric gives us the one-wag. He's sitting looking at me.
The one-wag sweeps the floor. The one-wag means something, like the helicopter-wag, when the tail goes round
and round instead of from side to side. There is absolutely
no way of knowing what these wags mean. Dog behav-
ioural therapists might think they know, but they could
never be 100% sure. My hunch is that he wants a walk.

Ferdie and Tania are high, buzzing with escape and romance too, it would seem. We walk up the river and Ferdie points out this and that, and I add my bit. Tania says
the Thames is beautiful, and it is. Covered in a blanket of
cloud, the city's darkness is tinged with a strange brown-
ish haze. Tania remembers learning about terrible fog in
London.

'That's right,' I say, 'pea-soupers. We don't get them now
though.' We get the brown orange glow of light pollution
and exhaust fumes, translucent; more of an onion souper.
I'm reminded of the foggy days on *Swan*, when through
the porthole there was nothing. We were in a cloud, cold
to the touch, swirling into the cabin like dry ice; a line of
geese appearing in phantom formation, then disappearing, silent; the fog turning down the city's volume, the end
of the bridge faded out like a rainbow's. Sometimes I'd
ring my driver to say I'd meet him on Cheyne Walk, just so
we could walk through it, feeling it catch on my eyelashes,
the fog making way for us, always just out of reach.

Come on, come on! The car is hibernating. Or sulking.
Eventually it starts with a resigned shudder.

Mica opens Carla's front door, rubbing her eyes.

'Were you asleep?'

'Nah, just getting bored to death by the word "Dean".'

'Shut up!' Carla appears, wrapped up and ready. Mica gets her jacket and we head off into the night. The car starts third time.

'So where is it again?'

'Up by the bingo hall, top of St John's Hill.' Mica fiddles with the radio.

'What does it say?'

'Wait and see. It's been bugging me for days. Bloody better still be there,' she says as she finds Choice FM.

We get to our location in no time. The streets are pretty quiet. It's after two by now. I can park here no problem. I stop directly beneath it, at the top of Plough Road. We get out and have a look: usual sort of thing but with a twist. A woman is standing, leaning, no, bending over a desk, sideways on, a city girl, just like me in South Africa. Her skirt is short, legs long, heels high, the sleeves of her shirt are rolled up; you can tell from her stance that the boss is getting an eyeful of cleavage. She has a pencil in her mouth as she looks into the face of said boss. They are sharing a joke, or talking flirty, whilst in the background, a man at another desk is looking on with a sort of 'phwoar' expression on his incredulous face. This is because the boss is virtually a mirror image of the woman leaning toward her, except for the fact of her hair being red, the other's being blonde. We assume the redhead is the boss because hanging down from her bosom is a tie.

There's very little more annoying at the moment than this fetish for what is known as 'Lesbian Chic'. Lesbian Chic = male fantasy². Two pubeless women at it for a man's benefit. Why ever else?

'Who says you can't mix business with pleasure?' reads the caption.

'But what's it for?' I don't get at all. It's obviously one of those clever, subtle ones that make you shrug to yourself as you sit at the lights, little knowing that you are being attacked subliminally, and two days later find yourself drawn to a particular product; a teaser, as they're known. You are taken by surprise by your own foolishness; the fact that you had been oblivious to your desperate need for a ... I don't know ... a foot spa, or something.

'I think it's a new series coming on Channel 5,' says Mica.

'Is that what it's called?' says Carla, getting her spray can out and handing it to me as she prepares to get on Mica's shoulders, *Coming?*'

I hand the can up to her when she's ready. I'm on the *qui vive*, hopping from foot to foot to keep warm.

'What shall I put?' Carla seems to have vandal's block.

'Anything, just hurry up! Have you put on weight or what?' Mica is steadying herself against the wall, one foot a pace behind the other. Carla shakes her can, the ball inside it rattling noisily.

'Think I'll just sign this one.'

'Just get on with it!' Pleads Mica. I walk up to the lights, look left and right, then down Plough Road a bit ... Shit!

'QUICK! Police! Get down! HURRY!'

'Ow, fuck, that hurt!' Carla lands hard on the pavement. She's managed three big drippy ♀s, has got black paint all over her trigger finger and is hobbling. Mica goes back to help her.

'Come on! Come on!' They must be almost ... I turn the key in the ignition frantically, knowing after the fifth or so time that it's futile. The bloody thing is absolutely dead to the world. In a final 'what not to do' moment, Mica reaches down for the spray can that is rolling towards her then drops it as the Police car pulls up behind me. They get in anyway. Two officers get out and approach the car. We should have taken the opportunity to get our story straight. Instead, we start giggling hysterically. DA always has this effect on us and tonight it's even worse.

'Just a one-off then?' The policeman raises an eyebrow.

The duty solicitor reminds me that I have the right to remain silent.

'That's right, you know, spur of the moment.'

'Just happened to have a spray can handy?'

'Yes.'

'You're an actress, aren't you Miss Jameson?'

I am given a date to appear at the magistrates court, told that I shall get a bill for removal of my vehicle and let out on police bail. They give me back my stuff. The whole thing is not quite so funny as it was to begin with. I don't know quite what I expected, a warning maybe, whatever they call it, but not to be arrested and charged with criminal damage. Seems a bit drastic. It was still funny in the back seat of the police car, less funny when they separated us, made me empty my pockets, hand over my phone and take the belt off my jeans, and totally unfunny after the eternity in the cell that it took for them to get round to the questioning. I wonder what the others said. I think I probably got it wrong. I half-walk, half-run home. I turn my phone on again and it rings immediately, it's Carla. Bloody hell, it's almost half-five.

'I told them the truth! Course I did. Said it was a protest against the exploitation of women. Why? What did you say? Hang on Rach, my mobile's going off. It's Mica.'

We have a poor man's conference call, Carla relating Mica's version of events down her land line to me. I should have told the truth. But then Mica says that if we'd all said it was just a mad moment, like I did, we'd have probably got off with just a caution. I feel vindicated, slightly.

'I wonder what your agent will think about it,' says Carla. Fuck, I hadn't even thought of that.

'How's she going to find out?'

I must have fallen asleep on the sofa, because the next thing I know I'm woken by the doorbell. Last night floods my consciousness as I sit up. It rings again, insistently. Oh please, not Teresa, not now. Badric is going mad, so I drag myself over and open the door, at which point a foot, yes a foot gets in it and holds it open. A hail of clicks and flashes hit my ears and face before I realise what's happening.

'Rachel, when did Shiraz turn feminist?'

'Were you responsible for the other similar protests in the area?'

'Rachel, is it true you've just come back from filming an advert in South Africa?'

'... that you make your money...'

'... a bit hypocritical?'

'... out of adverts like this...'

'... surely *Chefs' Wives* is funded by...'

I think I hear the words 'Haden Marshall' but by this point I've to shut the door. The phone rings.

'Is that Rachel Jameson? I wonder if I could just ask you... ' I slam the phone down.

Oh blimey.

Ferdie and Tania come down the stairs, bleary-eyed and in dressing gowns.

'Rachel! Are you OK? What is happening?'

I collapse back on to the sofa. Ferdie peeps out from behind the curtains. Tania puts the kettle on. We sit in the darkened room and I tell them. Ferdie can't believe it. I'm not sure that he gets it, but Tania does. She's nodding as Ferdie translates what I have just told him.

'I think this is very good, Rachel. In Brazil many women they look like porno film stars, you know?'

My house is under siege. Thank goodness I went to the shops yesterday. Ferdie and Tania take Badric out. I hear Ferdie pushing through, saying, 'Please move now!' I feel it's too early to ring Carla or Mica, then decide that I'm being ridiculous.

'What? No, I was awake anyway... WHAT? Bloody hell!

Have you told Mica? Some bastard from the Police station must have told them. How do they know you've just been to South Africa? I'll ring you back.'

Yeah, how do they know I've just got back from South Africa? My land line rings. It's Eleanor.

'Rachel love, oh thank goodness, you're alright. I thought there might have been an accident. Why? What did you do? Oh.' Longish pause. 'Don't worry, I don't understand you young people anyway. Yes I did. I'm sorry love, some man just asked me when I was getting some sugar. I forgot to get it in Asda. Do you know how much it co... I'll go and have a look.' Eleanor puts the phone down then comes back. 'About five of them. No, I won't say another word!'

Carla rings again. She's just spoken to Mica. Mica's really excited now and reckons this is a fantastic opportunity for a bit of publicity for the cause. She wants me to ring her. She can't ring me because she's out of credit, and she's getting the bus to work soon. Mica works in a care home in Clapham. I ring her number. She says we've got to make a statement saying why we do it. I tell her I'll think about it. She says, 'Time to put your money where your mouth is, darlin'!'

I sit down on the sofa feeling sick. Maybe it'll all blow over by tomorrow. Ferdie and Tania are back, the minute the door opens I hear, 'Come on, Rachel! Just a quick word love!' Ferdie and Tania have arranged to meet a couple of the guys from *Danse* at Camden. They say they'll stay if I want, but I tell them I'll be fine.

I make a cup of tea and smoke a cigarette. I think about what Mica said. I don't know if this leaves me any choice. I feel as if I'm just about to be outed. I can see an image of myself in that white shirt on the beach with Dean ... of Shiraz in her negligée. Of little Miss *Pasta Perfecto*. Of Jenny's face. Please don't let her find out. But if Mica and Carla want to make something of this... And isn't that why we were doing it anyway? Oh well, teaching is getting more appealing by the second. But I've got a criminal record now. Shit. OK, actors refuge on Stornoway time. The phone rings. I screen the call.

'Rachel, it's David.'

'I'm fine, really. Please don't worry. It was ages ago now ... I worry about you too... Listen David, something's happened ... em ... it's just, well ... I think you'd call it a spot of bother.'

I hadn't heard David laugh like that in ... well, ever. Which made me laugh. And we laughed for ages.

'OK, let's,' Carla asks me if I'm sure, then says she'll ring Mica. She rings me back. Mica has told work that she can't make it after all and is on her way back to Battersea. I have a shower and force down a piece of toast, get dressed and put on a bit of make-up. Oh come on, who wouldn't? I recognise that this is a seminal moment in my life, another one when I must make a quick decision and stick to it, whatever the consequences. I feel reckless, I feel free, I feel ... sick. Carla and Mica arrive and push through. Carla says we need to think about what we're going to say. She says I'll have to do the talking because I'm the only one they're interested in anyway, but I tell her that we all have to say something.

So we do it. Let them in, and say our bit about being sick and tired of these adverts, of being bombarded with images which are offensive on many levels, that in many ways things are just as bad if not worse than they used to be and that it's actually not just about women, but about selling dreams to people that don't make them happy, and that they can only afford on credit. Mica says that women are still enslaved by an ideal, a white one at that, and that this particular industry feeds off the low self-esteem of women that it generates in the first place and that until women embrace their nature, and that includes aging then we are as far away from liberation as we ever were. Carla quotes Mary Wollstonecraft:

> *Taught from their infancy that beauty is woman's sceptre, the mind shapes itself to the body, and roaming around its gilt cage, only seeks to adorn its prison.*

She adds that since *The Vindication of the Rights of Women* was written in 1792 it's about time we started getting our act together.

'Because you're worth it.' It just popped out, I couldn't help it.

When asked, I say that actors have to survive on this stuff unless you intend to live in someone else's spare room for the rest of your life, and add a bit about good parts on telly being few and far between, for women, especially the ones over thirty and that contemporary culture has been dumbed down to such an extent that people wouldn't know decent drama if they saw it. (Of course I don't add that I also do it because; a) I am angry, heartbroken, childless and still in love with someone who caused me an awful lot of pain; b) it's better than sitting in on my own shouting at the telly and c) that £55 pot of face cream didn't work. Joke!) Mica takes to it like a duck to water. They take some pictures and when they eventually go we sit there for a while and stare at each other in disbelief, then start saying things like, 'God!' and 'Shit!' and 'Bloody hell!'

28

What's up with Shiraz?

The rest of the day is a blur. Carla and Mica go home. Despite the full fridge and fruit bowl I find that cigarettes and chamomile tea do the trick, and when a decent hour arrives I move on to wine. I pace around, suddenly finding myself slamming my hand over my mouth and scrunching my eyes in a 'What have I done?' mime act. I have the urge to tell people, to confess, to, hopefully, get people on my side. I consider sending one of those annoying emails; the ones where the list of addressees with their whacky email addresses is longer than the message itself, and often makes more interesting reading.

When your parents die, who do you get the strong urge to phone when things happen? Your sister? Brother? What if you're an only child, and the only cousin you are close to is out? The Samaritans? Who? Friends, of course. But friends give you support of a different kind. Not love like your mum can give you, that convincing, 'It'll be fine,' that the child in you is more than happy to believe. The love that comes from your pain being theirs. Anyway, they're still alive, so why on earth am I wasting time imagining them dead?

'Hi Mum! Yeah, lovely here too! I know, just a week ago. Amazing isn't it? Listen Ma ... em ... tell Dad to get the extension, will you? There's something I need to tell you both, and I don't want to explain it twice. No, I'm not pregnant.'

Mum is worried about my future, but at the same time I hear something else in her voice, something other than the maternal. Something of the sister about it. Dad, unexpectedly, for he is the soul of caution, finds it absolutely hilarious. He roars with laughter. Dad did not like *Wives* at all. Nor did he relish seeing an airbrushed version of his daughter on the cover of *Bubbles!* He's pretty right-on, for a dad. Spends half his life behind the pages of *The Guardian* and makes it his business to abhor just about every aspect of contemporary life. Whereas Mum likes to indulge in a bit of ad slating and celeb-baiting with the rest of us, Dad won't entertain any of it. Suddenly I have not one, but two frightening flashes of insight: 1) In this respect at least, I am just like mum. 2) In this respect at least, David is not altogether unlike Dad.

'Just wait and see what happens,' is their response to the situation. That and, 'It'll blow over.' With just the one, loving, 'You idiot!' from Mum.

OK, who's next? Haden.

'You did what?! You've been doing it for ages? Really? That's so funny! God, what's Jenny going to say?'

The doorbell rings. I tell Haden I'll catch up with him later. I peer round the curtain. It's Teresa, holding my coat in her arms. I open the door.

'Hello, Rachel. Here, thanks. You've been away, haven't you?' She hands me my coat, avoiding my eyes.

'Yes.' She seems to be unaware of the earlier events.

'We're just back from Paris.' Oh right. Didn't realise it was a competition. 'Just wanted to tell you that Mark and I have decided to move, have a fresh start somewhere else.'

'Oh.' Well, it is the fashion. 'Getting out of London then?'

'Oh God no! Well, almost I suppose. We've seen a house

we like in Barnes. We'd like a family,' she says, as if you couldn't entertain the thought of one without the other. I hear my phone ringing.

'Teresa, I better go. Thanks for the coat.'

It's Carla, saying that she's going to do walkies in a minute. She fancies a kebab if I'm up for it. I am. I'm starving, and I'm due a free one after all. I feed Badric first, realising as I do that I have neglected him all day and that he looks very solemn and just a bit anxious, as if my career suicide could have some pretty serious ramifications for his stomach. I tell him not to worry, that even dogs whose owners are beggars on the street do OK. He doesn't look entirely convinced.

Ferdie and Tania are back when I get in. They've had a good day, first Camden, then a trip on a sightseeing bus. When I get to bed I sleep, sleep, and sleep. It's almost midday when I wake. I go downstairs. Ferdie and Tania are drinking juice. Ferdie says he made me one, and that it's in the fridge. He says that the phone has rung 'many times.' As if to prove a point it rings again. It's Nina; she says she's got loads to tell me, and wonders if I'd like a swim? She's just got to pick up a few things from the shops for Thai's lunch, then she's got the afternoon off. I tell her that Giacomo rang while I was away. Yes, she says, he wanted to invite me to an opening of a restaurant in Northcote Road. 'They' forgot I was away.

'How was it, anyway?'

'Fine-ish, I'll tell you about it later.'

About two minutes later she rings back.

'Rachel, what's going on? You're in the papers!' I feel faint. By not thinking about it I thought it might have gone away. 'I'm coming round.' I put the phone down.

'Rachel! You are gone white! Sit down, here,' Ferdie guides me to the sofa. I have turned to ice. My stomach is churning the juice like a Slush Puppy machine. Tania comes over and puts her arm round me. How embarrassing. She must think I'm nuts. I tell them what Nina said.

'This is not a bad thing Rachel,' says Tania. In a cosmic sense, I suppose she means. My answering machine bleeps accusingly at me. I can't face it. The phone rings again. It's Eleanor.

'Hello, dear, no, haven't had a chance. Been at the hospital sorting things out. Aunty May is going to The Pinewoods today.' Lucky her. 'You know, the one with the view of the petrol station. I know. She's not looking forward to it, I can tell you. Oh, alright, dear, I'll let you go.'

Nina is at the door. Ferdie says that he and Tania will take Badric out. They are so nice, I feel like crying. I feel like crying anyway. Before they go we spread out the papers on the floor.

'Rachel, you are famous again!' Ferdie holds up a red top.

'*WHAT'S UP WITH SHIRAZ?*' Underneath there is a picture of me in a micro-bikini, a still from the swimming pool party episode. *Just one week after being spotted dining out with Haden Marshall, Rachel Jameson, (35) is charged with trashing a billboard as a protest against being unemployed, despite the repeat of the popular series Chefs' Wives on Sky 1(Fridays 9pm). We ask 'Does the lady protest too much?'*

Another calls us the *Feministas*, as if we were a packet of Spanish panty pads. We are called 'self-confessed' feminists. Self-confessed? Blimey, just how criminal does that sound? Underneath there is a picture of the three of us and some column inches taking the piss, basically. They've turned the whole thing into 'fading star disguises jealousy with vandalism,' and their take on it is, more or less, 'stop trying to spoil our fun, you sad lezzies.'

They all get our ages wrong. Carla is Mica and Mica is Carla and everything we said has been turned upside down. It's as if the reporters were all ninety-two years old with advanced dementia, totally pissed, or just bastards.

There's one sentence about it in the broadsheets: words to the effect of 'Soap star charged with criminal damage.'

What a stunning victory this is!

I explain the whole thing to Nina, who is angry that I didn't tell her about it before, saying that she would have joined us. I tell her that I wasn't sure it was her scene. Ferdie, Tania and Badric head out. I send Nina down to the shop for some more fags. When she returns I tell her to tell me what's happening with Giacomo; tell me anything, anything.

She comes back. She says that she is going to marry Giacomo.

'What! Since when? Do you love him?'

'I'm not sure but...'

'Does he know that?'

'Yes, actually...'

'What do you mean, "Yes, actually"?'

'Well, he likes me. I like him, but... He thinks that after a while I will be in love. That it will grow.'

'Like it worked for Charles and Diana.'

'Well it's a chance for me Rachel. I can't wait forever.'

'But Nina, things have changed now! It's not as if you need a passport. Come on, you could get a great job if you tried, you're so clever!' She shakes her head. 'Yes you are!'

'It's not that easy Rachel. I'll always be a second-class citizen here. You don't know how that feels, but he does. We understand each other. These rich English guys ... they're not interested in me.'

I look at her. Her big doe eyes are filling with tears. She always seemed so tough, so resolved and business-like. I put my arms around her, feeling tears coming to my own eyes. Of course, she's just like me. She's lonely, sick of toughing it out. She just wants what we all want; for the Goddamn quest to be over.

She tells me she enjoys Giacomo's company, and hanging out with all the Italians in Battersea. They're going to go to Italy for a while to plan the wedding and meet his family, then they'll decide whether to stay or come back to London. Things might be better out there.

'You never know.'

'I hope so Nina, I really do. You better invite me to the wedding!'

'And you? What about David? And what about all this?'

The phone rings again. I let the answering machine take it. It's Carla.

'Have you seen the papers?'

'Yeah.'

'What are we going to do? I can't believe it!'

'I can.'

'Yeah, I suppose I can too. Hang on Rach, that'll be Mica.' I hear her opening the front door. Mica takes the phone. She is calm; she's taken control of the whole thing.

'Hi Rach, I know, what d'you expect from them? Bunch of sods ... yeah ... anyway, just spoken to a woman at *The Guardian*, and someone at the *South London Press*. They're interested. We can bite back, if we're all up for it, which we are ... aren't we?'

I think the expression is 'in for a penny, in for a pound'. To take the focus off me a bit, Mica has arranged for the journalist to go to Carla's.

'Not so effing middle-class then either,' she says, accusingly. I hear Carla protest in the background, saying that it would have been nice to have been asked first and that she can bloody well help her tidy up in that case. She tells me to be there by three. It's two o'clock already.

The minute I put it down the phone rings again.

'Gus! Hi! Look, I'll have to ring you back later...'

Gus won't be deterred and tells me that Mum's been on the phone to Uncle Rab and that he's seen a bit about it in the papers. Just to let me know that up there, they all think it's bloody great. I tell him that we're going to talk to someone sensible about it.

'Aye, you tell 'em Rach! Don't forget the party. Yeah, your mum said they're coming up Thursday, making it a long weekend. Come on, just come up wi' them.'

I feel better. My revolutionary spirits are rising. I am a hero in the place of my birth. My clansmen and women have rallied to my defence. Yes! Power to the People!

The phone rings again. For God's sake, give me a break! With my newfound bravado I grab it, put it to my ear and in loud and defiant tones yell, 'What now!' into the receiver.

'Rachel, I've been ringing you since eight o'clock this morning. I'm speechless, I really am!' Oh God. It's Jenny.

If that's her idea of speechless... The upshot of the tirade is that I no longer have an agent, and that the chances of me ever having one again are zero. That she's been trying to placate Foyle & Fagherty all morning, she's had Max shouting at her, as if it were all her fault, that apparently I snubbed him rather rudely in South Africa, that the ad may be pulled and if so, they may take legal action.

At this point I see that equity in my house, which Badric and I were sorely relying on, go up in smoke, along with everything else.

'Have you got anything at all to say Rachel?'

'...Um ... sorry?'

Breathe, breathe, breathe. Jesus, with friends like anxiety, who needs enemies? Tania, Ferdie and Badric reappear, I calm myself, press 'delete all' on the answering machine and tell them I'm going to Carla's. They point out that I'm still in my dressing gown. Oh yeah, so I am. I rush upstairs to dress. I wish I had time to call David. I need to hear his voice.

I stuff my hair into my baseball cap, hunt around for my sun specs and head across the park to Carla's. I can't believe this is happening. Why do I never think things through? What is it about me that attracts chaos? What the hell am I going to do? Two figures come jogging in my direction. Oh no, it's the Fag-arties. I see them see me. I watch in amazement as they rapidly change course and speed into the distance. Oh well. Looks like I'm off their Christmas card list, obviously. Still, I suppose it's better than the third degree. I rush onwards, turn down by the lake towards Carla's gate, as it is known, and with my head down I almost crash into Barry, who is walking with Ruff Guy and Mush.

'Rachel, Rachel!' I try to zoom straight past but Ruff Guy grabs my jacket. 'Hey! What's the story!' he says.

'Look, I can't stop now...'

'OK, OK, easy Rach. Whatever it is, nice one!'

Whatever it is, nice one? What on earth does he mean by that?

I reach Carla's, pull off my cap and collapse onto her sofa. She hands me a piece of toast and says, 'Eat!' I do as I'm told, and drink some tea. Mica is making a few notes and Carla is putting books into neat piles. I feel myself relax slightly, after I tell them about Jenny. My stress levels start to mount again as Carla says she wonders what will happen in court? Just a fine, probably, she reckons, or community service, but that's ages away. We don't have to think about that now. Oh right. That's OK then.

Funny thing is that the interviews go well, both of them. The guy from the *South London Press* is a cousin of a friend of Mica's, and the woman from *The Guardian* used to write reviews. A colleague of hers that she ran into earlier saw the Brecht at the Battersea Arts Centre way back, and remembers me in it. Seems like another life, someone else's. She's going to do a piece about us for the Woman's Page. That there are other women in the country doing this sort of thing, that there is a backlash, you just don't hear much about it. She also says that she happened to watch *Wives* the other night, the fondue episode, another of Riccardo's retro-nights. She wondered how make-up managed to make Mercedes face really look as if it was on fire. I explained about the dummy, and that of course Zsa-Zsa wasn't hurt in the process.

When it's over we don't really know what to do with ourselves. The emptiness of the evening is suddenly daunting. We have a group headache. Carla says she'll walk across the park with me, that Jessie could do with it.

'Rach, I'm really sorry if all this has fucked up your job. It's OK for us. It doesn't really affect us in the same way.'

I shrug, and say it's my problem, and add unconvincingly that it might be for the best. Please refer to **Rule No. 7.**

'What does Dean think about it?' I ask.

'Not sure really, maybe he'll run a mile. I said I'd ring him later. Shelley's cool about it. No such thing as bad publicity an' all that.'

I have the awful thought that if they pull the ad he might not get paid. I share this with Carla. She says that he'll get paid; everyone will get paid somehow. Except me, I think. And my house will be paying everyone else. When I get home, I see that an estate agent's 'For Sale' sign on a post has appeared outside Teresa's.

Ferdie and Tania are going out. Another friend of Ferdie's is doing a Tango demonstration somewhere in Convent Garden. They try to persuade me to come along. I tell them I just want to stay in and have a quiet night. Tania has a shower while Ferdie nips down to the shops to get some stamps so that she can send her postcards. Ten minutes or so after his departure I hear a scuffle outside my front door. I open the door to see Mark take a swipe at Ferdie, who ducks down, spins round and somehow, without seeming to touch him, sends Mark sprawling across the pavement. Tania has come downstairs, and she and I stand at the door open-mouthed. Badric rushes out and starts barking, bringing Teresa to her gate and Eleanor to Miss Jackson's window.

'You bastard!' spits Mark. Ferdie is offering him his hand but Mark refuses, staggering to his feet, fists flailing in Ferdie's direction. Ferdie deflects each blow with acrobatic grace. A member of *Danse de la Lune* does not make an easy target.

'Mark, stop it!' says Teresa, now by his side and pulling him indoors.

'Think you can fuck my wife and get away with it do you?!'

Oh my God. Tania rushes over to Ferdie, who is flicking a speck of dust from his cream cords. A rapid exchange of Portuguese ensues as we all go back inside. This continues till Tania runs upstairs. Ferdie turns to me.

'Rachel, I am sorry for this.'

'Ferdie, don't be silly. This is all Gus's fault. Mark even thought I was having an affair with her! They're mad, both of them. Just forget about it.'

'I didn't fuck her anyway.' What? I am taken aback. This seems like a very strange thing to come out of Ferdie's mouth. 'I only kiss her a few times. She wanted me to f ...'

'Ferdie! When was this?!' I'm amazed, I really am. Ferdie has just back-flipped off his pedestal.

'When she stayed here a few weeks ago. Remember? She was here when I got home.' I look at him. He looks at me and shrugs. 'A mistake, you know.'

I put my hand to my mouth.

'What is so funny?'

I shake my head, 'Nothing, nothing.'

Tania comes downstairs. They speak some more, and it seems that the crisis is over. Wait till I tell Gus just how special he was. They ask me again if I want to go out with them, and again I say no. As soon as they're out the door I ring David. I have so much to tell him. He tells me that worse things happen at sea, and that he'll be over as soon as he can. They've run into some problems with the barn and Nige is away for some reason, so he has to stay on until things are sorted. It'll be next week, definitely. Next week? My heart sinks.

'Not tomorrow then?'

'I'll take that as a compliment,' he says.

Badric looks at me as I pour the last of his healthy additive-free biscuits into his bowl.

'Look, I forgot OK? I thought there were loads left! I expect that Shelley gave you extra, didn't she? Come on, Mummy will get you a treat.'

I put on my disguise again and head down to FoodEtc for a tin of junk food for dogs. At the checkout the man looks at me with utter disdain.

'You stupid girl,' he says. I am taken aback. 'This is how you make your money, isn't it? You can't hate what makes you your money!'

I look at him, snatch the tin of food and my change.

'Well you do! Don't you?' I storm out.

'Badric, I need to walk for a bit, come on.'

The churchyard is quiet. The tide is coming up, slapping against the hulls of the boats. I pat the gravestone of my poor dry roasted friend, and lean over the railings. A mallard is surprised, his wings smack sharply against the water before he gets airborne. The Harbour Master passes, his bow wave causing a stir. Write that damn script, that's what I'll do. In Scotland, Ireland, wherever. I'll live with mum and dad if I have to. I look at the river and hear David's voice telling me worse things happen at sea, and picture us sitting on *Swan*, the sunset obscured by Chelsea Harbour, annoyingly.

29

Badric's Island
by R.L.Jameson

Badric, our hapless Saxon King sits by
the banks of the river, polishing his
shicld.

B: Forsooth, my heart is tired, I
am battle-weary. If God wishes me to
surrender my pretty Ege, and my heart,
then so be it. I give up. To Ireland I
shall go, to the hearth of my brother.
He will give me food and shelter. *(he
calls)* Hildelith! Come hither! *(Aside)*
Thou fiend in female form!
H: Thou call-ed, my Lord?
B: Take it woman, it is thine.
H: Prithee make plain thy meaning, Sire!
B: The Ege of my forefathers, it is
thine, take it!

To Badric's surprise, she turns away. He
thinks he hears a sob.
B: Woman, wherefore weepest thou?

H: Oh my Lord, I do confess, that after all these months of quarrel, I fear that without thee, this swamp would seem yet bleaker … I am quite dumbfounded by the murmurings of my woman's heart … Forgive me, I have no wish to take from thee this place … unless … unless … thee and I were to…

B: Damn thee woman! All this trouble and for naught!

Badric lets out a mighty roar, picks up his shield, holds it heavenwards, then hurls it into the murky depths of the river.

H: Badric! What in the name of Odin didst thou do that for thou stupide cnut! 'Twas all thou possess-ed of any worth!

Do you want to save the changes you made to Badric's Island?

I stare at the computer screen. No I don't. What's the point? Plan B is just not happening. I'm an actor for God's sake. Or I was. Now I'm just an unemployed person passing the time before a court case. I check my face in the mirror again. David will be here soon. Badric's asleep on the sofa, still exhausted from Scotland. We had a good time, even though the engagement party was cancelled. Gus told Helena about his little mistake with Teresa and she blew her top. I sat in with him as he got drunk, telling him that she'd be back, eventually. I visited Nana. She says she talks to Granddad all the time, far more than she did when he was alive. Aunt Ellie appeared while I was there and we were regaled with her woes, mostly concerning Dougie.

Things have gone strangely quiet round here. The spotlight's on someone else. Even the article in *The Guardian* went by practically unnoticed. Something else happened. That's life. There is some good news though. Carla rang and said that an A&R man came down to the studio and thinks he could get the band a deal. She's not going to get too excited about it yet. Teresa and Mark have had a few people look at their house but what with the credit crunch and everything they might be 'stuck here' for a while. Miss Jackson's still in The Pinewoods and quite enjoying it apparently, which is just as well, because it looks like she might have to stay. Her leg hasn't healed too well and she's not going to get mobile again quite so quickly. I went to see her this afternoon. Eleanor was there too. She told me she's got to go home. Her husband can't cope.

Ferdie and Tania have gone home too. There's a pile of Ferdie's stuff in boxes in his room waiting for a carrier to pick it up. The bongos or congas, I can never remember which, are still in the hall. He gave them to me, 'As a souvenir of the great times here with you,' he said, as I wiped my eyes. They got a cab to Heathrow. I offered to take them, but they said no.

My phone rings. It's nearly five. That'll be David.

'Jenny! No, I'm just surprised, what? Yes, I'm fine, I can't believe...'

I have to sit down to take this in. Badric, sensing a change in mood, rolls over and waggles his legs in the air. Looks like I'll be sticking to Plan A after all. Jenny wants me back on her books. Foyle & Fagherty are going ahead with the ad as it's for Europe anyway. What's more, she said, she's been inundated with parts for me, good ones too. Some theatre, and tellies. A new drama about some woman fighting against a proposal for a mobile phone mast next to a primary school in Huddersfield 'or somewhere like that.' Oh right, great. Maybe I could come in 'when it suits' and we could have a look at them together.

I run down to FoodEtc for a bottle of champagne and grab some flowers too. My enemy at the checkout smiles begrudgingly. As I hurry home I see a cab outside my house, a long-legged man-shape handing over some money. I feel myself lifted off my feet, flying towards him like a heron with a beakful of twigs.

Lightning Source UK Ltd.
Milton Keynes UK
UKOW05f1203241113

221637UK00002B/10/P